Invisible
Grace

Maureen Nery

To My Grandmothers

"Stay with it. The wound is the place where the Light enters you."

— Rumi.

1

GRACE

Grace moved like a fledgling bird, craving flight she could not yet achieve. Ma encouraged needlework and reading— 'ladylike things that will make your hands soft and lovely.' She stood over the stove humming "Too-Ra-Loo-Ra-Loo-Ra" to the boiling potatoes while Grace kneaded bread. Ma hummed when her daughter perplexed her. Grace had heard her parents talking on the porch after Da walked the long dirt path home from his blacksmith shop. "What kind of girl is this? Fifteen years old and shows no signs of womanhood. Who would marry her?"

Ma's mouth tightened a little. "I've raised my girls the same. Claire is kind and gentle, a perfect young lady. And she's been that way all her life."

Grace chuckled quietly. *She's been fooling you all her life. You haven't seen her with the boys at school, flirting and acting like Queen of the May.*

"Like a willow," Da said. "Tall enough to withstand strong winds but smart enough to know when to bend. And lovely.

He hesitated, smiling. "But the younger one…" The smile faded.

"She'll be fine," Ma responded, but she didn't sound too certain to Grace.

The O'Dowds lived in a town called Summervale, north of Pittsburgh on the Allegheny River. They owned their small drafty house and were not often hungry. Many families couldn't make this claim in 1915.

Ma finished with the potatoes.

"Grace, bring in some puds for the fire."

"Yes ma'am."

Grace ran to the woodpile wondering where the word "puds" came from. *Da probably made it up. He likes making up words. I wish he liked me.*

She piled the pieces on top of each other until she couldn't see. Six! The wood carrier sat near the stove but she'd invented this game, seeing how many pieces she could stack and carry. She teetered across the yard, up onto the old wooden porch. The second step tripped her up. One log landed onto her big toe and "that was all she wrote," as Da would say. She howled.

Ma appeared at the back door offering no sympathy.

"Grace O'Dowd," what were you thinking? The wood carrier is…"

As she pointed Grace nodded, holding her toe and forcing back tears. The pain pierced through her. So stunned by the force of it, she didn't even argue with her mother, just picked up some of the logs and started indoors.

When they got it stacked and Ma had started the fire, she put her arms around her daughter. Grace finally let a few tears escape. If she really cried, it would crack open the door to the inside of herself, her invisible self that nobody knew. She took the safest route out of her own secret place and rekindled a now familiar argument.

"I like sewing, making things, and I don't mind cleaning. Other than that, being a girl is boring."

Nora O'Dowd knit her eyebrows together, her mouth in a straight line.

"You're becoming a woman, Grace."

"Laundry. Taking care of sick people. Sitting around. No fun. Men have all the fun."

"Tis what we do. It is our duty."

"Well, who made up these rules? What's wrong with being out under the sky? Running? Watching birds?"

"You're supposed to be beyond that, dear."

Grace took one step toward the back yard before she heard her mother's sigh. When she turned back, Ma had her hands planted on her hips. "You're going to need someone to support you."

Claire entered the room, smoothing her hair and smiling. She took Grace's arm. You'll see soon, little sister. Men can be fun. They'll take you dancing and buy you ice creams…"

"They'll only do those things before you marry them and become their slave," muttered Grace. "Men are nasty. They stink and they only talk about themselves and they're lazy and stupid." She freed herself from Claire's hold, which felt a little too firm.

"Stupid is not understanding the world we live in. If you don't find a husband, you'll be poorer than this." She pointed her potato peeler around their tiny house. It crouched, tired and worn like the shirts they kept mending.

"I don't care. I'd rather be poor than with some ugly old smoocher."

"Putting up with a man's...em, advances, is better than being hungry."

Advances? Grace wondered what that meant. Her mother had not told her much about sex, except her monthlies and babies. She supposed it had to do with boys pressing against her, trying for kisses that left her cold. The boys were okay, playing games and running with them was great fun. Some of them counted as friends. But the kissing? No.

Claire is beautiful, and everyone loves her because they think she's so sweet. Still, I wouldn't want to be her. She's not too smart.

Da's chums ogled Claire when they came to play poker. If she lingered, waiting for her boyfriend to appear, the men forgot Grace except for a pinch or two. Sometimes she would smack one of them and they would infuriate her by snorting in their gross mannish way. Da didn't notice, or he pretended not to. He sat in his chair, concentrating on his cards and occasionally smoking a cigar. Ma hated the cigar, but Grace loved watching him— how his blue eyes locked onto the cards, revealing nothing, his voice soft and the rest of his brawny body relaxed and calm.

But Grace liked being around girls and women more. The smell of them, fresh bread and the perfumes they made from their herbs and flowers, their kind and inviting laps, their low voices, beckoning her and gentle.

A few days later, when Grace's toe had healed, she heard the knocker and ran for the front door. She hadn't gotten far when her mother called to her.

"Stop this minute, Grace Catherine O'Dowd. Compose yourself. The boy doesn't want to see you eager and breathless! He wants you calm and," her mother paused, "slightly out of reach. That," she added with a twinkle in her eye, "is what men want."

She pinched her daughter's chin, beaming.

Out of reach. That's no problem. Ha. Michael Curran had kissed her once. When he pushed his tongue into her mouth it tasted like day-old cream of wheat. Grace squeezed out of his grasp, surprised to see him smiling. "You'll get used to it," he murmured. "You'll like it someday."

I doubt it. But she had to admit that having Stephen Sullivan as a boyfriend made her the envy of all the girls at school. An upright achiever, his reports said. Dull, Grace would add.

Maybe he'll bring his sister today. A reasonable hope, since siblings often went to the annual fall school picnic together, trudging through the narrow streets of Summervale at least a foot apart.

Grace counted her steps across the living room and could feel her mother waiting to see if she increased her pace. When she finally opened the door the early afternoon sunlight blinded her. Shading her eyes with her left hand, she stuck her right into the brightness.

"Hello, Stephen," and she waited for one voice, not his.

"Hello Grace, you look really nice. Here, I brought you this."

He thrust some drooping daisies into her outstretched hand. Grace's heart skipped a beat. There stood Brid, grinning. She'd come! She'd made no attempt to manage her curly red hair the way other girls would. Her hands moved constantly. Feminine, according to Grace's mother, meant quiet and still. Brid appeared to be anything but.

"Hope ya don't mind I came along," she said. "Ma told Stephen he had to take me. Even though he didn't like it much, he's a good boy." Grace suppressed a giggle, knowing Brid loved to irritate her brother.

She led them into the living room. "Oh no, this will be great fun!"

Ma ambled in, her face flushed with pleasure. She greeted Stephen warmly and his sister less so. Grace knew she had so far listened to every word.

"Stephen, so good of you to escort both of the girls. I am sure your sister believes you are a prince!"

Grace cleared her throat before Ma could continue.

"Well," replied Stephen, "I do my best."

I do my best -- the most boring thing ever spoken. He would wag his tail if he had one.

Brid, on the other hand, would be her very naughtiest. They had so much fun together. More than fun. What more she couldn't name, didn't really know.

Never mind. The day promised delight. Stephen would drift off and leave them to their own devices. He always came back at the end and asked what they had been up to. They always gave him some version of the truth.

Grace understood their collusion. Stephen's other interests needed some cover. Today she suspected his flushed face had something to do with Nellie Neary, whose life and adventures were well documented by the town's busybodies.

They set off after interminable goodbyes, her mother keeping one hand on Stephen's arm far too long. At the doorstep, Ma held Grace back and whispered, "Pay attention to him. Ask him questions about himself. This is a boy from a good family and he is interested in you. This is your chance."

Grace softened at Ma's desperation, wishing she could oblige, but as soon as they were out of sight his attention wandered like a drunken man's car on Saturday night.

 "Stephen, what do you think you'll do after high school?" she asked him, "Oh, maybe become a doctor..." He gazed out toward the river.

They walked the rest of the way to the picnic in silence.

"Let's go over there." He pointed to a gaggle of girls surrounding the refreshments, pretending to eat tiny bites. Nellie Neary wiggled among them, waving to him.

Brid chirped, "Yep, you go right over there, Stephen. That is definitely the place for you."

He glared at her. Grace heard a slight snicker.

"We'll meet you, say at four? Over by the pony rides. Have a good time!"

Nobody argued, not Stephen with his need to appear the good boy, not Grace, lured by unknown desire and certainly not Brid. She grabbed Grace's hand and began running in the other direction, away from Stephen and his plans. Grace turned back once and glimpsed a mischievous grin spreading across his face.

The picnic took place at the town's only claim to a park, more like a patch of grass with a few trees and a view of the river. They brought a pony and some goats and pigs in from the Krushksad's farm but the kids didn't care about any of this since most of them had animals in their backyards. Sometimes they had a hayride or a swim in the river and always they had food. Plus, the day afforded endless possibilities for tricks and and trouble.

Brid specialized in tricks. Once she had convinced Grace they should put applejack into the cider provided by the Ladies Auxiliary. Grace had no idea where Brid got applejack. Surely they would be caught. What if one of their friends got sick or hurt? She convinced Brid to contaminate only individual cups, a much more time-consuming and riskier enterprise, and to alert their friends.

Kids who loved the taste came back for seconds, or thirds, and spent their afternoon whirling around the park, giggling and saying things only they thought were witty. Cathy Walsh, the spoiled, snooty class queen, broke up with John Sullivan and swore she didn't remember it the next day. Grace and Brid had a good laugh.

Brid appeared to have no plans for group antics today. She led Grace away from the picnic toward the hill behind the Krushksad's farm, and they climbed for ten minutes before either of them spoke.

Grace, shorter than her friend, labored to keep up. They stopped halfway up the hill overlooking the river. Grace panted, "So, what are we going to do?"

"We're going to run away of course!" Brid hooted uproariously.

Sometimes Grace felt timid in Brid's presence. Brid wanted to do scary things so Grace loved and feared her company. When they reached the top of the hill a half hour later, Brid stood with her arms outstretched, a mighty conqueror in the warm October sun. "We're...ha ha...we're going to run away! To Tibet! We'll climb to the top of the highest mountain and live like monks! We'll eat snow for breakfast!" She fell to the ground and rolled onto her back. Grace dropped down with Brid, feeling her ribs begin to ache and her eyes tear with hilarity. Suddenly Brid stopped, lifted herself onto one elbow and assumed an attitude of seriousness. "Do you want to know what we're really going to do?" Grace squelched her last gasp of glee because Brid's tone had changed everything, and she knew that whatever came next would be much scarier and more wonderful than running away.

She managed only "Uh-uh."

"We're going to kiss," and she bent over the startled face beneath her and put her mouth against Grace's. It felt so soft, so tender and forgiving that Grace kissed her back with her tongue, not just her lips. She made a sound she had never made and felt strong and full in her belly and below. Then Brid's arms were around her and she did not think of moving anywhere except on this small holy spot of ground.

They lay there for a long time, wrapped around each other, saying little. When they finally sat up and hugged their knees to their chests, the air felt cooler. Grace shivered, but not just because of the chill. "Well," said Brid, "I guess we should start back down." Grace had thoughts and questions but she knew words would only disturb the perfection of this moment.

They stood, brushed off their skirts and adjusted their clothes.

Brid said, "Give me your hand." Solemn as a nun and almost as frightening, she murmured, "This is only the beginning. Now we are bound to each other."

Grace held her breath. *Are we bound? And what does that mean?* She took Brid's hand and began to run, and they ran till they fell, then giggled. Brid had rolled right into a tree and stuck her legs straight up the trunk. Grace imagined some kind of giant deranged insect, and called, "You're missing your wings!"

Brid started flapping her arms and making a buzzing sound. They were high on their daring. They finally stood again, not far from the fairground where they realized things were starting to wrap up.

"Oh dear, we are very dirty," said Brid, without an ounce of concern.

Grace stared down at her dress. She couldn't worry about it. The day had been so perfect that a small thing like her mother's dismay could not interfere.

"Well, let's go see if there's any food left."

But there wasn't any food, only old Mrs. Kirkpatrick with her jowly face and her swollen ankles scouring the last of the pots.

"You girls–where have you been?"

An accusation more than a question. Surely Mrs. Kirkpatrick suspected something.

"We went for a walk...in the woods..." Grace said, trying unsuccessfully to sound innocent and apologetic.

"And how do ya get dirt on your bottom walking, I might ask?"

"She fell," chirped Brid.

"She did, did she? And you? Did you fall too? Because you're the end of the earth, young lady, and I don't think yer Ma is going to be happy when she sees what you've done to that dress she worked so hard to make for ya. Ya had boys up there with ya then?"

Grace shook her head. *If only she knew.*

"Why didn't ya stay here with the other girls and boys? They played games and had so much fun. And Stephen..."

Here she clasped her hands on her ample bosom.

She might swoon if old ladies could.

"Stephen won the prizes and what a joy he was to watch. And so modest too! He is the handsomest boy I guess I ever did see! Grace, I thought ya came to the picnic with Stephen."

Grace sighed. *Will I never hear the end of Stephen? His sister is more fun and exciting and she is a much better kisser.* Even thinking it made her blush.

Mrs. Kirkpatrick pursed her lips. "Run along. Stephen might be still waiting for you at the corner, and you could walk home together. It's getting dark. You know, he disappeared too, after the games. He probably went trying to find you."

He probably didn't. Escaping the old woman's glare and being alone in Brid's company changed Grace's mood again. She desperately hoped Stephen would not be at the corner, although conversation with Brid had by now come to a standstill. They walked along together, grinning as the air cooled and the sun lowered down over their little town. Soon they reached the corner where Brid had to turn. They stopped for a second. Then, a sweet embrace, which meant far more, but none of it could be said.

Grace past the house of the two old maids on her way home. Mrs. Pastorz and Mrs. Banek, whom everyone called "sisters", had lived together in Summervale for years. Everyone knew they weren't related. Mrs. Pastorz would receive a passing hello, but always with a slight grimace, as if the greeter were trying to figure out a problem. Someone might occasionally pick up a pear that fell from Mrs.

Banek's grocery sack, and hand it to her without a word. No one stopped to chat when they hurried down the street, covering their heads with babushkas. Schoolboys took pleasure in throwing paint at their house, or putting a harmless snake in their woodpile to hear them scream. The two women were peculiar, everyone acknowledged that. And boys will be boys.

2

GRACE

Grace hovered in the doorway, peering down the dusty street. She could hardly believe that Aunt Catherine and Uncle Jimmy were coming to dinner today.

Claire had asked her, "Do you remember the last time you saw them?" Staring into the mirror, hands on her hair, frowning. Grace didn't know if Claire's unhappiness came from what she considered to be her little sister's persistent ignorance or because she worried that her hair wouldn't do what she wanted. It always looked perfect. Claire talked, as usual, in that irritating way she had of letting Grace know she should remember, or should know, or should do something without being asked. Grace had recently learned the word. *Condescending.*

"Well, no. I was a little kid, maybe four or five."

16

"Let me tell you. Aunt Catherine and Da are not friends. I don't really know why…"

Grace couldn't resist. "You don't know why?" *How could you not know why? You know everything.*

Claire shrugged her shoulders and sighed. "The last time they were here Da and our aunt got into this argument…"

"About what?"

"I don't remember, but everybody sat staring at their food, and nobody ate much. Worst was that Ma had cooked roasted salmon with grated potatoes and apple cake for dessert. We never got to the dessert, at least not with our aunt and uncle. They stormed out before it ever came."

Grace put the toes of her foot on the floor and wiggled her foot around.

"Then why would they come back?"

Claire sneered. "Why do adults do anything? Now go. Brendan will be here in no time."

Brendan. The latest boyfriend. Grace had shuffled out of the room, wondering again if her sister thought about anything for more than three minutes. Now, lingering in the doorway, she hoped for a better outcome for this visit than Claire's report. *Maybe somebody hadn't been feeling well, that last visit. Or maybe Da had been mad about something at work, or even at Grace herself for playing stickball with the boys instead of cleaning the chicken coop.*

Ma called from the kitchen. "Grace, standing there gawking out at the street isn't going to get them here any faster!

17

Bring yourself in here and help me with these potatoes before time is gone. Come!"

Grace could hear the nervous tremor in her mother's voice. She turned toward the kitchen but saw two figures on the street just before she left the doorway.

In spite of anyone's misgivings, here they came! Grace noticed her aunt first, surprised to see how tiny she was. No wonder it had taken them a while to get here—walking from the train station down Pittsburgh Street and all the way to the house with those tiny footsteps must have taken an hour. Catherine's stride still managed to be full of purpose and determination, almost as if she had to make up for being small and short-stepped. Uncle Jimmy, tall and black-haired, sauntered along beside her.

Aunt Catherine stopped short about three feet from Grace and looked up. "Well, look at you! Aren't you the grand young woman!"

Grace looked around to find out who her aunt was speaking to, then felt a warm, pleasant blush descend through her body. No one had ever called her a woman, not even a young woman. She stepped forward, her hand extended as she had been taught. Aunt Catherine was having none of that. She pulled Grace down to her with a surprisingly strong embrace, then beamed up toward her husband.

"This is Grace! Wee Grace!"

Uncle Jimmy chuckled. "No longer wee, I'd say."

Grace would soon learn that those five words were close to being a speech for her handsome uncle. Aunt Catherine filled in all the gaps.

"We are so glad to see you, lass! You're what now?"

Grace knew what the question meant. It was always the same, from adults.

"Almost fifteen. Just two weeks!"

"My, my." And now she did look over Grace's shoulder. Ma had come to the door quietly, and stood there waiting, something her daughter had rarely seen her do. Another rare sight was Ma's broad smile. Grace extracted herself from her aunt's hug and stood back while Ma and her sister planted kisses on each other's' cheeks.

"Come in, come in!" Ma exclaimed! "We canna have ya standin' out here in the street, what will the neighbors think?" Catherine and Jimmy entered the little house, which Ma and her daughters had cleaned to a spit shine.

Catherine exclaimed, "Tis lovelier than I remember!" She turned to her husband again.

"Ay, tis."

"Well, sit down then. Make yourselves at home."

Aunt Catherine looked perfectly at home already. Grace couldn't imagine her not being at home, anywhere. Her ma, however, did not look at home. Grace knew why. Da would be in from work soon. After what Claire had told her, Ma had good reason to be nervous.

As if on cue, Claire made her entrance. She descended the stairs, her left hand resting lightly on the railing, her right fluttering out to the side like some lost butterfly.

19

Grace hid her smirk with a slight cough. *Oh for Pete's sake. Does she think she's coming down to a ball? It's our aunt and uncle, not the king and queen.*

Grace thought she shook her head quietly, unnoticed, but she saw aunt watching her with a small smile on her face. Catherine winked.

She winked! She gets it! Claire is such a show-off, and Aunt Catherine knows it.

The talk began, grownup talk that did not interest Grace: people she didn't know, a country she'd never been to, the quality of water in the city, how long to let the dough sit. The conversation floated in and out of Grace's notice like clouds. Claire sat smiling prettily but, Grace thought, she looked a little vacant. Nothing new there. Meanwhile, the woods were waiting. Maybe Brid. After ten minutes she started planning her escape, even if she could only get away briefly. She could plead that a chore needed doing, maybe the chicken coop even. No, that would make Ma suspicious.

Water. She would offer to carry water from the well. They would need extra for the company. Maybe Ma would even think Grace was being thoughtful. No, she probably shouldn't count on that. The important thing was to get out of the room.

The challenge would be to find her way into the conversation. "Children should be seen and not heard." Despite Ma's recent concerns about Brid, Grace was very definitely still a child. She cleared her throat, and Ma glanced toward her, briefly and not happily.

"What is it, Grace?"

"Excuse me. I'm thinking that we'll need water from the well, and this might be a good time to get it."

"Why, thank you dear." It worked.

Then, on the way out the door, came Claire's mellifluous voice, underscored by the taunting only Grace recognized. "And be careful, Grace! That is such a pretty dress, you wouldn't want to get it dirty."

A hand-me-down from Claire, of course. Grace decided to ignore the teasing. She had been released! Free until dinner. Surely no one would miss her.

Dinner was a crowded affair, the table being small for four, much less six. Spoons bumped up against forks and it took some care to keep glasses upright. Uncle Jimmy, left-handed and long-armed, sat at the end of the table, unwittingly taking the place Da sat in every night as far back as Grace could remember.

"Ah, ya just don't want to get in Jimmy's way when he's eating," chirped Aunt Catherine. "He does love his food, pays no mind to anything else."

Grace thought it a little odd that Aunt Catherine referred to her husband as if he wasn't there, but she guessed that was something some married couples did. They so rarely had company that she could not remember her parents talking with other adults.

Da, unseated, glared at no one in particular and Grace wondered if he would do that all evening. The room shrank a little more while Uncle Jimmy sat grinning and comfortable and Aunt Catherine questioned her nieces about their lives. Ma scurried back and forth from the kitchen, insisting no, she didn't need help and to just make themselves comfortable. Again. Grace could bring the drinks. Grace, felt herself lucky, this time escaping another dull conversation, this one involving Claire's boyfriend and social life.

The beer mugs were heavy, so she carried them one at a time and handed the first to Uncle Jimmy. He pretended to falter accepting and she cringed, but then, after a long swallow, he laughed. "Ahh, good work dear."

Da had finally seated himself in Ma's chair, making a big fuss pulling it out from the table. He took his beer in a different manner from his brother-in-law. One sip and then, frowning, "This isn't the Guinness, girl. It's Smithwicks. Jimmy likes the Smithwicks. I don't."

How would he know? He hasn't seen Uncle Jimmy in eight years. She guessed men remembered that sort of thing.

Jimmy spoke up. "Doesn't matter."

"It matters to me."

Grace returned her father's beer to the kitchen and put it in the icebox, retrieving a Guinness for him.

Ma served the food and Aunt Catherine continued her line of questioning with Claire, and then Grace, about her favorite subjects at school. She thanked Ma three times for "the loveliest coddled pork I've had in years—every bit as good as our Ma's." The cook demurred, and finally settled herself nibbling a little, while the men did nothing but eat. Uncle Jimmy had a second helping, at Ma's urging, and when Da finished the last of the meat, Aunt Catherine turned to him, smiling.

"So what do you think of this Sinn Fein, Cormac?"

Grace so rarely heard her father's given name (his poker mates called him Mac) that she had to look up to see whom her aunt addressed.

"Bunch of ruffians," he replied. "They'll bring the country down even further, as if it wasn't low enough already."

Catherine's shoulders lifted and she stiffened, although she did not seem surprised at the response. She turned to Ma, who had slumped a little in her seat, fussing with her napkin.

"I still hear from Kate O'Connor now and then."

Grace thought the conversation had turned to another boring but comfortable recital of updates on friends and family. She guessed wrong. Ma, apparently knowing what was coming, shrank a little further. Catherine continued, her voice calm as if they were discussing trivialities.

"Kate's husband Michael says that even though they've finally passed Home Rule, they will suspend it with war coming." She turned back to Pa. "And afterward they'll forget it ever happened. The Irish will be slaves to the English as always."

Grace gave Da a rare moment of credit. She could see his neck muscles tighten as he too tried to modulate his voice.

"These things take time, Catherine. All a crowd like Sinn Fein is going to do is lengthen that." He paused, drained his beer and indicated to Grace that he needed another, and to bring two. Claire stood to clear the plates, something she never did unasked. She obviously wanted to escape the coming storm, as did her mother and sister.

Uncle Jimmy stretched his arms overhead and excused himself, heading for "the jacks." Grace looked quizzically at Ma who shook her head and continued to squirm. She smiled feebly as her husband and sister prepared to enact some facsimile of the situation currently taking place in Europe. Catherine straightened herself to her full height, still barely half of Da's. She placed her hands on the table as if to anchor herself.

"Michael O'Connor is not a ruffian. And," she added as Da accepted his beer, "These men are fighting for freedom, which has been too long in coming. The English have starved, robbed and beaten us down for centuries. How much longer do we wait?" Da chose to ignore the history lesson, taking a different tack. "I doubt you can call Michael Curran an accurate reporter of the facts."

Aunt Catherine grimaced. "He is, in fact, a newspaper reporter," she retorted, pounding her fist on the table.

Ma looked wide-eyed. She tried to rise from her seat a few times. There were things she could attend to in the kitchen, but she couldn't quite make it to a standing position. Grace watched the scene, rigid with fascination and dismay.

Uncle Jimmy had returned, filling the doorway with his great frame. He stayed there, eyeing his beer on the table but apparently unwilling to cross the battlefield to get to it. Da took another swallow of his and replied only with a "harrumph," setting his glass back down a little too firmly.

Uncle Jimmy surprised everyone then by joining the argument, and not in his wife's support. "Michael O'Connor wrote one guest opinion piece for the Irish Times." He slid back into his seat. "One."

Ma took advantage of that small interruption to finally stand. She announced, smiling broadly, "Dessert is ready. And Claire made coffee!"

Grace thought that seemed a little too exuberant for the announcement of a small task, but she excused it in the name of peace-making on her mother's part.

Buoyed by her ability to insert two sentences into the ongoing dispute, Ma continued, "Why don't we take dessert in the living room?"

Chairs immediately began to shuffle, and a truce seemed possible. As soon as everyone sat again in more comfortable chairs however, Da violated the ceasefire with a low blow.

"At least the Sinn Fein is Catholic. You've got to trust that." he taunted. He glanced toward his adversary as if even he was uncertain whether this was an honorable declaration.

Grace knew the family lore: Uncle Jimmy prayed to a different God, in the Anglican faith, thus being the source of Aunt Catherine's estrangement from the family.

Da straightened in his chair, apparently feeling he had gotten the upper hand. "This keeps up, we'll turn into those barbarian Hungarians, fighting each other till the empire falls."

Aunt Catherine replied, "Ireland is hardly an empire. And history is a bit more complicated than that." She turned toward Grace. "Do you like history, dear?"

Grace stared at the floor. "Some." She did not wish to be drawn into the conflict.

Da took a long swig of his beer, followed by an exaggerated "Ahhh," then asked Jimmy what the football teams were like in the city. The argument appeared to have ended.

Ma came in with the chocolate pudding, Claire carrying the coffee cups on a tray, exaggerating the delicacy of her task with tiny footsteps and a furrowed brow. When she almost upended the works with a slight trip in the doorway, Grace hid her delight. But Claire, ever graceful, caught herself at the last moment and saved the day. The assembled family did not need a catastrophe.

Somehow dessert and the afternoon ended with no further assaults, and Grace's aunt and uncle stood to take their leave. Goodbyes and gratitude expressed, hugs between the women and little recognition of Da, who stood back, glowering. At the last moment Ma declared, "Grace, why don't you walk with your aunt and uncle to the station?"

"Oh, yes!" Aunt Catherine effused. "That would be lovely."

Jimmy nodded.

Grace could not fathom the reason for the suggestion, surely they knew the way? But getting outside, away from the house soured by ill feelings, appealed immensely, and she accepted the suggestion with enthusiasm.

They had just turned onto Pittsburgh Street when Brid appeared. *Of course.* Brid always seemed to just appear. She stood before them with her wide open grin while introductions were made.

"Grace is my best friend," she beamed, Aunt Catherine responding in kind, either in genuine joy at Grace's good luck or because she needed some positive outcome to the visit. "We've known each other since we were babies. We know all of each other's secrets!"

Okay, Brid, far enough. Their most recent secret did not need to be mentioned, even in the abstract. A few minutes more conversation, and Brid dashed away. Grace, wanting to make it clear that her exit was not a rebuff, said, "She can't stay in one place for more than a second!"

Uncle Jimmy laughed. "A bit more than a second."

His wife continued, "And she is delightful. You are so lucky to have such a friend."

Grace tried to will herself from coloring, but knew she hadn't succeeded. She mumbled, "Yes, I am," and they continued on to the train station.

3

GRACE

In the months that followed, Grace and Brid found places to hide. They accomplished this more easily by the new year, when the weather sometimes reached into the single digits. People were indoors and peering eyes were not likely to see them down by the river or in the old abandoned 'haunted house' up above Pittsburgh Street.

"It's colder than a witch's tit!" Brid snickered at her own vulgarity as they stood shivering against each other, burrowing under their woolen coats. "I can hardly find you under all these clothes!"

The old house held no furniture, just shelter from the wind and shadows to hide the girls. They'd met there before. Grace didn't care about the cold. With Brid she felt her true self, and contented in a way she never had been. She would put up with the weather or any discomfort to have that feeling. She knew Brid felt the same, else why would they be here together?

Brid cupped her hand over Grace's forehead, and smoothed back a few hairs. "I love you Grace." She kissed her lightly on the mouth.

Some small voice in her mind admonished, *A girl should not feel this about another girl.* She pushed that thought away like dirt on the kitchen floor, understanding nothing except this thrilling feeling, and returned the kiss.

"Again," whispered Brid. "Again."

Norbert Pusztai appeared just as they were saying their last goodbye. No one except his mother liked Norbert, a pudgy pest of a boy, mainly because he squealed on other kids as a hobby. Brid called him the Warthog.

Grace noticed him first, over Brid's shoulder. They stood facing each other, barely touching but still Grace thought it enough to incriminate them.

"What you doin' here?" he sniggered.

"Nothin'," said Brid. "Why don't you just go home to your Ma?" She glared at him. After a while he slunk away like a chastised puppy.

Grace stared after him. "He's going to tell. He's going to tell somebody."

"What is he going to tell, Grace? What were we doing wrong? He doesn't have anything to tell. He didn't see anything."

Grace didn't argue, since Brid would ignore danger as she always did.

They heard the high pitched, whiny scream a few minutes after Norbert's departure. It had to be him. The girls galloped down the hill, Grace in the lead and Brid following, loudly cursing the gods who had tripped Norbert's clumsy feet.

Grace thought only of what she would find, secretly hoping for any injury, even some blood. She felt strong nursing wounds: birds with broken wings, a puppy who had injured his paw. Once Claire got in the way of some disagreeable bumblebees. Grace removed stingers and applied honey. The pain subsided and Claire actually thanked her. Later that year a neighborhood boy plummeted ten feet from an old oak tree and tore his side open on the thorns and brambles below. Grace ripped off part of her shirt, wrapped his bleeding wound tightly and hurried to the doctor's office up on Pittsburgh Street without bothering to stop or inform his mother.

When reprimanded for this later, Grace summoned the courage her twelve years yielded and countered, "I may have saved his life, since we had to worry first about blood loss."

The mother colored and turned away.

Brid and Grace found Norbert belly flopped on the mossy green hillside, alternately moaning and bawling like a child. Grace knelt down closer and helped him raise his head, push up and roll over. No blood, but a good sized goose egg jutted out from his forehead. "Good God," whispered Brid. "Maybe there really are unicorns, because he could sure be one!"

"I'm going to die, aren't I?" Norbert wailed like a newborn screaming for milk. He reached to his forehead, felt the bump and howled even louder. "What is that?" he cried. "What is on my forehead? Oh, I'm going to die!"

Grace removed his hand and laid it, palm down, in front of him. He steadied himself. "You have a lump, Norbert. People get them all the time. You must have fallen, hit your head on something. Maybe that rock there?"

She pointed to a small boulder protruding out of the ground about five feet in front of them. "Me mither would call it a carraig," she smiled, trying to divert him from his trauma with her best attempt at an Irish accent. "Tis the parfect distance for you to have hit your head and tumbled back."

The diversion didn't work, so Grace turned back to Brid. She pulled a kerchief out of her pocket. "Down to the crick with ya, Brid, and get this good and wet. The water's cold. Better yet, if you can find some ice, scoop it up and bring it back."

Brid darted off like a leprechaun fleeing discovery. Grace turned back to Norbert, still sniveling but calmer. "Now,

Norbert, I need to check you to see what is wrong. Does anything else hurt?" Norbert renewed his moaning, pointed to his elbow. Ignoring his chubby, tear stained face, she examined the elbow, felt up and down his arms and legs, and put pressure on the back of his neck." Nothing, except a small scratch, a bit of blood.

"You are not going to die, Norbert. There is no possible way you're going to die. Now, what happened?"

"I saw a bear. A huge black bear tried to get me and I kept running (here a break for more sniffles, one moan) and I kept running and then…"

"Oh, for Pete's sake Norbert. It's January. Bears are hibernating. Anyway, I don't care why you fell, I want to know how you fell. Did you hit just your head? Or something else? Your stomach maybe?"

Norbert's extra weight padded enough that an injury could be hidden, at least for a while. He reached to his forehead again. "Just my elbow and my head. But what if my arm is broken? My mother will kill me! I'm going to die!"

I could easily agree with the likelihood of an early death by your mother's hand. At this point I could cheerfully throttle him, and I'm a peaceful person. She chose not to respond, instead lifted Norbert's elbow and said, "Bend it." He complied, wincing only slightly, which she counted as no pain at all.

Still she asked him. "Any pain?" Mistake. Norbert opened his mouth for the next round but she stopped him. "Okay, very little pain so I'm sure nothing's broken."

Brid arrived breathless from her errand. Grace felt her shoulders relax and took the cloth. "I found some ice!"

32

Grace smiled. She sounds like she's discovered Antarctica. "Thank you Brid." She positioned the dirty chip of ice on Norbert's forehead, and warned him it would hurt a little but not a lot, and to be brave.

She doubted anyone had ever suggested Norbert could be brave. He brightened a bit.

"Like a soldier, Norbert. Be brave like a soldier."

Norbert sat up, straightened his shoulders and allowed Grace to clean the blood off his elbow with not another whimper. More amazing, he put his hand to his head and moved Grace's away. "I'll hold it myself." This was fortunate for Grace, because keeping the ice positioned on the squirming boy's head presented a challenge.

"Now what? Are we just going to stay here?

Grace peered through Brid's impatience and noticed her unusually pale face. "Are you okay?"

The reply, "I'm fine," directly preceded Brid's slumping down onto the cold ground.

"Brid!" Grace quickly crawled away from Norbert and his agonies toward the fallen girl, cradling Brid's head in her own lap. A soft moan replaced 'I'm fine.' A sheen covered her forehead. Grace took the cloth from Norbert, leaving him only the ice, and wiped Brid's face. Norbert did not object. In fact, he forgot his own misery momentarily, and leaned toward the girls.

"What's the matter with her? Is she going to die?"

"There will be no dying here today Norbert," Grace retorted sharply. "Quit talking about it. You're supposed to be a soldier, remember?"

"Yes ma'am." Norbert backed away and assumed his straight backed pose. Grace, realizing she enjoyed being the boss, continued. "She's probably not keen on seeing blood, or people who are hurt. Lots of people don't like that."

Brid stirred, tried to sit up and eventually managed it.

"You mean she fainted for me?" Norbert's eyes were wide, and he now appeared positively cheerful. Partly, Grace wanted to give him another rough and vigorous response, but something stopped her, perhaps Brid's beautiful head resting in her lap.

"Well, I guess you could think of it that way. Now keep that ice up there on your forehead and the bump will go down."

The darkening woods alerted her, past time to be home. Grace helped Brid, insisting again, 'I'm fine,' to her feet. Together they resurrected the soldier to his upright position and escorted him out of the woods and toward his mother's house.

"She's gonna kill me."

Grace sighed. *Will he never stop?* "She's going to take care of you Norbert. Just tell her you fell in the woods. It could happen to anybody. Make sure to keep ice on your forehead a while longer, and stay awake for a few hours. You're going to be fine." She gave him a little shove. Halfway into his backyard, he turned and gave a salute. Grace knew he would not be a problem for them again.

The girls parted near the park, midway between their houses, at dusk. Brid put her hand on Grace's arm. "You were amazing back there. How do you know that stuff?"

"What stuff?"

"Like the ice and staying still and checking his bones and putting the cold cloth on me."

Grace waved the compliment away. "Oh, that. Well, I've gotten hurt lots of times, playing outside you know. Some of it I learned from Ma. Guess that's why I started to talk Irish!"

Brid's face softened. "Well, I don't know any of it." She brushed back her hair. "Let's go up to the mountain tomorrow. To the top." She bestowed a quick peck on Grace's cheek, and began to walk away. She turned around once. "I think I might have seen a bear. A big black one, down by the crick."

Maybe, but probably not. Brid always has to feel bigger and braver. Still Grace had learned that Brid feared something she did not: injury and blood. Grace knew how to help. Her pace quickened, the power of that spiraling through her body and soul, all the way home.

They always wanted more: more time, more comfort. Brid kept finding new hiding places, mostly out in old buildings or in the woods. Less safe, Grace thought. She argued constantly with herself. *Why do we have to hide? Still, I could not give up one bit of our time together.*

As winter's darkness and cold gave way to the promise of spring, they stole away to the hills as often as they could. Ma failed to find Grace repeatedly, although she couldn't complain about the chores. Grace had become a diligent and reliable worker; her duties attended to quickly and efficiently. Ma discovered them once in the shed, where Da stored his tools. Late afternoon shadows made it hard to see. Grace's hands were on Brid's waist, about to pull her closer, to kiss her. Only later did Grace realize what an ally the darkness had been.

Ma called out. "Grace? Brigid? What are you girls doing in here? Grace, I need you to help me with supper. Brigid, it's time you got home."

The girls emerged, smiling brightly. Ma frowned and dusted hay out of Grace's hair. Later, after Brid scurried away, Ma repeated her question. "What were ya doing in there, Grace?"

"Just talking."

"Talking does not dishevel your hair, nor put those silly grins on your faces."

Grace did not speak.

"There are unnatural things in life, Grace. Don't go playing with them."

"I don't know what you mean."

"Ya know what I mean."

 One unusually warm, cloudy morning in early March, Brid came to Grace's house, where Ma welcomed her. Grace, not impressed, understood that her mother only wanted to encourage her connection to Stephen. She finished her chores and Ma excused her, giving each of them a scone fresh out of the oven.

An hour later, deep in the woods beyond the house and garden, Grace heard a sound. Brid, busy undoing the many buttons of Grace's dress, noticed nothing else.

"Listen! What is that/"

"A twig, a squirrel. Nothing." Brid continued her work.

"It's something! I think it's a person! I hear footsteps!"

At that moment Ma stepped through a break in the thick brush surrounding the girls.

"Saints in Heaven! What is this now? What are ya doin'? I never!"

She seemed incapable at this point of uttering anything but short, rapid sentences. Grace and Brid, not completely clothed, froze.

"I'm after the goat! Have ya seen the goat?"

Grace thought the question unimportant at this point, nonetheless she knew her mother to be a woman of concentration and resolve. Ma focused on the goat, a safer, saner strategy that in light of the drama before her, unfortunately couldn't last.

"What in the world?"

Then she shouted, "G'way! G'way!" over and over, like she was chasing errant chickens.

The girls began frantically righting their clothing. Ma discourteously dismissed Brid. There followed a brief but painful session, Ma scolding while Grace stared at the peeling bark on the old oak in front of them. At eye level, a burl protruded, ugly in itself but able to be formed into something quite beautiful. Da had done that, many times. Grace said "Yes'm," and hoped her mother's furor would subside.

"Grace, listen to me. I love you. You are my daughter, my wee one. Please listen. I don't know what you think you're doing. This girlish adventure will not get you a husband or family. It will not make you safe."

"What if I don't want to be safe?"

Grace expected a sermon to begin again. Instead her mother offered only one brief piece of advice. "Fine when you're young, love. But when you're old, safe is a blessed thing." She turned to go, took a step and turned back, her face wet with tears.

"One more thing. I know I will break your heart, but you canna see Brid McQuaid again.

But there are more things for us to do! She didn't know exactly what, just more pleasure, leading somewhere.

4

GRACE

They spoke no more on the subject for a week. Grace ached with the loss of Brid. Then one afternoon, Ma took Grace to the back porch, where they sat, doing nothing. Grace stared out at the trees, remembering her time with Brid. Ma interrupted her reverie. *Ah, the time for the talk has come.*

"I went to see Father Larnagan yesterday. So understanding and kind. He helped."

 Grace said nothing, *Why are clergy members who can't get married always the ones people ask for advice about the very thing they would never do?* She shoved the question back in her file of curiosities so she could try and listen to her mother.

Nora O'Dowd's voice quavered a bit. "I told him you were...you did..."

Grace gazed at the garden. The tomatoes were getting soft, more had black spots, and the beans hung like tiny sticks from their stocks. She sighed. *How can she have talked to him when she can't even said anything to me?"*

Ma spoke gently. "He made it easy, sitting there in his long cassock, so quiet and wise. Christ-like, you know? Forgiving. Holy."

Once Brid told Grace she had seen Father Larnagan stumbling out the back door of Mike's bar early on a Saturday evening, before the crowd of regular drinkers arrived for their weekly festivities. Brid said the old priest had spotted her watching him and first tried acting naive. "Bless you my child," he whispered. He proceeded to step down over the curb but tripped and only great effort (and the Lord?) kept him from pitching head first into the street. He grew solemn.

"Remember the trials of the Lord, child," he muttered, and began weaving his way back toward the rectory. Brid told Grace she expected him to enhance his departure with something like, "Remember how Jesus was silent," or even "Keep this to yourself." He had no need to say anything else, knowing the pecking order. A young girl with not much credibility and no power would be wise to know her limits. Brid told Grace, no one else.

Ma had no such image of the priest. She tried again. "I told him what went on with you and Brid. That I know you are a mostly good girl, and he nodded and said yes, of course." She frowned, her hands twisting in her lap.

"Mostly good? Where in my life did 'good' become 'mostly good?'"

"Grace, please don't make this any harder for yourself or for me. You know exactly what he meant, what I mean. It's difficult to find words to describe, uh, what you were doing."

Grace made circles with her toe on the dusty porch floor, and again did not reply.

"I have never seen such a thing as what went on between you and Brid McQuaid. No one ever imagined that. So, I have nothing to go on except my own conscience, and what I could learn from Father."

That's quite a combination. Ma's conscience prickles like a raspberry bush. She gets mad at the neighbor's dog because it tears up her garden, and the neighbor's been asked, begged even, to tie it up. Nothing changes. Still Ma feels guilty for her frustration, and beseeches the Virgin for forgiveness each night.

Grace felt stuck to the porch swing. She wanted to believe her mother, to follow her direction. This woman had borne her, nursed her and taught her. Until now, she represented everything warm and stable in Grace's world. Even her constant admonishments endeared her to her daughter now, for Grace momentarily appreciated her good intentions. But the shelter her mother offered did not embrace the latest developments in Grace's life.

But she wavered. What if Ma is right? What if this love I believe is good and proper is not? How could it not be? I have never felt love like I feel for Brid. Never felt a draw to any man or boy. If this is wrong, then I am wrong.

Her heart and her body belonged to Brid, whether that was wrong or not, and despite all assertions to the contrary. Brid, beguiling, confusing, exciting, held Grace's love and trust now.

Nothing about this conversation with her mother boded well. Still, the time had come to hear Father Larnagan's pronouncement. To hear her mother's plan. She leaned forward slightly, then turned and gazed directly into Ma's eyes. Surprisingly, Ma cupped her face with warm hands. "I love you." Then she stood, hands on hips, turned away a little.

"Father Larnagan agreed you are a good girl. No reason not to believe that. But, he said, you are also a young and innocent girl who has been led astray. What we need, along with prayer, is to give you a reason to make your way straight again."

Years later, when the terminology became more specific and sophisticated, Grace would remember that pronouncement and think how perfect the use of the word 'straight.' Probably just as well she didn't know it then.

Her mother now clasped her hands to her chest. She began speaking and inhaling more quickly.

"Father Larnagan believes it's time for you to marry. You have these 'urges.'" She hesitated here, and cleared her throat. "They are actually, he says, urges toward motherhood, which is our sacred duty. With a man to protect you, someone for you to love and serve, you will become a happier and more wholesome young woman." Her hands were now unquestionably at prayer. She glanced down at her daughter.

Grace, silent again not of her own volition but because of the stunning message she had just heard, felt her skin tighten like she had been lying in a pit of salt for hours. There were so many things to say, to scream.

Marriage? I'm only fifteen! I haven't finished high school! I'm about as ready for marriage as one of your baby chicks!

She said nothing.

"Is there a boy, Grace? One who has perhaps expressed an interest? Stephen…"

That's perfect. Ma wants me to marry Stephen and then Brid will have a place in my life forever! Too good an idea to ever actually work.

"Stephen is not interested in me."

"How do you know?"

"I know."

Grace's words and tone did not deter her mother. "Perhaps if you tried a little harder. He certainly has paid some attention."

Grace could contain herself no longer. She flew out of her seat and ran into the back yard, arms flailing, hair flying, shouting.

"That is not the point! I don't want to marry Stephen McQuaid! I don't want to marry anyone! And I certainly don't want to have babies! I want to be a nurse!"

Ma turned to her daughter. "Calm down, Grace. Please. You'll make yourself ill."

Grace, instead of feeling ill, felt stronger than she ever had. "I want to be a nurse!"

"A nurse? Where in heaven's name did that come from?"

Grace jumped back onto the porch steps and glared at her mother. "Actually, I want to be a doctor! That's what I want!" Her heart pounded, she could feel the warmth of her blood rushing through her.

A shadow fell from the back door. Grace turned to see Da, standing there, arms crossed in front of him, the way he always stood. As a child, she could beguile him into just about anything: a ride on his horse, a new toy he could build, a push on the swing. It didn't matter his mood or obligation, she would convince him. No more. His gloomy face destroyed any hope of understanding.

"Grace," he began, taking a few steps toward her. "You are not hearing what your mother is saying. We want the best for you. A good life. Not to be lost in a bog of confusion and loneliness. You are young. Listen to us. We have learned some things. We Irish are known for our wisdom as well as our wit." His face hardened. "You will marry. It is the only way. You will work out the details with your mother."

He has never spoken that much at one time before. The crushing cascade of his pronouncement threatened to drown her. Her energy vanished. Trapped by her parents' best intentions, she dropped her head and tried simply to breathe. Then, gazing up at the sky, she watched her dreams disappear as Ma and Da returned to the house together.

That summer, Ma steered her toward the sons of her friends, like Brendan McCarthy, a waif of a boy two inches shorter than Grace whose only words were' "Yea," and "Dunno" and Davin Quinn, a presence like the pope himself, who brooked no argument from Grace on any score. Those each lasted about two weeks. Ma didn't push.

Dominic Cierc lived only two streets away from the O'Dowds. The line between the Hungarians and the Irish ran steadily from the river up to Pittsburgh Street, and no one challenged the housing situation, although people constantly crossed the neighborhoods. At nineteen, Dominic interested lots of girls with his handsome face. He could exude power like a young wolf, but always appeared courteous and friendly to Grace and her mother when they met on the street. "Hello, Mrs. O'Dowd. And Grace, nice to see you." Grace could see Ma, impressed with his manners, smiling back, but doubted his integrity. Likeable perhaps, not loveable.

He asked her parents if he could take her out, to a football game at the high school. Grace could have cared less about football. Still, Dominic could be funny sometimes, the life of the party and always the gentleman. He took her to the movies, to dinner, where he'd have a beer or two, never more. A few times she trekked up the river to New Huntington to watch him play football in a sandlot league. Dominic had lots of friends. In fact, they were never alone.

Curiosity caused her to ask, "How about going for a walk?"

"Walking. What fun is that? Let's go up to Pittsburgh Street, see who's out, what's going on today."

Grace didn't much care. Being alone with Dominic was not at the top of her list, to say the least. They never talked about anything interesting. They hardly ever laughed.

Once, Brid appeared as she and Dominic turned around a corner. There, bright as day, beautiful as ever. Grace held her breath.

"How are ya? Long time…"

"Fine," replied Grace. "You know Dominic?"

"Of course. Nice to see you Dominic." Gone again, with Grace's heart. Brid had never even tried to get in touch after the fiasco in the woods, just disappeared like a shooting star.

They'd been seeing each other four months when Dominic abruptly announced, "So you're graduating this June." Dominic never stayed long on a subject that did not involve him directly. She nodded her head, cursed herself for studying hard enough that she could graduate early. She trembled about what might be coming.

"I think it would be a good time to, you know…"

Grace felt sweat under her arms and fear all through her body.

"I'm asking you to marry me, Grace. Do you hear me?"

He had never stroked her hair back from her face, never softly whispered her name, never said he loved her. Brid had done all of those things.

"I need to think about it."

His face turned hard, nostrils flared. "Then think. But don't think too long."

He took her home and left her abruptly at the door, before Ma could appear and ask him in for fresh rolls and coffee.

The next week, Dominic did come for Ma's coffee, but he didn't stay long. He departed after informing Ma that he desperately wanted to marry Grace.

She started her protest before he left their yard. "I can't! I can't marry him! I don't love him."

She stood in front of her mother in the kitchen. *Desperately.* Grace did not believe that.

Ma stood erect, hands on her hips. "Love is overrated, child. You can't love a man you know so little of. Marry him, get to know him. Love comes with time, patience."

Grace, brought low by this injustice, sat down on the steps, head in her hands. Ma didn't quit.

"Dominic Cierc likes you because, thank the Lord, you are pretty and lively. And Irish, which is a step up for him. You will bear his children, work hard, and he will provide for you." "And you will lie down in his bed and give yourself to him, take him back if he wanders. Love will come."

Grace regarded her mother, saw her blushing. *Marriage meant she would be forced to do those things?* Grace recoiled. Her insides were crumbling and she needed her mother's love and forgiveness. Ma spoke again, her voice softened and choked with sadness.

"Do you…do you understand, Grace? Have you begun to understand what it's like to be a woman? You cannot make choices like this one you've made."

Her mother covered her heart with her hands. Her tears, refusing to be held back any longer, rolled down her face in tiny cascades. Grace wanted to dry them and hold her tight, but her future and the thought of Dominic Cierc turned her arms to lead.

"I can't do this, Ma. I won't. I'd rather throw myself in the river. I'd rather go in the convent. I'd rather starve. She stood in the doorway, hands clenched like a boxer's, arms straight at her sides. "I have dreams. I will not give in."

"What dreams?"

"I told you, I want to be a nurse."

Ma's shoulders slumped. "Nurses go to school, girl. School costs money, money we don't have." A pause, where Ma rubbed her fingers together, a familiar gesture to Grace that meant nothing good. "No. You are only sixteen. You need to understand this is your best choice."

"Why is it my best choice? I choose to live alone, not to marry anyone."

"It is your best choice because..." She couldn't speak it, but Grace knew. Because of Brid. Her mother moved on, headed for bigger artillery. "How will you eat? Surely you want to have children? Who will protect you? No, my child, this is best. I have lived much longer, and I... (the tears again) I love you."

Ma paused, regarding her back yard.

How could this much drudgery, so gray and dull, be the best she could hope for?

Her mother's shoulders straightened. "You will marry him in September."

48

"So soon! Why September? " Grace knew there were bigger, more important questions, like, "Why this?" but she couldn't sort it out.

"Because that's when he wants to get married."

A cold chill spread through her chest. For days she did not speak and ate little. She spent hours in the backyard in the days before her wedding. Ma left her alone. Grace rested on the still warm grass, dreaming of Brid and wondering. how something that felt so good could bring her to this end.

She walked the streets of Summervale, searching for Brid, no success. What had happened to her? Were they marrying her off to some dope as well? Would they never see each other again? One afternoon Grace collapsed on the bank of the river, holding her aching stomach tight and writhing on the ground. She felt she could no longer stand this horrible pain in her heart. Death. Please. Here, in the river.

Then there were gentle, familiar hands on her. Brid spoke right through her pain. "I am here. I am always here and I will always love you." Helping Grace to her feet and holding her tight, she murmured, "I can't stay with you now, Love, and I don't know how any of this will ever work out. Only I know we will be together somehow." Grace opened her eyes to find her pain had disappeared. She gazed around the shoreline, and realized with another ache that Brid had vanished as well.

Back in the house, Da said nothing, his silence worse than Ma's recriminations. Grace knew Ma would not discuss the wedding with him. Men didn't concern themselves with such things. Grace believed she had never pleased him, but now she thought he wanted to make her disappear. Then he would only have one daughter, the right kind of daughter.

49

One morning he worked on repairing a lcak under the kitchen sink. She sat at the table, pretending to read. He liked reading.

"I need a screwdriver." His voice was low and gruff.

She hurried to the shed, where his tools, various sizes of wood chunks and shavings were piled on the old wooden table. He had never been organized. She finally located the screwdriver, and rushed back to the kitchen. He hated to wait.

He took the screwdriver and turned back to his work.

Grace wandered down to the river alone. She watched the current drift past, wondering again if her life could get any worse. This time Brid didn't appear to comfort her.

5

GRACE

Grace married Dominic Cierc at St. Ladislas, the Hungarian Catholic Church on September 27, 1916, when the trees were already beginning to change color. The day dawned chilly enough that she had to wear her old navy coat over her wedding dress. She had made the dress herself out of blue wool, which she knew set off her eyes and fair skin. Why not be pretty today, she thought, after obsessing for weeks about this sham of a marriage. Maybe, somehow, Brid would see her.

A few friends and relatives of the O'Dowd family watched, smirking, wondering how a girl this beautiful and spirited (maybe a little too spirited) could marry this man. Admittedly handsome, but a Hungarian? And why marry before her sister Claire? They spent the wedding ceremony conjecturing instead of listening.

There must be some explanation. They searched for the small, telltale bump on her belly, and speculated on a due date. Were her own poor parents so stupid as to think she could do no better than this Hungarian? Surely not. But her father had come round door to door passing out the customary handwritten invitations with the same pride and bearing he did when he'd forged and placed the beautiful and intricate metal decoration for the City Hall gate.

Surely she is pregnant. So young, so pretty, what a shame. They shuddered as they wished the young couple good luck and prayed for her immortal soul, then moved downstairs for cake and coffee. The few Hungarians, men from Zoltans, the bar where Dominic's father Tamas spent his evenings, kept to themselves as though they were still in church with the aisle dividing them. They sidled to the back of the church hall away from the Irish, surreptitiously handing the flask back and forth. Unnecessary, the Irish men were stealthily sharing their own.

The Irish went home unsettled in body and mind. Did the Hungarians make the cake? It tasted almost like heaven. Too much butter maybe, or too many eggs. Sinful, actually.

Grace accompanied Dominic to his parents' two story frame house, a converted barn that had been carelessly repainted twenty years earlier. Chipped paint ornamented the window frames, and wind whistled through the old clapboard frame. She and her husband would share the attic room, where he had always slept. A small lumpy mattress constituted her bed . Dominic preferred to sleep alone.

Even though the Irish were in the minority, they were one step up in the town, having come earlier and suffered their share of exploitation. The newly arrived "Hunkies" worked the mine and mill jobs, were the maids and other servants. Irish families like Grace's scraped by. Lack of luck, talent or connections kept them from advancing any further. Still, in their minds they were a little better off, a little better.

Dominic started immediately to prove his personal superiority over Grace. "Yea," he told his friend Lazlo, after he introduced her. "She's not too bright but she is lively." He swatted her rear and winked. "If you know what I mean."

"If you were any slower you'd be going backwards. Hurry up, you little *lustasag bukott* (lazy girl)." Grace bent down to her husband's feet. *I'm tying a grown man's shoes.* Shame engulfed her.

This Hungarian world smelled of paprikash and violence. She only saw Ma every now and then, and missed her soft brogue in the morning.

And yet, there were occasions when Dominic could be nice, even humane. Once, in the spring, he took her on a picnic. They walked down to the river with a basket full of sandwiches and cookies his mother had baked. They had no beer. Having fallen out of a bus the day before and knocked his head on the cobblestone street, he had vowed to quit drinking. Grace doubted it, but decided to enjoy this brief respite from her regular life with him.

They sat under an old willow that hung over the broad river. It drooped down so much its leaves almost touched the water in the summer. Now it only had bare branches. She thought of the times she sat on the ground, with Brid...

After they ate, almost in silence, Dominic stretched out his long frame. Grace wondered if she should do the same, to please him maybe. Too cold.

"Did you like having a sister?" he asked, suddenly.

Her eyes widened, she couldn't immediately reply.

"I mean, did you like her? Or not?" His face eyes crinkled , disavowing her notion that he planned on some cruel joke .

"She was alright. We were different."

He played with some small pebbles on the ground in front of him, and looked away from her, toward the river.

"I wanted a brother," he said. "I always wanted a brother. My friends had brothers, or sisters. Big families."

Grace had noticed a tightness in the back of her throat recently, making it painful to swallow or talk. If she were still, it would go away. Today she feared she would say the wrong thing and the tightness returned. Dominic had made himself vulnerable for the first time, and anything she could say might crush him, or worse, enrage him. She too kept her eyes on the river. It quickly became obvious she did not need to respond.

He sat up, leaned his elbow on his knee, and his body grew rigid. He threw the pebbles into the river. "She lost six babies. Six. Couldn't keep a single one." A pause. "Except me."

Grace wanted to shout at him, "She couldn't help that!" His words and manner suggested his mother should have prevented it. Again, Grace held her tongue.

He turned to her. "And you know what the old man said? Each time? Every time? He said, 'Just as vell, vee couldn't afford anudder one.'"

Dominic shook his head and threw the last pebbles at the water, where they hit and sank immediately. His perfect imitation of his father caused Grace to peer around to see if the old man had actually appeared.

It ended as quickly as it had begun. He jumped up, grabbed the picnic basket and her arm in one jarring gesture, and said nothing more. When they were almost to the house he turned to her, his brown eyes flashing like the new neon signs she'd seen on the bars on Pittsburgh Street. He hissed, "Don't you dare ever say a word about this to her. Or anyone. Ever. You understand?"

"Of course not."

She knew she had placated him and the tightness in the back of her throat loosened a bit. They returned to the house and went their separate ways.

She learned to read his moods and stay out of his way when they darkened. The first few times they did, before she knew when and where to hide, his eyes darted like lightning bolts in the night, searching for failures he could blame on her. It usually involved whisky, often late at night. His drunkenness could be an advantage because sometimes he couldn't find her, and if he did he couldn't get close enough to hurt her badly.

His parents never said a word about the muffled sounds of his ferocity, nor of its residue in their house. Grace wondered how early her mother-in-law rose to set the house to rights. Tables and chairs that may have been upended in Dominic's path were upright again, and any that had suffered real damage disappeared into the shed until they could be repaired. Tamas repaired them, not Dominic. Never Dominic.

Her mother-in-law, Marta, seemed to Grace as old as the hills around them. She worked constantly, wringing chicken necks, carrying water from the well, cleaning the guts out of a slaughtered pig, repairing fences, and cooking. Always cooking. Her husband and son's appetites were insatiable. She excelled at baking. Her arms were long and muscled and she tied her thinning hair up into a bun on the top of her head. She rarely spoke and only appeared content when she rolled out the dough for one of her delectable desserts.

Despite her new life, a triangle of boredom, loneliness and fear, Grace did not give up. For one thing, there were chores to be done. At Ma's house, she tried to escape work—here, she clung to the distraction of it. She found pleasure first in the animals and offered to feed them and clean their cages. On winter mornings she trudged outside and through the snow to do her chores. She didn't mind the cold. It gave her an excuse to be outside, under the clear blue sky and away from the dense, dark history of the house. She gave the chickens names: Deirdre, Kyla, Nora, Nessa, Aileen, Claire. The prettiest one she named Brid, but she only whispered that name. That made another triangle of happiness, thrill and sadness at the same time. Sometimes, after she whispered that name, she skipped from the chicken coop to the pigpen, singing an old Irish ditty Ma had taught her.

It's a long way to Tipperary,

It's a long way to go.

It's a long way to Tipperary

To the sweetest girl I know!

Goodbye, Piccadilly,

Farewell, Leicester Square!

It's a long long way to Tipperary,

But my heart's right there.

She had never minded cleaning, now it actually helped her to feel better. If windows were clean, the light could come in from outside. If walls were clean, they reflected that light. And at least she could move. One Saturday afternoon she began cleaning the grime off the walls of the small, dark kitchen so she could whitewash them. Ma always said "too proud to whitewash and too poor to paint."

Marta had reluctantly agreed that Grace could use the leftover whitewash from the barn.

"Not too much! Is not good, too much," Marta admonished on one of her many inspections. "And remember. Dump! Dump!" This confused Grace until she realized her mother-in-law's accent made her insistence that Grace wet the walls first ("Damp") to sound like she wanted the buckets of whitewash spilled out on the floor. Little did either of them know what a prophet Marta would turn out to be.

The sun reflected a rectangle of light through the window onto the wall next to Grace, where she had just finished painting. She had been daydreaming about being in the woods with Brid as her brush went round and round. Grace felt calmed, grateful for the peace of the quiet room and the warmth of the sun on her back. She got a small ladder and began working up higher on the walls.

First she cleaned the dirtiest wall, stained with mold, smoke and drink. She imagined invisible stains of fear and despair, hunger and anger. Perhaps dejection at the expectations her in-laws' new country had failed to fulfill.

Her bucket sat on the floor when Dominic appeared, as always, like a dark cloud. Grace knew better than to ask what he wanted. He leaned against the doorframe,

58

steadying his large frame. She knew he had already had a few nips from the bottle he kept 'hidden' under their bed. She wondered how that would feel, especially at this hour of the day, even wondered if she should try it herself.

"I'll get you some more." Dominic turned around and exited, walking like a toddler. Grace watched him and wondered why he would offer to help with women's work. She guessed the alcohol had already skewed his thinking.

Shortly she heard sloshing and clanging. He reentered the room with a full pail. The clash of the bucket and the sound of whitewash splashing across the wooden floor startled her. Then she heard a thud and turned to see Dominic sprawled on the floor with one foot in the bucket.

Grace stared. *How do you get one foot in the bucket as you fall?"* Whitewash everywhere, creeping into the cracks and corners of the slanted floor and even spraying up the walls. Most of it landed on Dominic. Cursing, he attempted to stand, but he had only a meager ability to balance and fell again.

Grace turned back to the wall stifling her laughter, knowing that would have been a very bad idea. She didn't ask if he needed help; it would only be an affront to his pride, the last thing he or she wanted. His father appeared at the door.

"Vat the hell?" He bellowed and his gaze went to her. He took two steps toward Dominic, one too many. He always wore slippers until he went out to the barn. In a flash he lay thrashing on the floor beside his son.

Grace had seen a fishpond once, two trout in too little water, hoping for depth but unable to find it. She briefly considered throwing her bucket of whitewash on them, which pushed her further toward silent and dangerous convulsions of glee. She painted harder, faster, up and down, up and down. The sunlight had moved higher in the room and she tried to concentrate on its warmth rather than the ridiculous scene below her.

Then she heard the most unexpected sound, dry and hollow like the last inhale of a dying creature combined with the snap of a tree limb as it breaks. Grace held herself steady on the ladder, her astonishment almost overcoming her effort. Her mother-in-law stood in the doorway chortling, pointing at her husband and son, throwing her head back so that some gray hair escaped from her bun and fell down her back.

Not daring to be caught thinking it funny, Grace turned slightly. The ladder rocked like a rowboat, and only her own sure balance kept her from falling into the dark waters of this family's torment and trouble.

The strange sound continued. Grace remained on the ladder, painting, holding in her heart and her glee. Her mother-in-law gasped, actually honking, as she pointed to her spouse and offspring trying to regain their manhood and unsuccessfully rise from the floor.

"You look like couple of drunk chickens," she cackled, and Grace had to turn and see them. They did indeed. She joined her mother-in-law, realizing the other woman's rare mood would protect her. The men struggled to rise, finally upright, righting their long bodies from the mess they had created. Marta glanced at Grace.

"Let's get to it, is only going to get vorse as it dries. The valls are good." The men silently exited the room. The question of their cleaning the mess they had made did not occur to anyone but Grace. But she didn't care. She had never found praise more moving than Marta's four words: "The walls are good."

Her spirits lifted for the first time in months. She felt some happiness and gratitude fill her as her mother's warm soup once had.

She had seen Ma last week when she ventured to her parents' house to return some plates used in the wedding. The visit went as usual. She and Ma sat in the kitchen, occasionally talking, often silent.

After a while her mother said, "Are you helping out in your new home?"

Grace nodded.

"I'm sorry we haven't seen you, but I know you are busy."

"I would come more if I felt welcome."

Her mother did not argue with that. She opened her mouth, and closed it. She twisted the hem of her apron. Then she took a breath, and stood. "Well, your father will be home soon."

Grace grasped her meaning and left quickly. They hugged at the door, Ma clinging as Grace pulled away.

Still, there were times when she needed to return. "The washboard for the laundry is broken. I'm sure we...I mean you have an extra one. Could I borrow it until there is money for another?"

"Why sure and they could buy one! They're not so dear..." Then Ma understood what Grace really needed. She fetched the board and they sat and talked. Despite the discomfort

Grace could not stay away. Once a month or so, miraculously caught up with her chores, she would walk to her parents' house in the afternoon when Da was at his shop. She couldn't face him. Anger and love fought an unending battle in her heart.

Eventually, Ma stopped at the Cierc house, acting like she did this often. Marta, hesitant but polite, made an offering, Ma's first taste of retes. Marta's delicious Hungarian dessert, considerably warmed her to Grace's mother-in-law.

"Why, 'tis lovely!" "I don't think we have anything like this." Grace glared at her. The "we" meant "we Irish." Ma considered. "Well, scones maybe…" Marta stood waiting.

"But the pastry is nothing, nothing like this. So light! How do you do it?"

Marta sat primly, but Grace noticed the air becoming lighter, like the pastry.

"Time, patient. Lots of vork with hands."

"I really shouldn't be eating this," Ma sighed, patting her noticeable tummy. "But 'tis lovely. A labor of love, we would say." She took another bite.

Grace cringed slightly at the "we would say," a reminder that her mother-in-law, not Irish, warranted a bit of condescension.

"Maybe," Marta said, her expression unchanging. "Maybe love from mother. Long time ago. She teaches me how to make retes. Hard worker." Marta sat, hands tightly folded in her lap, her thin lips tight.

Still, the afternoon wore on and the women talked of food and cooking: how to keep the flour safe from bugs, (lids, and a cold place in the house) how long to fry bacon (depended on the freshness of it) whether milk or water improved the bread dough (water). Grace sat and listened until she got restless, then stood up.

Ma rose slowly. "I'd best be going. I've had a lovely time. Thank you."

Once, Aunt Catherine came to the house with Ma. Her aunt seemed completely at ease, which was not surprising to Grace. Catherine settled her small frame onto the rocking chair, which engulfed her. Marta protested, urging Catherine to the threadbare but more comfortable armchair. Catherine rose up to her full height and insisted the chair suited her perfectly. Ma sat back in the armchair with a sigh and a smile. The women's conversation flowed, Catherine asking most of the questions.

"Do ya remember the old country, now?"

Marta beamed. "Oh ya, vas beautiful. Mountains green and everything grew. Very good food."

"And what do ya think of the States?"

Ma frowned, knowing the United States had not been good to Marta. But Marta smiled slowly and said, "Some good. Some not so good." She paused, took a tiny bite of one of the rolls she'd brought in from the kitchen. Then her eyes lit up. "I like always people trying to get better."

Grace noticed Ma and Catherine exchange a small glance, but her aunt recovered quickly.

"Yes! Yes, I think you're right. This country is more open, and people want to improve their lives. There wasn't much chance for that, in Ireland anyway."

Ma added, "If you were a farmer your son farmed after you. If you worked in the shipyard your sons did too."

Grace had not heard her mother talk much about the old country. Ma seemed different with Catherine around. More confident, maybe.

Marta nodded. "Same in Hungary."

"Well," Ma continued. "We can hope for the best. And...these rolls are delicious!"

"Is called beigli. Here, I guess, nuts roll. Sugar, milk." A shy grin. "A little rum, if you have it."

"Mmm," said Catherine. "So that's the secret."

The women stayed until Grace started worrying about getting dinner before the men got home. Her mother noticed her squirming and glanced over at Marta. "She never could sit still."

"Still doesn't. Always vorking. Good helper."

Catherine added, "And an intelligent and lovely young woman."

Grace blushed. Compliments were rarely part of either family she had inhabited. But her mother nodded.

"But we should go. I need to get you to the train, Catherine."

So Catherine would leave before Da returned from the blacksmith shop. Nothing had changed there.

The women encountered some confusion at the door, with each of them unsure whether to hug, kiss or shake hands. Their countries differed in the practice of farewells. Catherine solved the dilemma by finally wrapping her arms around Marta's waist and quickly releasing. Everyone including Grace followed suit.

Ma's last words were, "May your bed be made in heaven," and Marta eyes shone. Grace thought how senseless the divisions between people were. In a small way, they had been defeated for a moment.

6

GRACE

Marta continued to warm to Grace, always with 'Jó reggelt' ('Good morning') when they first met each day. She taught Grace how to make goulash, chicken and dumplings and maranitos, pigs in the blanket. Strands of her hair fell down in her face in her kitchen, where her face lit up and energy poured from her. She didn't care about her appearance. Grace wondered if she wore her apron to bed.

Grace took on more household tasks, sewing curtains out of old, worn sheets, doubling them over to cover their spots or tears. Hanging rugs over the clothesline and beating them stifled anger, momentarily.

"Slow down," Marta yelled from the kitchen. "You break hole right through them!

Grace cleaned. Dust as thick as plywood on the furniture, where more than once, she wrote Brid's name. Little else deterred her from her task. The windows were a challenge – they hadn't been cleaned, maybe ever. When she dragged the ladder outside, balanced it against the house and began to climb with the bucket in her left hand and the rags in her right, Marta called out, "Careful! You fall off there and we spit and ha ha again!"

Grace nodded and continued to climb, and in two days the windows were gleaming. Tamas, squinted and remarked to Grace, "I see things in house I haven't seen in twenty years." She thought too late to thank him for his praise.

Marta always had flour on her hands, spending whatever spare time she had in the kitchen, after finishing the grueling work of transforming the vegetable garden and small farmyard into not only edible but delicious food.

The house became a more comfortable place. The beauty of small things appeared when the grime disappeared: a rounded window ledge, where Grace placed some decorated hollow eggs, and a few photographs, frayed at the edges. She mounted them in little wooden frames and displayed them in the living room. One morning, Marta picked up the picture of a young, smiling woman Grace assumed she had once cut out from a magazine.

"Anya," she said. "Back in Hungary. They had farm. Milk cows. Many cows. But she wants better life for me. Not so hard work."

She placed the frame down and walked away. Grace watched her go, then examined the picture again and saw some resemblance, masked by the fact that the young woman in the picture had perhaps known happiness in her life. *'Anya' must mean 'mother.'*

Despite the lack of money they always ate well: goulash, gombapaprikás (mushroom soup—Marta gathered mushrooms in the woods, knowing which ones to leave behind) lecso, a vegetable stew and jókai bableves, a bean soup, Grace's favorite. The first time she spooned the broth and beans up from the steaming bowl into her mouth, the spoon stopped in midair. The soups her mother made were bland, mostly white.

"This is delicious!"

Marta exhaled and returned to the kitchen. She never sat down at dinner, always scurrying and waiting on her husband and son.

Grace felt as if she had sprouted horns. Nobody praised Marta's cooking. Ever. She put her head down and ate.

Marta produced fresh breads and desserts at least twice a week. Her mother had taught her to bake as a child, on the farm outside a small town in Hungary called Jolskva. Only a wood stove for cooking. First the wood had to be gathered and the fire started, no small task in itself.

Grace, standing quietly in the doorway, once found Marta holding her bread, pressing on it gently and studying it.

She had perfected things Grace had never heard of, much less tasted, like retes. Flitting around the kitchen like a hummingbird, gliding to the icebox for butter, pausing to collect some eggs from the counter near the sink, she produced a smooth ball of dough the size of a melon. She kneaded and stretched it to the size of the dining room table, by respectfully reaching under it with her forearm and pulling it towards the edge, a smidgeon at a time. On a dry day, she would add extra pork fat to help it stretch. It was like watching someone pray, Grace thought. At those moments, liberated from the prison of her life, her gray eyes lit up. Totally absorbed in her work, she appeared to be at peace. Over and over she would reach under the dough and slowly pull it toward her and toward the table's edge. If a hole appeared, she methodically repaired it, pulling the two fragile sides together, producing an invisible seam.

She would hover over the table for an hour, her tall frame bent, her long, veined hands kneading the dough, then adding fruit and nuts. The fillings came from the trees outside: pears, apples, plums or cherries, walnuts. Grace envied her fierce concentration, and paused, her mouth watering. Her mother would have called it sinful, but sins can become less damning after a taste of them.

Marta's recipes had been handed down through generations of Hungarians, who had continued to produce them despite millennia of invasions. They poured their sweetness and sadness into food that caused happiness. The only need for pastries in a poor, dominated society is the joy of them. Pastry so thin it barely held itself together, covered with light sugar and best eaten hot. Bread with finely chopped nuts mixed with brown sugar, cinnamon, butter and some other ingredient that Grace could not identify, until Marta finally, taking a great risk, told her. Ginger, just a pinch.

In spite of this, Marta never gained a pound. She did not seem to take nearly as much pleasure in eating her creations as she did turning them out. Dominic and his father would come in from the mine in the evening and sit down at the newly scrubbed kitchen table, (thanks to Grace's determined hand, displaying the walnut wood it had shown when new.) The men would sit in the small, warm kitchen after they removed their boots and jackets, and eat a piece of bread or a roll. Grace heard only sighs from them, or

"Mm mm, Ahhh," and contented breathing. Then they would go out to the bars, and come home grumbling.

"Where is dinner?" Grace would hear Tamas' bellowing voice before the door opened.

"Just coming, husband," Marta's voice soft and plaintive. She ladled soup into large crockery bowls and hurried them to the table, where her husband and son awaited, frowning. The soup should have been on the table when they arrived.

"I wanted garlic have chance to add little more flavor. Just extra minute." Marta murmured.

Her husband grunted and he and his son began to eat. Grace brought a small bowl and joined them, sitting at the end of the table, as far away as possible from any trouble.

Dominic finished his soup in less than three minutes. His cheeks glowed. Grace knew he'd had an extra beer or two.

"They elected me to City Council."

Tamas added, "Important job."

Marta put her hands on her son's shoulders, and although he grimaced, he allowed it. "Important man!"

Tamas scowled and a moment as close to happiness as Grace had seen fled like an errant schoolchild escaping the strap.

"If I have more sons, I have more important men."

Grace looked down into her lap, feeling her chest and arms begin to shake, hoping that was unnoticed. She heard her mother-in-law's steps scurrying toward the kitchen.

Dominic put his hand on his father's wrist, sneering. "But none more important than me, huh Pup?" Half declaration, half plea.

When his father did not answer, Dominic pounded his fist on the table and yelled. "Where is the meat, woman? Hard-working men need to eat!"

Marta returned just in time, bearing a plate with skirt steaks and boiled potatoes. Only she could make such a meal delicious, as far as Grace knew. The men said nothing, just bowed their heads and forks to the task. Dominic again finished first.

"I'm gonna give those idiotas something to think about," he uttered, watching his father. Grace knew idiota was a Hungarian word, its meaning stronger than its English counterpart. She wondered how much of 'something to think about" her husband could give City Council, being younger, poorer and less educated than any of them.

A long pause with Dominic never taking his eyes from Tamas. Finally his father finished the last mouthful.

"You will. Now let's go look at back fence, finish it before sun goes down."

They left the table without another word. Grace cleared the plates and helped Marta clean up.

Then, a short respite while the men worked, or more probably wandered back up toward Pittsburgh Street. What seemed to descend on the house as the sun set in the smoky sky couldn't be called happiness, but perhaps a moment of contentment. The two women sat together with a cup of coffee. Marta told Grace stories of the old country, and her life growing up on the farm.

71

"Once I met bear on the bridge."

Grace thought she had misheard. "A bear?"

"Yes. Very big. Spooks the horse. I almost fall off!"

"What did you do?"

"I talk to the horse. Good horse. I pet him. He is big horse. Bear goes away."

"You must have been so scared,"

"Very scared. Most scared ever. But then bear is gone, we go home."

"Did you tell your parents?"

"Oh yes. Papa goes out and shoots bear."

"Oh, too bad."

"No, good. Bear is very scary."

They were both silent, imagining and remembering. It was early spring, 1917, still cold, even snowy. Marta had added coals to the stove so the house would be warm when the men came home. They listened to the fire crackle. In the quiet, Grace's life seemed a little better. If her husband and father-in-law weren't in the house, it could have been bearable.

The snow finally melted and spring arrived. One morning, buoyed by their growing friendship and new life returning everywhere, Grace approached Marta after the animals were fed and the eggs collected from the hen house.

"Sometimes I get so scared..." Grace said. Not surprisingly, the night after the whitewash disaster found Dominic drunk and mean. She had escaped only by hiding behind the pig sty, with its horrible smell, but better than what would inevitably take place if he found her. She felt ready to burst with distress and fear, coiled snakes inside her, ready to strike at any moment.

Marta's eyes were cold. "You, girl," she snapped, "vill never speak like that to me or anyone in this family again! This is good Christian home. You vill live vith my son and be glad to have roof over your head. Keep to your vork, and honor my son. Vat you get is vat you deserve."

Grace understood. She realized the unpredictability of this potential ally. Marta's only son remained the pride of her life, no matter what. She had made a few concessions to this young woman now living in her house, but she would never side against Dominic.

Grace plunged this new pain into a walled-off chamber in the blast furnace of her heart. *A part-time ally seems a better option than an out and out enemy.*

She kept to the house and the housekeeping—the cleaning, the kitchen, chores in the yard. Most evenings after the supper dishes were done and the yard chores at an end for another day, she set out for a walk in the neighborhood. She wandered past houses marked with beautiful Hungarian geometric designs over the doorways, or curtains with colorful floral prints. Her house had no such décor.

Still, her steps lightened, remembering Brid, longing for the feel of her hands, her skin. Then one evening as the light began to fade, Brid appeared. In typical fashion, she popped out from behind a tree, grinning like nothing had changed and they were on their way to a new hiding place. She had torn the hem on her old dress and her red hair flew in every direction.

"How are ya, Love?" She grinned. Grace felt anger welling up inside her. She pulled Brid behind the tree and prayed they wouldn't be seen.

"What do you mean, 'how are ya?' I'm married to a boar and I work like a slave every day. These Hungarians hate me for lots of reasons…" She paused here, and her face reddened. "My husband is brutal. That's how I am. And how are you?"

Brid's happy countenance faded. Grace saw a rare hesitation on her face. Brid stared at the ground, her hands clasped in front of her.

"I am about to marry John Boyle."

"No."

"Yes."

Brid had once called John Boyle a mouse of a man. He stood barely five feet tall, already stooped with age. Brid would tower over him by a good eight inches. His overbearing wife had succumbed to pneumonia two years ago, and admonished him with her dying breath: "Fix the…" He therefore spent his free time in deference to or in fear of her spirit, fixing everything he could think of in his sizable old house in the hills just outside of town. The Boyle Hardware store on Pittsburgh Street, which he owned and managed, constituted his one other interest. The only other employee, Mrs. Cavanaugh, kept the store neat and clean, did the books, brought her employer casseroles after his wife's death. John Boyle had done well for

74

himself, and the town gossips speculated that Mary Cavanaugh bore a grudge at not being asked to be his second wife. Brid would have willingly forgone the opportunity, but her choices were few. Though the rumors about Grace and her were not specific, they were still harmful. Grace knew Brid would not be a wife. She would be a maid and, before long, a nurse.

She stared at Brid's drooping shoulders. Her full lips pressed into a grimace.

"I will marry him. It won't be horrible, I guess. He's kind enough." She forced a smile.

Grace felt a wave of nausea, brought the palms of her hands to her face. Not Brid. Brid would never give in. Brid had strength. "But…"

"But what, Grace? What are my options? Live to an old age in my parents' house, eating what little food they have? Or simply starve?"

"You always had answers."

"The only answer I have ever known to be true has been loving you."

"I have to go." Grace choked on the words.

"I know, love. I'll see you around. That will have to be enough, for now. I love you."

She planted a quick kiss on Grace's cheek. "I'm sorry. I wish I could make it right." She walked away, her shoulders slumping further. She turned once and waved. Grace stood, rooted, wiping her own tears in vain. They should run away, she thought. Somewhere no one would know them, or care. She wished she could be brave.

What harm had they ever done to anyone?

Grace returned home to find the house quiet. In the living room, she picked up a jacket she had been sewing for Dominic and draped it over her arm. She knew he would like the rust colored, thick corduroy. He had no sports jacket, and when he went out with his friends he often claimed his clothes made a bad impression. She had never sewn anything so complicated before, but she managed and had just to sew on the buttons, which she planned to do before going to bed.

Dominic usually spent his evenings at the pool hall on Pittsburgh Street, arguing politics in front of the old City Hall building, just as he had done as a bachelor. His late night returns were fine with Grace, the less of him the better. Sometimes though, he made demands. Then she closed her eyes and hoped it would be over soon.

Tonight the quiet fooled her. Dominic leaned on the side of the doorway to their bedroom, trying to steady his bulky frame. "Where the hell have you been?"

Seeing his cold eyes, fear gripped her. His sagging skin brightened a little and she knew a storm threatened. Trying to slip past him into the room, she glanced at him with an attempted mixture of respect and nonchalance. He jerked his knee just as she neared him, and the jacket fell from her arm onto the floor.

She bent to pick it up and the blow came so quickly, so violently, she didn't realize that she lay on the floor on her back, completely vulnerable, until she saw Dominic's foot hovering close to her face. Surprisingly he moved back, and she stumbled up onto her feet, only to be pushed against the wall. He grabbed the jacket. "This is the ugliest thing I ever saw." He hissed at her, his enraged face looming closer and closer. "You know what I'm gonna do with it? I'm gonna throw it in the garbage. Cause it's garbage, just like you. Thas wha you are. S'why you don' want me in bed. You can't handle a real man. Garbage."

She backed up against the wall. "Please, Dominic. Please stop. Please."

No response. Her plea only seemed to anger him more. His face, beaded with sweat, loomed menacingly close. He grunted as he fought to stay upright. The excruciating press of his hands on her neck made it harder and harder to breathe. Her body sagged toward the floor. The grip of the whisky pulled him down with her, and his hold on her loosened.

Then she heard Marta's voice coming from the next room.

"Dominic."

Not hearing it yet, he raised his open palm over Grace's face. Just before he brought it down the voice came again.

"Dominic!" Marta sounded strong, commanding. The terrible huge hands disappeared and the shaking stopped. Grace sat up slightly and watched him stumble out of the room, knowing he would go back to the bar. His brutality had been satiated, now his thirst needed to be. Every part of her body hurt.

When he says 'garbage,' he means my love for Brid. Despite all the sneaking and pretending, it must be obvious. Was she garbage? She fought constantly for her goodness in her mind.

77

After that night, he seemed to drift away from her and from the house for a while. Even his nightly demands lessened, he would come to her bed only once or twice weekly, and often he would fail to achieve what they both expected. She felt a little relief and guessed the alcohol did that.

7

GRACE

Less than a year later, one spring morning when the slightest green had appeared on the trees, Marta shuddered and fell softly to the kitchen floor, landing like a luna moth. Grace rolled her mother-in-law onto her back and sat quietly for a few moments, thinking how odd Marta appeared, silent and reclining. Flour still covered her hands.

Then it became real. Marta was dead. Grace thought her heart would break through her chest. The day before she had announced to her mother-in-law, even before she told her husband, that she had new life within her, and that her baby would be born before the year ended. Marta had beamed, taking Grace in her arms for a rare hug, and assuring her that she would be here to help. No sadness evident about her lost babies. Just joy.

Now this. Grace had never seen a dead person before, or witnessed life leaving a room, a dark cold hole in its wake. Shivering, desperately wanting to flee, she stayed. Marta needed her.

Grace had listened to Ma's stories of death and what the women did afterward. She tied a scarf around Marta's face, to keep her mouth closed when the coldness set in. The hands were easy. She wiped the flour off and crossed them over the Marta's lap, proud of the way they appeared so peaceful and still for once. She closed Marta's eyes, covered her like a sleeping child, and left the house through the front door for the first time ever.

Three miles to her mother's house in a trance, not seeing the blue sky, not hearing the voices as she crossed Pittsburgh Street. Panting her way up Coal Hill, she stopped momentarily to breathe, and found herself staring across the street at the back of a woman's head. A curly red-headed woman. The sight of her made Grace's heart stop. Not now, she could not face both of these things: death and her only chance for life. Brid. No. She clenched her fists and continued up the hill. The woman vanished into an alley.

Grace opened the back door of her childhood home, crossed the threshold into the kitchen and stood watching her mother at the counter, deboning a chicken that had no doubt been squawking in the yard earlier that morning. Ma's hands moved so quickly that Grace stood spellbound by the sight of them. She watched until the chicken had been made into something for dinner, ready for soup or dumplings.

Ma turned. Her face showed no surprise, only happiness and sorrow simultaneously. She crossed the kitchen and held her daughter close.

"I need you," said Grace.

She could feel the tenderness rising in her mother's breast, the same breast that had given her life.

Grace had no time for long explanations.

"Marta is dead. She died this morning. I need your help preparing the body."

Ma backed slightly away from her. "Oh, my sweet girl. I canno do that. Her people, her husband, they would be outraged. Me, an Irish woman? No! The Hungarian women must do that. Her people."

Grace pulled herself away from the embrace. "You know she has only an uncle and two cousins here. Male. You were at the wedding. You know."

Her mother did not reply, only continued shaking her head and staring at the floor.

"It's not her husband you're worried about. It's yours. It's Da. Worried that he might be angry that you violated some stupid rule that depends on the country where you were born. He hates me and Dominic and his family. That you had something to do with dirty Hunkies, besides sticking your daughter with them, he would hate that too."

Grace turned back toward the door, her face hot and her heart beating fast. As she opened it she heard Ma's voice again, softer than before.

"Is it that bad then?

"Yes, it is that bad. And I am trapped in it. Now even without Marta."

Halfway across the yard Ma caught up with her.

"Ya can't do it yourself. I'll come with ya."

Relief flooded through Grace like a soft spring rain. They made their way back through the town, noting the oddness of a brilliant blue sky and unseasonably warm weather. They passed the place where Grace thought she had seen Brid. When they reached the small shops and bars on Pittsburgh Street, Ma let out a sigh.

"Remember we used to stroll here, seeing these shop windows and dreaming?"

Grace did not reply. They hurried to the house. Once inside Ma exclaimed, "Ah, but the house is lovely. Would this be your doing, Love?" Grace merely nodded and headed toward Marta's body.

Ma expressed no surprise or dismay. "Well then, let's get to work." They lifted Marta, carried her to the couch and began to undress her. At this point Grace felt her stomach begin to churn. The old, naked dead body made her head swim, but she calmed herself, breathing long breaths. Ma insisted that Grace do the washing.

With a warm, damp cloth Grace traced the lines of Marta's face, neck and ears. She cleaned her ropy arms, the hands with their raised purple veins, the rough elbows, the bony shoulders. She made circles on the breasts and stomach, and then proceeded down to the legs.

Ma helped her here by holding up one leg at a time, so Grace could gently, slowly (Ma insisted, slowly) wipe them with the cloth. The next, most difficult, private part of her seemed a violation to Grace.

Ma knew. "Remember, Grace, the woman is dead and beyond caring."

They turned her on her side, to wash the back of her and finish the job. Grace, still in the trance that had descended when Marta fell, remembered how good it could feel to be touched by another person. Maybe even the dead savored it.

"What is her best dress?" asked Ma. "Hmmm?" Grace stared down at Marta's half-covered body.

"Grace, listen. We need to finish. Bring her best dress."

Grace approached Marta and Tamas' dark and forbidding room, the one place in the house she had never entered, never cleaned or painted. She had been like a tractor all day, forcing herself to do the things that needed to be done, despite obstacles. She went to the closet, pulled down the light green dress Marta had worn to their wedding, and brought it to the living room. Dressing the body presented more of a challenge than Grace had imagined. Uncooperative dead weight.

Afterward, her mother stood for a moment, twisting her hands and then attempted a few words.

"Her husband will have to put her on the table…"

"Yes," replied Grace. "And thank you."

Ma gazed at her, straightened the errant hairs that had fallen over her forehead during the work. For a brief moment, the last year fell away and Grace felt like a girl again, waiting for Brid to appear at the door.

"My sweet lass. What a hard life has been given to you. And what a beauty you are. I'm so, so sorry."

They embraced and Grace again felt her mother being pulled back to the safe life she knew. The Irish life, full of stories and potatoes. And tea, of course, in the late afternoon, a "wee break," from the chores of the day. As she watched Ma leave, Grace wanted to run after her, clutch her skirt like she had as a child, crying for refuge and some bit of happiness.

She wondered about heading to the mine and giving the news of Marta's death to Dominic and his father. Erring on the side of caution seemed her best bet. They did not like interruptions and they would be home soon enough. Marta had never ranked high on their list of priorities.

She sat beside the old woman for a long time after her mother left, then left her alone to consider eternity. Grace had other work to do.

She began to clean the small house again, removing miniscule pieces of grit behind the kitchen sink and dusting baseboards in the hallway. It didn't need to be done, but it helped her fight anxiety and stop herself from considering her future. She couldn't. It loomed like a summer storm, waiting to pour havoc and destruction upon her.

Marta had lived in this house since her wedding day, over forty years. Her imprint was everywhere. What flowers grew in the garden, what breed of chickens was in the coop, what color the curtains were and how the dishes were arranged on the kitchen shelves. She had given birth here six times, and buried five babies in the back field with her own hands. Town gossips said her husband spent those holy hours, both the births and the deaths, at Zoltans, getting drunk and staying that way. Grace once told Marta that it didn't matter, he wouldn't have been any help anyway. Marta had frowned and Grace knew she had overstepped her bounds again.

Her dusting had become hand wringing, and she stood in the hallway talking to no one alive. *I've got baking to do. I need to bake the retes.* She felt panicky, having never baked bread alone, much less something as complicated as retes. But she felt that to have that sweet, warm smell in the house would be the only way to bring back some semblance of normalcy. To bring back Marta.

Then she clapped her hands. First there must be flowers, and that she could do. She hurried to the back yard, stopped by the chickens who were hungry and squawking to announce it. She spread the chicken feed carelessly and then cleaned their coop, weeded the nascent garden and hung up the men's underwear, socks and stiff work clothes. Then to the back field to gather flowers. All of this, still in a daze.

When the flowers were safely in the glass jelly jars, perfuming the rooms and making them quite lovely, she thought, she tiptoed back into the parlor where Marta lay exactly as she had been left. Grace carefully eased one solitary small purple flower into her top buttonhole, and stepped back to admire her work. That caused a problem.

As Grace rose back up away from the body, Marta's right arm fell off her lap toward the floor. Grace replaced it but as soon as she stepped away it gave way to the pull of gravity again.

She put her hands on her hips. "Well, for gud's sake Marta." She heard her mother's voice then, intoning, with that pinched Irish'o'. "For gud's sake, just put yourself back together. Sit up straight there and quit dwelling' on yer troubles. Yer no child, ya know that don't cha?"

Grace knew she talked to a dead body, since she never would have spoken this way to a live Marta. She lifted the arm again and pushed it further into Marta's lap, then sank down to the cold floor.

"What do you expect me to do? I've got retes to make and then dinner and you're not even going to help. This is pretty sudden you know."

Marta still offered no assistance save finally keeping her arm in her lap. Grace began to feel like an unwanted guest who has already said goodbye twice but is still standing with the screen door open, letting in flies. She headed to the kitchen.

I need flour. She began frantically pulling ingredients off the shelves. *Did every Hungarian recipe have sour cream? Eggs, butter, baking powder. I remember that she kneaded the dough for a really long time. I don't have that much time, I still have to get the fruit and figure out dinner and..."*

She put the ingredients in the bowl and began trying to mix them. Unfortunately, the cold butter and unbeaten eggs were at a disadvantage. Eventually she created a floury disaster. She decided to start over and reached across the milk jar for the flour. A thump in the front of the house startled her, and as she started to the living room she knocked the bowl off the table onto the floor.

Marta lay face down on the living room floor. Grace scolded her. "Marta! Really! This has gone far enough! You are going to have to start behaving! I have too much to do!"

She struggled to lift the body back up onto the sofa, and did her best to resituate it, but Marta ended up in more of a prone position than she had been. "Now, stay there." She pointed her index finger toward the corpse, and returned to the kitchen.

Grace hurried to get some rags and the mop to clean the soggy mess on the kitchen floor. At some point she began to shake. Her chest felt tight and the room seemed to be closing in on her. Coming back to the kitchen she promptly kicked the flour bowl and spread its disaster even further. Defeat seemed certain. At that point a copper-colored glass bottle, its shine dulled by shadow, peeked out at her from behind the kitchen curtain. Dominic had forgotten his whisky.

Throwing back her head as she'd seen the men do, she tossed the first swallow down. Her throat immediately screamed "Fire!" and she vowed not to drink again, but the delightful, soothing sensation that followed changed her mind. She sipped this time, and could feel the liquid travel slowly down to her belly, where it rested and warmed her cold places. The third 'drop' (what Ma called it) offered her energy and a confidence she had not known in some time. She followed that with a full-fledged swallow, and by then she exited through the front door for the second time that day, the bottle lodged in her apron pocket.

By the time she arrived at Brid Boyle's house she understood that while whisky might help some things, it did not help walking. The one-mile trek seemed to take hours, especially when she began trudging up the long hill outside of town. She sang to keep her spirits up, the old Irish songs: 'Toora Lura Lura,' 'The Rose of Tralee' and of course, 'When Irish Eyes Are Smiling.' Standing in the yard, down the hill from the house, she warbled:

"When Irish hearts are happy

All the world seems bright and gay

And when Irish eyes are smiling

Sure, they steal your heart away."

At some point she lost track of the words and 'steal your heart' became 'peal your star' but Grace didn't care. It felt so good to be outside and singing!

Descending from the house, the young Mrs. Boyle apparently did not experience the same emotion. Shortly after Grace's sad, flat attempt at the high 'E' in 'smiling,' Brid came flying down the hill. "Stop, you little fool! Stop that racket right now!"

Grace turned, ceasing her serenade. The sun shone through the trees and she saw something like a sapling, branches extended and fluttering at the ends, adorned with reddish-orange leaves. Wrong season for that, she knew. *The tree seems to be coming this way, and sounding like a whooping crane! None of this makes any sense.*

No stationary tree, Brid had always been able to run like the wind. She reached Grace just after her last note ended.

"What are you doing? What are you doing here?"

"Oh, Brid! It's you! How wonderful that you should appear right at this moment!"

"Who else would appear, you lunatic? This is my house!" Brid shook Grace's shoulders. "What in the name of all that is holy are you doing here? Jesus Mary and Joseph, you're drunk!

Grace ignored Brid's remarks. "I thought we could play!" Grace turned, pointed toward the sunlit water. "We can play in the river!" She loosened herself from Brid's grip, stumbled down towards the water and dove in. She came up close to the middle of the river. Danger had sobered her some. The current pulling her downstream seemed to have the strength of a tornado that had once raged through their town. Her desperate strokes achieved little, and her dress obstructed her attempts to swim. She had less and less air to breathe, and the lovely, light feeling of recent moments had completely disappeared.

Brid galloped into the river. She stood waist deep, holding something in her hands, and yelled "Catch this!" A long, spiraling rope landed an arm's length in front of Grace, who grabbed it and held on, white knuckled. Brid hauled her out of the river while Grace continued to try and breathe. They climbed up the bank and collapsed, breathing like asthmatics.

The cold river water had sobered Grace. Her first words were, "Where did the rope come from?"

"We keep one down here, in case somebody does something stupid."

"Like me."

"Exactly. Like you."

They giggled. Neither one knew why.

After a bit, Brid took Grace's hand.

"We have to get you home." She pulled Grace to her feet and they embraced: the quick thrill of being in Brid's arms, where warmth and safety enveloped her. Still, she shivered.

Brid steered her up to the house and gave her dry clothes, several inches too long but otherwise fitting fairly well. Grace, pulling on underwear in one of the many bedrooms, trembled. Brid waited just outside the door, she knew. *She has never even seen me like this.* Grace stood, staring at the dress she held in her hands.

The alcohol still had just enough of a hold. She thought, "Why not?" and dropped her dress to the floor. Exiting the room, she opened the door clad only in her brassiere and underpants, and found Brid hovering just on the other side.

Eyes wide and drawn up to her full height, she gasped, "What in the name...lord, the state of you!"

Grace quickly began to retreat. *Well, that was a bad idea.* From the safety of the bedroom, she heard Brid clearing her throat.

"It's not that, I mean, you are tempting, but, time and place, ya know?"

Grace knew. She had just been drunk for the first time in her life, and almost drowned. Her mother-in-law lay dead in her home, which needed a great deal of attention. Not the time for romance, surely. But when? She wondered, and sighed.

"Yes. I do know."

An anguished sound, not quite a word, constituted the reply from the other side of the door. Grace grimaced, thinking that this was the first time she had proposed some rash act, the first time Brid had sensibly refused. Grace wondered if there would ever be a right time, because as usual something more pressing summoned her.

They took the back way across town and snuck into the house, where Marta still lay on the sofa, not much worse for the wear. Brid helped Grace clean up the kitchen, gave her a quick kiss and exited. Feeling nauseous and sweaty, her head pounding, Grace folded herself into the chair beside Marta's cooling body and dozed. Ma would say she was knackered.

8

GRACE

An angry, familiar growl scared her out of her sleep. Her heart hammered in her chest as fear enveloped her. Dominic. Were the blows about to start again? But he stopped as soon as she awoke and shortly her heart calmed. The living room, where Marta lay serene and, Grace thought, looking a bit stupid, had darkened, too much for the party she had planned. Maybe she could light candles.

Dominic's fierce bark jerked her back. "What the hell's the matter with you? What if someone had walked in?"

She didn't bother to answer, instead noticing the red stain on the sleeve of his work shirt, wondering how it got there, and more importantly how she could get it off.

"I'm certainly not going to get any help from your mother now that she's decided to sleep all the time."

 Just as his hand started its downward arc toward her face she ducked and slid down to a crouch on the floor. She held herself there in a tight ball, her hands over her head, waiting. After an eternity of minutes she heard him walk away. Her breath returned.

She stood and tiptoed to the lamps, lit them and tried to exit the room like moonlight, sliding out with no attention drawn to herself. No hope of that. Dominic's father stood in the doorway, his huge frame blocking most of the light from the kitchen. He spoke, but his voice seemed to come from far away.

"There will be few neighbors and cousins and uncles. You need to cook food."

Grace felt panicky. Cook food? Meals? Baking was hard enough. Had he seen her attempts to cook? Marta always came to the rescue. And Tomas didn't mean sandwiches, the only thing she could produce competently.

He gestured toward the body. "We move her after dinner. It will only be one day. We bury her on Saturday." He turned to go.

Grace, incredulous, stood like stone. "This is your wife," she said, her voice flat. "You've been married to her for forty years. And you have nothing more to say than that? Like this is one of your pigs, or turkeys! The old man turned back to her. He came close, closer than he had ever been, put his face in her face so that she could see every whisker and smell the liquor on his breath.

"She is dead, girl. Your tears don't bring her back."

Marta's features had stiffened, her hands were crossed exactly as Grace had arranged them. Hours ago? Or days?

Marta, dead? Her only ally in this godforsaken place, gone? How would she survive? She felt fear surging through her chest and arms, down to her fingertips. She didn't really even know how to make retes, or anything for that matter. Suddenly it seemed as if a thousand lamps would not lift the darkness from this house. She touched the purple flower, then headed toward the kitchen, trying to breathe. The house might collapse on her if she didn't remember the recipes: how much lard remained from what they had rendered last week, and whether it would be enough for the baking she had to do. More baking than she could imagine. Her heart beat faster.

She stood still in the kitchen for a few minutes, waiting for calm, hoping the panic would settle. But her heart kept beating so quickly she thought she might faint. Sweating, she paced the room, intoning the alphabet to keep herself calm. A-B-C-D… She didn't know why she did it, but it helped. The sight of her garden and spotting new blooms on the snow peas helped her begin to breathe more slowly. After a long while, the dreadful feeling passed and she reached for the lard jar.

Claire attended the funeral along with Grace's parents. They were the only Irish, plus about ten Hungarians from the bars or the church. Dominic stood beside Grace and wept, surprising her. She had never seen any emotion from him toward his mother. One of the Hungarian women chastised Grace later for not crying, but Grace had been trying to remember if she had ground the coffee. She knew better than to offer that excuse. She had been imagining Marta could take care of the coffee. No. The casket brought her back to reality. Marta would not remember the coffee. Tamas would supply the whisky for those who needed it; at least she didn't have to worry about that. The men lowered the casket into the earth, and people threw dirt and then flowers. Grace and her mother's eyes met and then Grace felt lost. She would remember not the dirt or the flowers or the casket or any of the words, but the empty space above them, where there should have been forgiveness and love.

Her mother's words echoed: "You will work harder than you ever imagined and you will not complain."

She rubbed her raw, chapped hands, felt a small surge in her belly and knew she would do exactly what her mother had said. It seemed the only choice left.

Did she glimpse Brid's face in the back of the crowd? Did she give a little wave? Grace knew it could have been only her imagination.

Somehow life continued. At first it seemed impossible: no Marta, only these two grumbling men with their hunger and hateful words. She felt grateful that their exhaustion prevented them from bothering her more. They earned their pay not for how long they worked, but for how much coal they produced. Ten hours in the dark holes of the earth, at least six days a week, to make enough to hold bodies and souls together.

Grace mentioned Mother Jones once. She'd heard tales from her father. He had told her, "If that woman still fought for the miners' rights, it wouldn't be like this."

But Tamas and Dominic shook their heads. A woman? And Irish? No.

Tamas often came home, ate dinner, took his bottle and went straight to bed. If he did go out he came home early, and Grace noticed his body beginning to bend, the creases in his face and neck deepening. His eyes dimmed, and his old self often seemed more pitiful than frightening to her.

Even Dominic seemed to soften a little after his mother's death. She would find him on Sundays, sitting in the yard, staring at the trees. For a brief while his drinking lessened. When he took to the bottle again he became enraged less, and it seemed important to him now that she forgive him afterward.

"The drink makes me a different man. And if you could keep the house clean, make the bread like Ma used to…I would be happier. I wouldn't drink so much. It wouldn't happen, I swear."

A different man? *No, the same man, unleashed.* She tried to keep her stomach from heaving, tried to reach out and touch him, smooth his hair, but she couldn't. His embraces smothered her. He repelled her. She guessed her house, cleaner than any other on the street, did not cause or intensify his drinking.

All through her pregnancy she longed for Marta, partly because her workload had more than doubled, but mostly because there was no one to ask about all the things she didn't know. *What about the birth pangs? How do I know if they're the real thing? Am I getting too big, or am I not big enough? Is the baby okay? And where in the world did you put the canning jars?*

The birth almost killed her. The contractions came closer and closer, then, after an eternity her mother and sister appeared. Grace had been alone for hours and she barely knew them, barely knew herself, and did not know or care why they had come. Sweat-drenched hair, cold, clammy skin. Almost senseless. Only pain.

The men were gone from the house and didn't hear her screams. "I am a mountain. Mountain begins with 'm.'" Her eyes, barely open, formed two short straight lines across her face. "You begin with 'm.' You are a mountain too. M M M M M."

Ma gently put her fingers to Grace's lips and whispered to Claire, "Go and get Chloe Burke."

"But Ma, she won't come here."

Grace opened her eyes. "I am a big coat. Coat begins with 'c.' C C C C C. Claire begins with 'c.' " She clutched her stomach and arched her back, as the next contraction started and the pain took her again.

"Go," Ma repeated. "Tell her it's Nora O'Dowd who needs her. Tell her to come." Her voice sounded like a mill boss, louder, stronger. She was not asking. Claire threw her coat over her thin frame and fled.

Chloe Burke appeared quickly, an older woman whose stout body and huge hands made her well suited for her work. She had been delivering babies in Summervale for forty years and knew her job as surely as a coal miner working a seam. "Ah, he's just a bit twisted around. We'll get him right. Push girl. Now stop a minute." She pulled at the slippery feet, gently but firmly, pushed her hands up into Grace's body, and finally found his thighs.

After an hour of this Claire sighed. "My family. My husband is waiting for supper. And my children."

Ma glanced at her beautiful, uncomplicated daughter. "Of course. Go then. I'll see you tomorrow." A quick kiss and Claire disappeared.

Thirty-eight hours of labor produced a ten pound infant in the early evening. The baby finally emerged, feet first.

"Thick thighs," Chloe declared. "He is a Hungarian, to be sure."

Grace heard his screams, full of outrage. It seemed he had been forced out. Ma exclaimed, "Ah, I've never seen this! Is she going..." Blood splattered over the rumpled sheet. Grace, lying on the bed, barely conscious, heard Chloe say, "She'll be fine. Let's clean things up here, and then keep her in this bed for a day, if you can."

Ma held him before leaving, tears in her eyes. "I should come to see you more often. I will. I promise."

Grace gazed up through her exhaustion, and mumbled, "Promise begins with 'p.' P P P P." Chloe heaved a sigh, and hugged Grace's mother. "Go then, Nora, and come back soon. She will need you."

Ma met Tamas and Dominic at the door. Through her haze Grace heard her mother say something like, "She will stay in the bed until I return. Make sure she is fed, or the baby will not survive." Nora struggled into her coat and headed for the stairs. Tamas steadied himself in the doorway, glanced at the baby squalling in Grace's arms, and said, "We call him Andras. Means 'Man.' He will be man."

Dominic added, "He will always fight. He's already fought for his life."

Grace slept until her milk came in. When Ma returned the next morning, she was sitting up in the bed, nursing Andras. He sucked like a starving creature, pulling at her until she winced. Grace managed only a few sentences, the most coherent being, "How did you know my time had come?"

Ma continued to concentrate on the pile of rags and dirty sheets, and said only, "Brid."

The one word Grace wanted to hear. She didn't question how Brid knew.

The second baby, born exactly one year later, came quickly and easily. Grace's mother and Chloe attended again. This one was a girl, so the men didn't even notice. Grace named her Eileen, from a song called 'Eileen O'Grady' Brid had sung to her once. Two years later another boy, and Grace again thankful for not having the terrible struggle of Andras's birth repeat itself. They named this boy Itzaak (to laugh), and he slipped into his place in the family.

Early one January morning Grace felt a low rumbling deep in the earth. The Fenwick mine. She knew another life had begun in her body—swollen breasts, every smell assaulting her nostrils. She grabbed coats and scooped Itzaak into her arms, ordering Andras and Eileen to hold onto her coat. They began the long frantic run toward the train, joining dozens of other women pulling their young ones, half dressed and screaming with delight or terror. Feet stamping on the dirt road. Hushed voices, occasional moans. Running, walking, hobbling, however they could get to the train yard, where they jumped onto boxcars (Grace heaved herself, with some help) that would carry them to the mine. The temperature could freeze a man's mustache. Later she would remember nothing of getting there, only being there. Women without gloves or hats, they had come so quickly, shivered violently in the bitter cold. The Fenwick mine had exploded, their husbands trapped inside. They could only wait and pray.

Grace wanted to flee, but a voice in her brain kept saying "Stay." The cold and the horror of it were a double-edged sword, stabbing like a crazed murderer. The few bodies they had brought up were freezing on the pallets where they lay. Methane gas poisoning, due to a fire exploding in one of the coal seams, spread through the mine in less time than water takes to come to a boil. Ice blocked the air vents, blocked air from the men. Anyone could guess how long they could draw a breath, though everyone knew it could not be long.

By mid-afternoon two rescuers had been killed in their attempt to reach the miners. The families were told that many of the bodies probably would not be brought up. Still they stayed, only leaving when a pallet carrying their dead husband or son appeared. The mothers tried to shield their children, who would stop and stare at a body. Grace watched them.

They probably think the man is only sleeping. I hope.

To her relief, the little ones finally ran off to play. Andras, five years old, charged out onto a frozen field near the mine, where he led a game of chase and capture on the ice.

There were muffled cries and pleas as people stumbled back and forth across the frozen field, words that were not yet words uttered from the mouths of the bereft. They did not grieve; they did not yet comprehend their loss.

Grace stared at a coffin, rough and assembled quickly with coarse pine boards. It sat there in that frozen hell, so small, and yet so full of anguish and fear that she could not understand why it hadn't burst. Despite its size it possessed a power. When people went close they quieted.

The few other bodies still lying in the yard without families to claim them seemed only to want some dignity in death, to be prepared, to be lifelike and fine as possible. The women prayed, but that seemed meaningless to Grace. By late afternoon it seemed likely every man in the mine had died. They could see it, the smoldering caves in the entrance, bodies brought out a few at a time, white and silent. Still they prayed.

What God could they beseech? The same one that had allowed this hell to erupt? Grace and the others learned later there had been virtually no air in the mine that morning. The ventilation had been nonexistent due to ice and consequent blockage. Dust in the shafts forced the methane gas to streak through like lightning. For some unknown reason, the ventilation had not been checked that morning like it usually was.

Grace could not understand what the women were praying for. That this same God would reverse it? That suddenly these broken bodies and lives be restored to life, so these wives and mothers would again be at home feeding chickens or washing sheets?

Three men emerged, carrying three bodies, stumbling in the light and cold. The crowd sucked in their hopes, holding them until the men gestured 'No.' There were no more down there. They had barely escaped and the fire was spreading too fast.

One of the men, Dominic, carried his father's lifeless form.

They brought the body home and Grace prepared it for burial. Tamas had died quickly, Dominic told her. He himself had escaped only because he had been halfway out already, going for some forgotten tools. Tomas lay only twenty feet behind his son, where he had been felled when the explosion occurred. Dominic managed to get back and pick him up. Since his chest still rose and fell it was worth the risk, but by the time they reached the opening, Tomas' breathing had ceased.

Grace did not lose her mind to fear or dread the way she had when Marta died. Dominic helped her lay the old man on the table in the parlor, and then left to drink and cry publicly at the bar. Grace knew he needed that.

Washing the old man's body, his penis laying flaccid as the rest of him, she wondered why this most unattractive organ ceded to men enormous and often monstrous power.

She tried to hate him, recalling the times he had belittled and demeaned her. But now she felt nothing, not even pity. Tamas had had his share of fun in life, those nights he and Dominic spent doing God knows what. Clapping her hand to her father-in-law's belly, she chuckled. "Can't be sitting around here daydreaming, you old goat. There's work to be done."

Her children, born of Dominic's clumsy demands, stood at her side like little soldiers at the gravesite. She felt nauseous and only wanted to sit. Four year old Eileen held her hand lightly, her tiny fingers barely touched her mother's palm.. Itzak, barely walking, and Andras were both delighted when the time came to throw dirt on the casket. Grace quickly subdued them, then suddenly had to hide her own chortling, which kept trying to escape like errant children. Dominic squeezed her hand hard, fingernails digging into her skin like dull knives, but it didn't help. People glared at her. She put her head in her hands and pretended her giggles were sobs born of grief.

9

GRACE

Then back to the house and the yard and the baking and cleaning and cooking. Rendering lard and washing clothes, hand wringing them and hanging them out to dry. She added manure she hauled from Mr.Krushksad's stables to her garden, pushing it in a crude wagon made of planks and tires that went flat almost every day, working the ground till the soil turned black and fine. Potatoes, tomatoes, beans, onions and more had to be weeded. She cared for them as if they were gold, because they often were--the only food to put in her children's hungry mouths. Jozef, her fourth child, came the summer after the mine exploded. As if to offset her other troubles, he cried little and slept well.

She sat nursing him when Dominic's friends carried him into the house late one afternoon, in the fall of 1923. Grace had just thwarted Andras' attempt to hit Itzak over the head with a cleaver he had somehow unearthed in the kitchen.

They had hauled Dominic home from the bar many times before. The men tipped their caps. One volunteered, "Mule kicked him, ma'am. I'm always telling him not to get too close, but he never listens. Teased that animal till it got mad. And when a mule gets mad, well, you know. We tried to clean the wound. Probably ought to see a doctor."

They left quickly. Dominic lay white-faced and still, blood trickling from near his temple. Grace traded a chicken and two dozen eggs for the doctor's services, which turned out to be negligible.

"Probably has a concussion, and he's hurt a disk in his neck. That will be a problem for the rest of his life. Close call, but he'll be alright. Just needs to rest for a few days. Keep him awake for a while. Give him some of these pills when he starts moaning. He's going to have a heck of a headache. And these will stop him up, too. Don't give him too many, no matter how much he demands."

Grace's mother had taught her about the old medicines: herbs like aloe vera for constipation, turmeric for stomach problems, ginger and garlic to fight pain and infection. She put them to use immediately and never bought more of the doctor's pills, which would have cost them several meals at least.

Dominic lay in bed for a month, helpless, demanding and still wanting her at night when her exhausted body fell into the bed. When he reached for her, wordless, she did not resist. Daytime always found her working. She grew fruit trees, pruned them, picked the fruit and made jellies and pies. Late at night she sewed and embroidered for the wealthy women of the town, ornamenting fine jackets and dresses. That brought in much needed cash. The lamplight turned low made her squint until she had to admit she could not see the fine stitches. One of her customers complained, so she sold one of the turkeys and bought a pair of eyeglasses.

Dominic recovered but did not go back to work for over a year, and drank "to ease the pain," he said. He slept a good deal of the time, less abusive although still belligerent. Despite her efforts she could not keep the house clean and tidy, socks and toys everywhere, the smell of sweat and the street. Her children were growing. Andras now six, big and temperamental like his father. Eileen, a sweet child, buoyed by her mother's strength, already helped with the chickens and the cleaning. Itzaak, thin, reedy and sneaky as a cat. Jozef, still a baby, was big like Andras but happier. He still crawled into her lap whenever she had time to allow it.

Grace didn't mind when Eileen slipped into the back yard, away from her brothers' constant fighting and noise, and played in the dirt. Sometimes she found a flower and brought it inside, put it in a glass. Grace knew young children needed time to play, but she needed their help, as tiny as they were. Andras had already mastered slipping through the cracks between his chores--taking out the garbage, feeding the pigs. He disappeared toward the backyard and then out of the sound of her voice before Grace could stop him. She would stand at the back door and call his name until her throat ached. One day she didn't stop calling for a half hour, and a neighbor, Mrs. Nyilas, came and found her pulling at her apron and weeping. The kind woman took her inside. "I can't do it," Grace moaned. "I can't do it alone. It's too much."

"Yes dear," her neighbor replied. "I wish I could help, but I've got my own brood and chores. It's endless."

She stayed a few minutes, patting Grace on the shoulder, then left, but returned on Saturday and helped Grace render the lard and make a special retes for Dominic. He let her go out with Mrs. Nyilas the next afternoon, and they walked up to Pittsburgh Street.

Mrs. Nyilas bought them each a soda at the drugstore, and they sat at the booth, sipping. Grace told her about nights when she couldn't sleep, days when all the children were crying at once and exhaustion rendered her almost unable to move.

Mrs. Nyilas began to tell stories of growing up on a farm in Hungary, and how for fun she and her eight brothers and sisters would hide the pig.

"Hide the pig?"

"Yes. It would take the nine of us to carry him out to the far pasture. He kicked and squealed, mad to be taken away from his pen and his slop. Hard work, but fun. My father had a fit, but he never thought we could do it so we didn't get in trouble."

Grace laughed in spite of her life, then felt an ache in her face: her muscles, unused to curving upward. Mrs. Nyilas told her another story about her mother getting the laundry mixed up and her father trying to fit into her brother's pants in the half-light of dawn.

"Did he get angry?"

"Oh no. How could he not see how funny it was?"

I can tell you how he could not. Dominic would bring out the belt.

Mrs. Nyilas gently pushed Grace's hair off of her forehead. "You are different when you have a smile. Pretty."

"My children don't recognize me when I'm happy."

"I doubt that's true, dear."

Mrs. Nyilas covered Grace's small, rough hands with her own. Grace's permanently furrowed brow exposed her distress. Tears sat in her eyes like small ponds about to overflow. Grace pushed back memories of two young girls in the woods above the town, running like captive birds freed from their cages, certain this world of love and delight would last forever.

"The house just keeps getting messier, I can't keep the clothes clean and Dominic yells and curses. I think I'm going to crack open like an egg, and my self is just going to fall out."

Mrs. Nyilas chanced a chuckle, but silenced it quickly. "You need help, or you will, how did you say, crack? Your mother?"

Grace cast her eyes down to the soda glass. "It's hard because she's across town and has her own work to do. She comes more than...she used to."

"Mmm-hmm," replied Mrs. Nyilas. "I saw her a month ago, I guess."

"She hasn't much cared for my choices. But at least she comes, every now and then. She likes the children."

Mrs. Nyilas didn't reply. After a while, she leaned across the table. "Little Mike Krushksad has grown some whiskers."

She nodded to a table in the far corner, and Grace rose up in her seat a bit to see the lanky young man slouching there, pulling at the minimal hairs on his chin.

"He's trying to cover that chinless chin, but it's not working," she murmured, continuing to keep her voice low. Mike had a temper and did not appreciate ridicule.

"A chicken with a pig's chin," Grace whispered back. They kept their giggling quiet.

Mike started toward them but checked himself at the last second and bent to tie his shoe. An old, transparent move, familiar to Grace. She had become invisible when she married Dominic. In the eyes of the town she simply didn't exist; she had disappeared somewhere as a teenager. Where she went, no one knew, and certainly no one wanted to follow.

Another round of seasons, winter always the worst. The house never warmed, no matter how much coal they burned, and the children shivered in their thin clothes. Always hungry mouths to feed. She gave the children bread and beans, but that much did not stave their hunger. She began to slip back into her imaginary world more often, leaving the boys playing in the street, walking away from the house in the late afternoon. Once Dominic found her down by the railroad tracks.

"What the hell are you doing?" he demanded.

She gazed at him, her blue eyes dulled. "I am waiting for a train."

"These are freight trains, you idiot. Now get home to your children! The house is a mess, a damn mess. Get going!"

He began swatting her behind and continued the whole way up the street to their house. Neighbors peeked from behind their curtains and tsked.

Another day she sat cross legged in the garden, throwing mud clumps at her children while they gleefully threw them back. Brown streaks dribbled down pants and dresses and the back of the porch. Everyone except Eileen thought it hilarious, until Grace stood and began to cry. Howl really, like a coyote. Eileen went to get Mrs. Nyilas, who got

Grace inside. Eileen cleaned things up before their Pup got home from up the street.

It had gone on for months, growing worse and worse. Dominic's Aunt Sofia came from New York in the spring to help. Unfortunately, her assistance consisted of befriending and gossiping with every meddlesome wife on the street. She deemed housework not fitting for her talents.

One evening Dominic sat in the living room moaning, as Grace peeked from behind the door. His aunt perched beside him on the sofa. Sofia didn't mince words. "The neighbors say she talks to the chickens!" Here she raised her hands to her mouth and belted out "Bwaaak, bwaak, bwaak! But too she has names for them! Nora! Nessa! Child is not right!"

Dominic frowned at Sofia. He sat hunched in his chair. "You think I don't know that? I live with it! Guys at the bar snicker when her name comes up. Say things like, 'Hey Dominic, that pretty little Irish thing you married ain't turned out so good. My wife says she sees her dancin' in the backyard, by herself. Guess them Irish ain't exactly what they seem. Crazy Irish fairy!' They think it's funny. Even my friends. They call her the 'crazy Irish fairy.'"

"She is crazy. Does you no good. She walks around like ghost, we have no dinner or we eat slop. Children running around in rags. You need to get rid of her. I stay a little longer, then you need help."

"What do you mean? Throw her out? Divorce her? Or..."

"Shush. I just mean she goes somewhere, where someone takes care of her. We can't. Maybe she gets better with rest. In old country, old woman..."

"This ain't 'old country'."

Sofia ignored his mocking her accent.

Dominic scowled. "Who you got in mind? Who you think's going to take this pathetic wreck and just keep her? Nobody. Our people aren't going to take her. And her people, they gave her to us, remember? They won't take her. We're stuck with her."

Eileen had been sitting in the corner, supposedly immersed in her book. No one noticed her until she spoke. "I know someone who would take her." She paused until her father looked at her. "Mrs. Boyle."

She was six. Dominic ignored her, but not her comment. He addressed Aunt Sofia again. "I can't let that woman take her. She's crazier than Grace. You know she lives out there in that old Boyle house by herself? No decent woman does that."

"Okay choose. Either joke, or starving man, eating swill every night. Living in pig sty, children like wild horses." Her wig slipped as she shook her head, rendering her scowl ineffective.

Grace walked into the room, her hair bereft of its neat bun, drifting toward her shoulders like a deserted bird's nest. Her eyes were bright, her dress dirty and worn.

"Well, I guess Marta is sleeping again tonight! So, Grace makes dinner again."

She hadn't slept in days. A strong wind could have knocked her down. She could see Dominic eyeing her and tried hard to ignore him. Things were not quite right, she knew that. The light that had always lived somewhere within her had gone and she could no longer prevent herself from falling apart. The children seemed to be everywhere, dressed in any way, fighting or crying always.

Dominic stared at the floor. "Okay. I'll talk to her."

Brid Boyle stood on the rickety porch, Grace cowering beside her. Dominic's movements were quick and jerky. Grace recognized his humiliation and rage, so close to the surface they could easily erupt and spread like lava. She had seen the empty whisky bottle and kept her silence.

Grace sensed Brid, who stood placidly waiting, stifling her amusement. Dominic shoved the cardboard suitcase toward her, never making eye contact. "Jus' take her then. Take them."

Her children stood with Grace, wide-eyed. Eileen in the front, straight and determined. Andras with his fists clenched, Itzak and Jozef trembling. "I don't care what ya do with her. She's a wreck. Don't bring her back till she's right."

Brid hid her furor like a goddess who could destroy this human in an instant, but wouldn't, because it would not amuse her. She answered calmly.

"She's a wreck because you and your father wrecked her. I will take her and heal her, but she will decide whether or not she comes back."

"Ya can't keep her, you wicked woman. She's my wife. You'll bring her back." He rose up to his full height and glowered down at her. His aunt positioned herself at his side, clutching his arm and nodding as though she were the final authorization.

Brid turned and led her charges down the front steps. Eileen continued, first in line. Itz clung tightly to her mother's skirt. Joe's tiny fingers clutched Brid's as she gripped the suitcase in her other hand. Andras, the seven year old warrior, strode ahead, his short, thick body straight and tight and Itz followed, mimicking his brother as best he could.

A grueling hour's walk through town and out into the old forest They entered Brid's house. She slipped her arm through Grace's as they approached it, the birches around them nodding like kind grandparents.

"Ahhh," breathed Grace. "Tis lovely." Brid gazed at her, and knew she had already begun to heal. She hadn't heard her speak like an Irish woman in so long.

The children collapsed onto soft beds upstairs after Brid fed them bread and hot chicken broth. They were dirty but it didn't matter. They had been dirty for weeks, baths could wait.

Joe fell asleep with his hand clenched. When it opened, a small black stone fell onto the floor. A child's treasure. Brid picked it up and tucked it into his shirt pocket.

"I remember the last time we kissed," whispered Grace as Brid laid her down on her bed in the front room of the cottage.

There were tiny pink flowers sewn into the bedspread. Cherry blossoms, Grace thought. So pretty.

"Not now love." Brid pulled a blanket from a closet filled to bursting and covered her friend. "Rest now."

She stood over Grace, who had already begun drifting into sleep.

"How did I let you go?" she whispered. "How could I let them take you and do this to you? You are my Grace. You are my saving grace."

Grace surprised her by answering. "It doesn't matter, my love." she said. "Grace remains."

Grace and her children returned home two weeks later. She approached the porch with a 'spring in her step,' as Ma would say, having determined to make the best of her situation, for her children. Dominic, apparently at work, had left traces of himself everywhere in the house. She set to work cleaning and cooking. Leaving Brid had been hard, very hard, but Grace knew where her loyalty had to lie. Her children wandered around aimlessly. She imagined they craved something familiar and safe in the climate of fear that had been created here. She missed Brid's touch more than she had ever missed food.

10

GRACE

The years disappeared into the continuing vat of poverty, struggle and longing. A world war came and went, and along with a flu epidemic the likes of which none of them had ever known. It killed tens of millions worldwide. Young men from their town had gone to war and not come home. Friends and neighbors sickened and died. Then, came the worst time of all. Some were calling it the great depression.

President Hoover had just left office, and many people thought the new president, Franklin Roosevelt, would set things right. Grace believed he was the one to solve the great problems and alleviate the suffering of the country. Pup thought he was a socialist. Just another reason for them to disagree, Eileen thought. She listened and read, and, at fifteen, began to form her own opinions.

Despite all of the world's suffering and their own poverty, Eileen and her brothers thrived, thanks, she knew, to all of her mother's efforts. Joe was only twelve but big enough to be a teen, although Eileen thought his soft heart belied that, sometimes he acted more like a ten year old, and sometimes he seemed more mature than Itz and Andras. Lots of times, in fact.

In the late afternoon she observed her mother, sitting stoop-shouldered in the kitchen. Rare, to see her sitting. Mum flicked her eyes to the floor when Pup and his whisky stink walked in demanding supper. Rising like a reluctant soldier, she did not look at him but straightened he back. She wrung her hands and murmured, "Just a few minutes," and turned to her daughter. "Eileen, I need you."

Mum always needed her. They stirred the pots and pans in the small, dark kitchen.

Later, Mum began to climb the narrow steps into the darkness of the second floor. Eileen stopped reading when she heard the step creak. Mum leaned on the rail and placed one hand on the small of her back just as she took that first step. Eileen realized her mother's exhaustion for the first time. She had never thought about that before, but in that small moment her life began to change like the slant of sunlight coming through the window, moving toward darkness.

The house smelled of cabbage. Eileen sat on the couch, its fading rose-colored cover almost threadbare on the seat and armrests. Her brothers didn't sit on furniture; they wrestled with it, just like everything else. But they were out now, playing football or finding some kind of trouble, so the house had mercifully quieted. Eileen whispered a word of thanks, and read her book.

Later that night, she heard the grunts and groans coming from her parents' bedroom down the short hallway. Mum let him do that to her, Eileen thought, hating it. She tried singing a song Mum had taught her, but she could only remember "it's a long way to…something." The sounds in the other room ended abruptly, then the bed creaked. She didn't want to think about this but imagined her mother, lying there with her eyes open, planning what they'd have for supper tomorrow.

An hour passed. Eileen heard Pup get out of bed. That meant Itz had snuck out of the house again and Pup heard the window crack. She went to her window, waiting for the soft night air to be broken by his bellow. He was such a sucker for Itz's game, every time.

Hearing the first few words, banging the quiet like a sledgehammer, she stepped back a bit. "Izaak, come back to the house. Now."

Then the train whistle blew, clear and distant but coming fast through the town like a dog after a bitch in heat. She chuckled. Itz had done it again. He probably hadn't gone far, just crouched hidden in the neighbor's yard, smirking and making Pup furious.

Back in bed, Eileen pulled the covers up over her shoulders. Joe had rolled off his mat on the floor, still sound asleep, snoring. If Pup heard any other noise, he would storm into the room, yelling, since he didn't want to yell out the window any more.

She dozed, dreaming of Mum's retes, almost tasting it in her sleep. When she awoke, her first thought brought her back to reality quickly. Mum would not make retes tomorrow or anytime in the near future. Desserts were rare in their house; there hadn't been any extra money in a long time.

Retes, their favorite dessert, took hours to make. Mum rolled out the thin pastry and stretched it, then she rolled it up and out again. Over and over, around and around the table. She reached under the dough and pulled it out a little farther till it fell over the sides like a tablecloth. Finally, when it spread out as thin as an old penny, she trimmed off the edges with her hand and added nuts and sugar and fruit. Into the oven, and a sweet and salty aroma filled the house. Joe still denied it, but once he actually cried for joy when he took the first bite.

Eileen knew Mum had learned to make retes from her mother-in-law, the grandma who had died long ago. Once she asked Mum how she could just keep working and working that dough. It seemed so boring. She didn't talk the whole time, but after she finished she said, "Sit down here with me."

Eileen perched on the edge of her chair. "My mother named me Grace because she knew from the moment I came into this world that I would have a hard time with that." She hesitated, her eyes lowered. "With being graceful. She told me once that part of gracefulness is patience, and part of patience is acceptance. When you quit fighting so much, quit believing the world should go your way, you will find some happiness." Mum nodded, almost to herself.

Eileen understood that she wasn't talking about the retes only, but she wondered where Mum had found some happiness.

When the boys smelled retes baking, they surfaced out of their various holes, running. They waited to see whether Mum would cut the pastry or save it till Pup got home. It depended on her mood.

116

Sometimes when no one fought or whined or needed something, Mum, almost happy, told them about the old days. Back then there were no cars and her father made horseshoes. Eileen and her brothers had never met him. He had died before they were born. Once Mum whispered to Eileen, "He didn't much like me." Eileen felt Mum's sadness fall over her like a blanket.

Pup's old neck problem acted up and he missed work, and lounged on the couch ordering everybody around. "Somebody fix these pillows. I'm in agony." Somebody usually meant Eileen. She didn't mind, because then he said she was the only good thing in his life. But she did feel sorry for Mum.

Pup did not get paid until he went back to work. They ate watered down chicken soup. The fruits and vegetables had just begun to blossom, or had just been planted. Only a few potatoes and beets were left in the basement. The boys had each lost weight and Eileen sometimes felt a little weak-kneed.

Pup's pay at the end of his first week back to work was almost nothing. Eileen watched him from her corner chair. *You can't stretch what's already so thin you can see through it, like the soup.* And that's what their money was—so thin it could be seen through. Mum appeared to be stretched to the point of breaking. Joe would say "she goes away," and she really did. If anyone asked her a question and she wouldn't even hear it. Sometimes she talked to herself. Words no one understood.

Mrs. Boyle came to visit every so often, never when Pup might be home. Eileen didn't know why he didn't like her. She could be so much fun, Irish as a shamrock, Mum always said. Once, she showed Eileen how to find

117

shamrocks in the grass. Said they'd bring her luck. Eileen thought maybe it they didn't bring her luck because she was half Hungarian.

When Mrs. Boyle visited they sat in the living room and talked about old times. Well, Mrs. Boyle sat. Mum hopped up and down for more tea. She straightened the little crocheted covers on the sofa at least twice. They were beautiful and they didn't need any fixing. Mum could make anything beautiful. When Eileen was little she sewed two dresses, real cloth and tiny red flowers, one for herself and one for Eileen. They wore them together everywhere: to the store, to a picnic once, even just to go for a walk.

But when her friend arrived Mum couldn't stop fidgeting.

Mrs. Boyle brought scones. Eileen thought scones might have been the best thing the Irish had ever done. The dough resembled Hungarian pogacsa (biscuits), but better, she thought. Blueberries or cranberries baked in with a crispy sugar on the top.

"What is that other taste?" Eileen asked.

"What other taste, love'?"

"I don't know. It's like nothing I've ever tasted. Sort of sweet and warm."

Mrs. Boyle and Mum both chuckled. "Let's just call it my secret ingredient."

Eileen didn't care that much as long as Mrs. Boyle brought them and she got to eat one. She knew just enough about baking to help Mum when she needed it. She'd rather be reading.

Her brothers didn't know about the scones. She told Mrs. Boyle to hide them if the boys suddenly appeared. Mrs. Boyle nodded and said, "Ha! Sure 'n we'll be accomplices in that." When Eileen found the word in the dictionary, she thought she would be happy to be an accomplice with Mrs. Boyle.

The two women had been friends since they were kids, a long time. Eileen liked to be there in the living room with them, sitting sipping tea. After she settled down, Mum acted differently than any other time, but it never lasted. When Mrs. Boyle left, she would be sadder than ever. And then she'd go back to work.

11

JOE

They would have started earlier, but Mum stopped them in the backyard. "You're not going anywhere until that wood is chopped, Andras. Winter will be here before you know it. And Jozef, the job takes two. Itzaak, I've been telling you about that garden for days. It's so full of weeds I can barely find the vegetables.

Joe studied his mother in the sunlight. She had always been a puzzle to him, coming and going like embers in a fire. Sometimes she would tweak his cheek, even give him a little hug. Other times she seemed to not even be there, going about her work without being aware of any of them. Eyes somewhere far away, hands moving, then she stiffened at the approach of another person, whether child

120

or adult. Like the robots Joe had read about in a book Itz lent him.

"Quit dreamin." Andras snarled. "We'll never make it to the river if you don't get to work." He was sixteen, bigger and stronger than anyone else Joe knew.

Andras held the ax above his head like a mountain man. Joe knelt on one side of the log, watching his brother and hiding a chuckle. Scary and funny at the same time. *He should be in the movies. Always the big guy.*

They sliced back and forth with the cross saw for an hour, stacked the wood, then headed the quarter mile down to the river with Itz, stopping briefly at Old McManus' house to throw stones at the windows. Andras had splintered one a month ago and today, a long crooked crack still snaked up the glass. Sometime in the near future it would shatter noisily. Joe thought he would like to see that–shards falling to the porch floor, a small but interesting explosion, something to pass an odd moment or two. The unshaven, smelly McManus, huddled with his bottle, might not notice it until he stepped on a piece of glass and then no doubt he would curse. The boys had learned from him.

Early May, late morning, warm but not yet hot. Mum said there had been some rain last night. Joe dragged one foot through disappearing puddles, leaving lines on the sidewalk. Andras took the lead as always, followed by Itz. They understood Andras needed to be the leader and they knew he could beat the living crap out of any of them if offended, or sometimes just for the sheer fun of it.

Out of the corner of his eye Joe spotted Old McManus tripping off the second rickety porch step. The guy didn't so much fall as careen, descending like a stray firecracker ember. Joe didn't say or do anything, knowing McManus hadn't been hurt because he'd seen this happen ten times before. McManus' muscles and nerves, coated with whisky, probably protected his bones. Joe hurried on, catching up with his brothers. Then he heard shuffling behind him. McManus, from the sound and smell. *Darn. He's going to follow us to the river again.*

Joe nudged Izaak. "Itz, he's behind us."

"Aww, shit." Itz slowly turned his tall, skinny frame toward the old man.

Itz rolled his eyes but spoke softly. "Sorry you old souse, you can't play. Go home. "

Itz' chest puffed out as he spoke. The old man didn't even seem to see, much less hear him. He continued his shuffle, veering close to the street sometimes, and onto his neighbors' yards. Joe couldn't help but sneak glances back at him. He tripped once again but didn't fall down, just fell behind.

They crossed the railroad tracks. The mountain that loomed over the town on the other side of the river dwarfed even the giant mill. Andrew Carnegie owned the steel mills where many of the town's men worked, slaves to the enrichment of him and his henchmen. If the workers were lucky enough to escape injury or death in its maws, they emerged old before their time, and poor as when they went in. But few of them complained--thoughts of the misery of the old country kept them meek in the workplace.

For the boys, work in the mill or the mines, where their father worked when he and if he worked, lay the distant future. For now, the river beckoned. In the early spring, when the water could still bite with cold, the river was a test of endurance, and each of the brothers had their need to withstand it. Two hawks circled overhead and Joe shuddered on top of his shivering. Hawks always reminded him of death, so casual about their killing, swooping down and back up again. Just lunch really, for the hawks.

McManus wheezed up behind them as they shed their clothes and strolled toward the water, Andras headed toward the big eddy closest to the bank, the other two just behind. They eased themselves in, knowing from experience its depth did not permit diving. Itz started swimming fast out into the river. Andras yelled, "Slow down you idiot," and Joe's heart started to pound, because Andras wouldn't worry about his brother any more than a hawk would cook you dinner.

Lots of days the boys could make it across the river by starting up high on their side. They would swim diagonally upstream toward the other side, trying not to be pulled downstream by the current. Today though, the water surged toward the dam. They must have had a lot more rain upriver in Marville and decided on an unusual summertime release from their dam this morning. The river ran as swiftly as an unbroken horse.

Itz disappeared into the sunlight, so bright on the water that at times the dancing ripples of light were all they could see. The noon whistle blew its cruel and strident song, taunting the workers, "It's only noon, you still have six hours to go." Joe watched Andras yelling at Itz. He felt numb even as he began to realize the short distance between his brother and the dam.

For centuries the Allegheny River zigzagged through western Pennsylvania, creating towns and economies. Twenty miles downriver from where the boys swam, it merged with the Monongahela and formed the Ohio River, giving birth to the great, groaning industrial city of Pittsburgh.

The brothers loved the river, but like most lovers it did not always behave well.

Itz vanished. Joe swam back toward the bank and stood in waist deep water, staring. His body would not move. *Get the rope, get the rope.* But he couldn't remember where they kept it. Finally he pushed out of the water and ran up onto the bank, grabbing the rope from underneath a fallen oak log. *How could I have forgotten?* He ran back toward the bank with the rope coiled over his shoulder. Joe knew he couldn't pull this off. The river had already pulled Itz too far downstream.

Itz's head bobbed to the surface, his light hair dark with water. Just before he went down again, about twenty feet offshore, he opened his eyes and stared straight at Joe, who heard a silent plea breathe out of every pore in his body: "Help me. Please help me." Finally Joe uncoiled the rope and hurled through the air toward Itz. It traveled in slow motion, like a long fly ball sailing out toward centerfield. *It seems like there's so much time, and you catch or miss it and it's over. One split second and you're a hero or a fool.*

Anyway, where is Andras? Always the big hero. He should be taking care of this.

The throw hit the water at least fifteen feet from Itz's flailing arms. Joe retrieved it and heaved it out again the water, this time further but it landed just upstream of Itz. Joe's energy and strength melted like wax from a candle. He saw Itz's head bob once more to the surface as his body rushed toward the dam. His brother gazed ahead at his fate, knowing the dam meant death.

He would not be the first of the dam's victims. Drowning in the 1930's in Summervale, Pennsylvania was an undesirable but not uncommon fate. Bill Doherty had gone over just two years ago, swimming out there by himself one gray winter day. Some said Bill had done what he meant to, having endured the blows of his drunken father's stick long enough. Bill hadn't said anything to anybody that morning, just went down to the water and did the one thing he could do without parental recrimination. The body had bruises everywhere. The family said they must have been caused by the dam, and nobody disagreed except old McManus in the bar that night.

"No dam ever did that to a boy. No dam would be that mean."

Everyone got quiet then because they knew he spoke the truth. Too many of them had inflicted the same kind of punishment, often and hard. They called it discipline. Fewer blows fell for the next few days, but boys knew they would return.

What would Mum say if I have to go home and tell her I couldn't save Itz? Would she drift even further away?

Joe reached the bank and turned to see Andras swimming upstream toward Itz. He felt a hallelujah force its way up through his body and softly out of his mouth. *But it's impossible—the current's too strong. He'll never make it.* Besides, Andras hated Itz more than he hated anything. Three years apart, he and Itz fought for lead dog until they were almost teens, when Andras started growing into the body of an offensive lineman and Itz began to bring home books from school and read. The nighttime backyard brawls lessened when Itz learned to step aside from Andras' anger, but the feelings between the brothers persisted. No such thing as brotherly love. They avoided each other and spoke, when necessary, in grunts and groans learned from their father. When Itz wanted to taunt Andras, when his daring overcame his common sense, he would make fun of the older boy's lack of brainpower, using words that Andras didn't understand.

"You are such a cretin you make imbeciles smart."

Itz continued the diatribe even after Andras threw punches, always smiling like some martyr seeing salvation not in the valley of the Lord, but in his own intellect.

But now Andras muscled his way out into the river, his smooth, oily body moving through the water with the confidence of a seal. Joe knew Andras could swim, could do any sport better than every boy and practically every man in town. He won the awards, taking the trophies with a grimace and almost always smashing them later. Nobody ever clapped for Andras. Nobody wanted him to win.

By sheer act of the will Andras possessed in abundance, he fought his way upstream until he could throw the rope effectively. When Itz caught it, Andras started to pull against a current stronger than himself, stronger than Pup even, and he won. He grabbed Itz's arm and gripped him around the chest. Joe half expected Andras to choke his brother or pull him down under the water. Instead, Andras swam out of the current toward the shore, directly past Joe, not a word, just swimming with his last ounce of strength.

Itz, motionless and white as snow, was still breathing. Joe still stood shivering in the water, thigh deep, feeling like a fool. He should have, could have offered to take over and pull Itz the rest of the way to the shore, but he hadn't. Even exhausted, Andras wielded control, and watching them, Joe felt the familiar demons of failure and shame on his

126

shoulders. Andras reached the water's edge, pulled Itz up and left him lying there while he crawled further up onto the shore.

Joe waded up ad onto the bank and helped McManus, sobered by the scene, drag Itz out of the river. The old man, his skinny ropy arms totally unfit for the job, nonetheless did it quite well. He held Itz's shoulders while Joe dragged Itz's sagging white body and laid down there with the same delicacy Mum took when laying scones in a baking pan. Andras had collapsed to his hands and knees, his chest and belly rising and falling more swiftly than the hawk. He gulped in air and almost collapsed on each exhale. But he didn't. Wouldn't.

Joe stared at Itz and imagined what Andras would say when his breath returned. *"You're pathetic. This old drunk could do a better job than you. Standing there like a little girl. Not worth a shit."* Joe could hear him say it, could feel what he would feel when it had been said. But even worse, Andras said nothing.

Itz hadn't moved or even opened his eyes. Joe had never seen him be still for more than a few seconds. He never sat in chairs, always on the edge of them, poised for flight. Always with toast in his mouth on his way out in the morning, slinging one arm, then the other, into the jackets and yelling goodbye.

Joe reached for his and Itz's shirts, laid them over him. Andras panted a little more slowly now, trying to rise from his knees, keeping his eyes on Itz. Finally he attacked.

"Well, what do you think, hero? You've done so well so far––tell us what we should do now."

Joe croaked, "We should take him home." Andras nodded his head and Joe realized the big guy had actually been a little bit afraid. Unbelievable, but Joe could see the slight tremor in his hands and chin, like McManus after a day without drink.

Then Itz burped the loudest burp they'd ever heard. Water gurgled up and spilled out of his mouth and ran down his cheek and neck like a pot boiling over. He opened his eyes and they all breathed one identical breath. Joe watched Andras. Itz sat up and vomited, and Joe saw Andras' expression change from concern to disgust. The Andras Joe expected.

"Jesus Christ, idiot." He sounded like a cat, ready to pounce, that low growl in his throat. "You're a moron, a f-cking retard. First you make us almost kill ourselves because you still don't know how to swim in this river. Now you've gone and messed yourself. Sickening." He spit for emphasis.

Itz sat up and shook his head. Water sprayed out in spiral. "What happened? I swam out there fine and then, I don't know, it just broke up."

Seeing Itz at a loss seemed as odd as imagining Andras being kind. Nobody knew how to react.

McManus stood there whittling a piece of driftwood. "You just lost your bearings, boy. You went out a little too far and got in trouble. You're lucky for your brother."

He pointed his knife toward Andras and then went back to his whittling. The boys had never heard old McManus string that many words together. Joe wouldn't have been surprised at this point if Andras began to fly.

They all stumbled back up to the house, with Andras and McManus half-carrying, half-walking Itz.

Joe, hurrying to keep up, couldn't help himself. "Why'd you save him? You hate his guts."

Andras still panted slightly. "Because he's my brother. You don't let your brother go over the dam. You just don't."

They took a few more steps, then Andras spoke again. "The son of a bitch."

Joe saw Mum's friend Mrs. Boyle leave the house as they were coming up the street. She tucked her head and her shoulders in like he did when he snuck away from trouble. Why would she be sneaking? Joe squirreled that away in his nest of uncertainty.

Mum's face froze when her sons dragged their groggy brother through the back door. Joe tried to assure her. "He's alright." The boys waited through her moment of shock, then her rush toward Itz. She cradled his face in her hands, studied his slitted eyes.

"What happened?"

"He swam out too far," Andras began the story in a calm, low voice. "He got a little crazy."

"Andras saved him." Joe thought stating Andras' heroism early might help.

Mum took Itz's shoulders, then helped him lie down on the floor.

"Joe, go and get the pillow from the sofa. And bring a blanket."

129

Joe could see her fighting for control. He flew to the living room and back, handed her the blanket and pillow. She placed the pillow under Itz's feet, then took the blanket and covered him.

"What are you doing?" Joe asked.

"She's checkin' him. Shush." Andras took his eyes off Itz as he spoke. Joe knew he wanted to act like he didn't care.

Mum murmured, "His skin is warm, even though he's wet. That's good." Joe saw her hands quiver, just like Andras' had.

"But he's awfully pale, and still breathing hard. Did he vomit?"

She asked Joe, not Andras. He didn't know why, but it made him feel a little better. Then Andras had to butt in.

"Yea, but mostly river water."

Joe stared at his brother. *That's not true. But maybe I remember Itz puking more than he had.* It seemed a little hazy already.

"He's pale, but not much more than usual. And his breathing is calming down already." She pressed two fingers into his neck. "Pulse is a little rapid. Stands to reason he's weak." She studied him. "How are you?"

Itz raised his head, and immediately lowered it. He nodded but didn't speak.

"I think we'll have Doc Torok come over and look at you."

At this, Itz murmured. "No. M'fine. Pup finds out you paid a doc, kill me."

"Your father does not have to know. The doctor will be here and gone before he punches the clock. And you will pay me back out of your newspaper money, plus chores you'll find to do around the neighborhood." She glanced up at her sons, relenting. "I'm sure everybody did what they could. Thank you for that." Itz allowed her to take his arm. Before she helped him up she spoke again. "Itzaak, you have a brain for a reason. Use it more." No yelling, no blows. Mum.

Mum bit her lip. "You need to spend some time in bed. Joe, how about taking him upstairs?

"You think you can handle that, Panty-Legs?" Andras stood sneering.

"Then Joe, I need you to get to the doctor's office and ask him to come. Find out what time. If he can't come before two, get Dr. Meany. Remember, no later than two."

"Yes. No later than two."

Joe knew she had asked him to make him feel better, but he didn't. Panty-Legs.
Andras knew how to hit where it hurt.

131

12

EILEEN

Late July, and the cherries were ripe. It surprised Eileen when Mum made retes. She seemed so tired and distant, and she never had enough time, always cleaning and cooking and worrying.

Just enough flour, and Mum begged some sugar from the grocer. The retes sat there gleaming in the kitchen, long gleaming rolls just barely holding the fruit. Mum held up the first slice. "Let's see," she cackled like a witch. Eileen's heart skipped a beat.

It had been a while since Mum acted strange. Once, right after Joe was born, she started lining up the chairs in the kitchen and telling them to behave or she would have to put them out on the street. Another time she told Andras to bring the chickens inside. The younger kids didn't remember that, and they never talked about it. For three days Eileen cooked and cleaned and waited on Pup while Mum lay in bed and stared at the wall. Pup behaved better toward Eileen but he never said thanks. Eileen had never heard him say thanks to Mum either.

Mum held the slice of retes up higher and cackled louder. Eileen watched everyone's faces register fear, like rabbits when the hunt begins. Andras headed toward her and tried to put his arms around her. She shook him off like a wet dog.

Joe whispered, "I'm scared."

Mum heard that and she seemed to come back a little. Andras tried again, approaching her slowly and talking softly. Eileen remembered her mother's unseeing eyes from that other time.

"Mum, you're tired, let's have us a rest now. C'mon, here's a good seat for ya here on the sofa. Won't this be fine?" Andras' affected brogue seemed to soothe her. She put the piece of retes down and let him lead her into the living room.

The rest of them stood there staring at the pastry.

"We might as well eat some." Itz reached toward the table. Joe didn't lose any time either. "She meant to give it to us before she got, uh, confused."They were on it in a second, tearing it and stuffing it into their mouths, devouring the retes like wolves.

In the living room Mum, who was always there and always working, who hardly ever got angry, would normally ask them to settle down please and then went about her work. But Mum had just cackled like a witch and withheld the prize pastry. It was frightening and upside down and they all knew it.

Eileen tiptoed into the living room, where Andras had helped Mum down onto the sofa. Limp, with glazed eyes, she chanted letters: "KMB KMB." Andras, having done what he figured was his duty, disappeared into the kitchen and left his sister with Mum. The sounds of the brothers arguing increased with his arrival.

Mum was still mumbling but calmer, and Eileen worried about what was going to happen in the kitchen. Fifteen feet away, and she knew exactly when Andras realized the only thing left of the retes was crumbs. Standing in the door way she could see both Mum and the circus in the kitchen. Andras stared at the table, incredulous.

"You didn't save any for me? Where's mine?" His brothers were gazing at the crumbs sitting sadly on the plate, like they were hoping looks might reproduce at least one piece of the retes. Joe attempted to secretly swallow his last bite. Itz traced the corner of a broken tile on the floor with his toe. Then he snickered, quietly but audibly enough for Andras to hear. Itz could never stop agitating.

Eileen screamed as Andras bolted across the room, hitting Itz hard and low. Itz's body plummeted toward the floor. There wasn't enough room for a good fight. If Pup were there he would yell, "Take it outside," from behind his newspaper, without so much as a glance, so that's what she did. Mum started mumbling and shifting around again. Eileen sat down on the sofa and began to stroke her

134

mother's arm. It seemed to soothe her but the furor of her brothers' fight increased and there was no choice but to return to it.

They had taken it to the back yard. Andras was after Itz, who hadn't tried to escape so much as relocate in a more advantageous position. He climbed the plum tree where he proceeded to hang from a branch and kick Andras in the head with both feet. Andras bellowed but hadn't succeeded in scaling the trunk himself.

Eileen finally had enough of the sight of blood flowing from heads and noses or even the loss of consciousness, with somebody lying twisted in the sparse grass of the back yard. She knew why they did it. Pup had done it to them since they were small, and it seemed that males settled their differences with a fight. Still, this was too much. She ran upstairs to her parents' bedroom. Pup had shown her where the shotgun lay hidden a few months ago, probably because he knew it wouldn't be wise to hand his sons another weapon besides their fists.

It surprised her that Andras hadn't figured out the gun's location. She knew he suspected Pup owned one and it killed him not to know. Eileen could not believe she hadn't killed him with it, either. She eased the gun up out of the false bottom of the cedar chest Pup's father had brought from Hungary: Pup's one beautiful possession, with little filigree etchings on the top. He must have had dreams then. What did he do with them?

The gun weighed a ton. Pup had been drinking, "in his cups" as Mum would say, when he showed it to her. He did say only to use it in an emergency. Mum was sitting on the sofa half out of her mind and the boys were trying to kill each other over pastry. Eileen decided that constituted an emergency. She hoped she didn't shoot anybody. She just needed to get their attention.

The lid stuck and she couldn't get it closed again. This had happened before–a double curse. It slowed her down when she didn't have the time and if she didn't get back to it before Andras; he might see it and know. Fortunately he didn't focus or observe things well. She left the lid open and ran down the steps like a mad woman. The real mad woman still sat on the sofa, talking to some invisible person. Seeing Mum that way from the stairs scared Eileen even more. She slammed through the back screen door and got another shock. Joe flailed on top of the heap, trying to pull Andras off Itz. All three boys had blood somewhere on their bodies and clothes, and she saw no sign of any of the insanity stopping.

The sight of Joe in the fray of flailing limbs pulled her away from her fear. She'd always known she could and would do this if needed. Pointing the gun toward the sky, she shot once. The sound reverberated in the valley as the bodies untangled, pop-eyed and stock still within a second. Nobody licked his wounds; they just sat, legs splayed out in front of them like four year olds waiting for a snack.

"Andras, Itzaak, get off this property and don't ever fight here again. You can kill each other anywhere you want except within a hundred yards of this house."

They still didn't move, so she figured she had their attention and might as well continue. "Do you have any idea what you're doing to Mum? If I had to work as hard as she does and watch my sons fight like polecats and never have a decent word for each other, I guess I'd get a little loopy too."

136

They stared at the gun. Eileen suddenly felt exhausted. She pointed the gun at Andras, then Itz, who slowly and carefully moved away from her, hardly lifting their behinds off the ground. They pushed with their hands back through the grass. It would have been funny, but she had this cold metal pushing against her palms, waiting to explode again. Joe stood back in his standard position, motionless. She detected a glimpse of amusement in his eyes, as she lowered the gun farther.

"You. Come with me."

He joined her as she backed into the house, mounted the stairs and stood in front of the cedar chest.

"Why in here? Why not the basement? There's lots more places to hide it in the basement."

"Because they won't come in here, mostly. And if they do, they won't spend much time."

Joe hadn't been to their parents' bedroom in a long time, years probably. He gazed at the old wooden frame bed with its sinking mattress and Eileen knew he wanted to be outside, running and yelling in the sunlight with his brothers, no matter what they were up to.

"Why do they keep that little bed in here?" he asked, gesturing to the corner. "Nobody's used it in a long time."

She shrugged. "Sentimental reasons I guess." It was funny, but not really.

"I need you to help me with this now. I can't get the lid closed."

They fit the gun back into its hiding place. Joe broke a tiny piece of wood as he forced the lid closed. They hoped nobody would notice and straightened the cedar chest into its exact previous location. She dusted her hands–which felt as dirty as if she'd just finished sweeping the porch.

"That's that."

"Well, okay," Joe murmured, although she knew he probably wondered whether wielding a weapon against your brothers and shooting it in the air like Tom Mix in one of his Westerns should actually be concluded with "That's that." Still, it gave him his escape route; he disappeared in a flash.

She turned toward the bed, hands still shaking as she ran her fingers along the worn bedcover. Hand-stitched with beautiful minute flowers of many now-faded colors, Mum embroidered it before she married Pup. She taught Eileen when she was just a little girl; spending hours sitting on the porch in the evening after the three boys were asleep. Eileen's left-handedness made it hard for them both, but Mum knew how to wait and praised her daughter's efforts as if they were works of art. It seemed like a hundred years ago.

In the living room, she slept, snoring softly and occasionally mumbling in her sleep. Most of her words had to do with food or the scarcity of it. Things like "not enough yeast," and "more eggs."

Mum sat up and called 'Andras', sounding like a hatchling threatened by a hawk, then immediately lay back down again. Her eyes were still closed when Joe reappeared and started to walk toward her.

"No, let her sleep,"

"She needs some help. A doctor or something."

"We cannot afford that kind of help. The only thing we can hope is that sleep will cure her. C'mon."

Joe put his hand on the smooth round wooden disk at the bottom of the stair rail. Mum appeared peaceful, but the strain and exhaustion gripped her like a fist seem.

"Joe, one day you're going to start thinking less and moving more and the whole world's going to take notice. You are going to move mountains."

He rubbed his hands together, front to back, back to front, staring at her.

"You are."

His lips lifted slightly on one side. The Cierc smile. He started toward the back door.

After an hour or so, Mum sat up, rubbing her eyes. Eileen tiptoed toward her, and Mum grimaced. Months ago she had pulled one of her own teeth, fortunately on the side, not one of the two in front. They couldn't afford the dentist.

"I took a nap?"

"You had a long night last night, remember? Itz had a fever."

She frowned and her eyebrows lifted. "I stay up lots of nights with one of you kids or waiting for your father to...to get home from work. I don't take naps."

Eileen hoped she didn't remember anything else. Mum stood and Eileen attempted to distract her.

"How did you have such big babies?" Five feet tall, 110 pounds.

Mum's small, thin shoulders lifted slightly toward her puzzled face.

"Andras weighed nine and a half pounds, the midwife said. A big baby, hard birth."

She turned toward the steps, her face darkening like the woods at twilight. "And he gets worse every day. So now I'm going to have to kill him. Kill my baby."

Mounting the steps slowly, gripping the bannister, she tolled like a funeral bell. "Kill him. Kill my baby."

Eileen ran up the steps and grabbed her, whose face was blank. "Mum, where do you think you're going?"

Mum kept repeating those horrible words. Her shocked daughter led her back down the steps. The bottom step creaked. Eileen couldn't believe she would notice that, in the middle of this. She lay awake some nights listening; hoping Andras or Itz would be sober enough to remember to skip that step, so there would be no scene with Pup.

Mum did not resist as Eileen lowered her back down onto the sofa. Her eyes shone like the glaze she put on her cakes; she didn't seem to see anything. Then she started abbreviating her chant, using letters instead of words. "K My Baby. KMB." Her cheeks were flushed and her skin clammy. She had disappeared and an infant had replaced her, blessed or cursed with the power of speech and knowledge of the alphabet.

Eileen thought she'd heard the screen door slam. Maybe one of the boys was back. She prayed for it to be Joe.

"I could use a little help in here!"

Joe appeared at the door, and it felt like salve on a burn.

"I need you to get help. I can't do this alone. She's getting worse. Get someone."

His eyebrows lifted. "Who?"

Eileen groaned. "I don't know who. I don't care. Somebody. A woman. Not Pup."

Joe fled.

Mum wrung her hands and made no eye contact, trying occasionally to raise herself up, then lying back down. Once she seemed to return from her frightening journey and her eyes filled with tears.

"I'm sorry, honey. You should be dancing."

"Oh Mum." Eileen forced her tears not to fall. Not the time for emotion. Mum's shaking hand traced the edge of the sofa.

"ABC. A is for Apple, B is for boy, C is for Cabbage, A is for Apple."

"Sweet Jesus, what now?" Eileen moaned.

She decided to get her mother up off the sofa. They walked around the living room and into the kitchen where a fresh chicken lay on the counter, waiting to be transformed into dinner for six healthy appetites. Mum didn't notice it.

"EFG. E is for eggs."

"HK, HBM." Now she couldn't even keep the letters straight. Out of desperation Eileen tried to hold her, but couldn't. "HKBKRKFK."

She waved her arms like a conductor to the beat of her alphabet chant. The sun reflected patterns on the dull red oil tablecloth and broke up small bits of light as a breeze whispered through the plum tree, rustling its leaves. Mum ran her hand over the cloth. Eileen hoped again she had come back to herself.

But, "Time to kill the baby," she said, picking up the cleaver from beside the chicken. Eileen berated herself for not having noticed it there. As Mum raised it there could be no way of knowing who she might go after--Andras, one of her other children, herself or the chicken.

"Grace O'Dowd, put that down." Mrs. Boyle's thundering voice reverberated as she threw open the back door.

Joe stood at her side. "I saw her walking down our street." He shifted his feet.

"That's okay, you did fine."

Eileen stared up at Mrs. Boyle, the tallest woman she knew, who now lived on the other side of town. *What in the world was she even doing in the neighborhood?*

She moved toward Mum, patting Eileen's hand and saying, "I just sensed she needed me. It's always been that way."

Eileen didn't really understand but she didn't care. She needed Mrs. Boyle. She leaned against the kitchen wall, weak with relief. Mrs. Boyle approached Mum. She lay her arm around Mum's shoulders and spoke in soothing tones.

Mum nodded and slowly lowered the cleaver. Eileen watched Mum's tears run down her cheeks. She began to sob and between her gasps for air they heard, "NM NM NM."

Mrs. Boyle kept patting her shoulder and saying "There there, Grace." She glanced at Eileen. "I think she means No More. She has had too much work, too little money, not enough kindness."

Eileen wanted to be anywhere but in that kitchen watching her mother cry.

Mrs. Boyle gazed at Mum for what seemed like an eternity.

"I'm going to take your mum to my house for a while, darlin'."

Her hair in disarray and her face tear-streaked, Grace frowned and gazed at Mrs. Boyle.

"But but when will you be back? Pup will be home soon and he'll want his supper."

Eileen knew Mrs. Boyle had to decide between one bad choice and another. Leave Mum here or leave the rest of them alone with Pup. The two women moved steadily toward the back door, Mrs. Boyle's arm still wrapped around Mum, who shuffled like an old lady. She didn't even say goodbye.

Eileen repeated, "When will you–she, be back? How long will it take?"

"No tellin ', dear. I'll take care of her and you're going to have to take care of your Pup and those boys."

They turned away and continued out the back door and down the porch steps.

Eileen stood still but she couldn't help but notice the sunflowers blooming behind the garden, some of them opening almost to full perfection. Mum loved the sunflowers. They always seemed to lighten her spirit, but now she turned away. Mrs. Boyle slumped for just a second, something Eileen had never seen her do.

Then they were out to the street, good as gone, leaving Eileen in a daze, her hands hanging limp at her sides. She thought her life would be a lot easier if Mrs. Boyle had taken her brothers instead of Mum. Standing in the doorway staring, trying to take it in, she suddenly wanted to break things, run down to the river and jump in with her clothes on. She stomped back into the kitchen and pounded the counter with both fists, yelling, "No! No!" Eventually she felt her hands aching. Finally she sat and listened to the odd quiet of the house.

Maybe I could run away with my boyfriend. Get married, have a little house, just the two of us. No kids, at least for a while. But this is what I have to do, take care of this crazy family until Mum comes back.

She walked across the room to the counter, picked up the cleaver, and began to cut the chicken.

13

EILEEN

"Did you make this?" Pup asked, taking the biggest piece of baked chicken from the plate, then helping himself to the boiled potatoes. He took a bite of the chicken. Eileen was not sure how to answer. *Is it good that I made it or bad?* They were seated there, or what was left of them: Pup, the boys and herself. She'd only had a few minutes to tell her brothers what had happened, where Mum had gone, before Pup came in, and for once they were smart enough not to ask any questions. In fact they were behaving so well at dinner that Eileen would have been surprised, except this whole day had been one long string of the unexpected.

"Where is your mother?"

He addressed the question to the open air.

"She's out walking," said Andras, and Eileen wondered how such a stupid lie could cause anything but more trouble.

Itz's answer was about as bad. "She's over at the Masons taking care of the grandma." Great, Pup would love hearing that Mum was taking care of someone else's relative while he ate rubbery chicken.

Joe stared at his empty plate, saying nothing. No surprise. So she told Pup the truth, including the alphabet talk, the nap on the couch and the cleaver problem. She stared right at him as she spoke.

Pup chewed as he listened. He frowned a little but maybe it was the chicken.

"She'll be okay Pup, and I can..." but Eileen stopped as he raised his palm toward her. He poked his finger into the roof of his mouth, trying to get something out that was stuck, probably the chicken. His fingernails were black around the edges and underneath. They were always black from the mine, so he didn't see any sense in cleaning them. They would just get grimy again. His face and skin were dead white with only the black residue, and he always smelled like coal, dirty and oily. The mine came home to their house every night.

He put his hands down on the table and stared at his children. "Eileen will cook. We will eat whatever you cook but I'll expect it to get better. Andras, you will keep this house in order."

"But that's women's w..." Andras started, but Pup's eyes bored into him. "Yes sir."

"Itzak, you will see to the outside–there's still the root vegetables and we'll need them to get through the winter."

Itz nodded, and Eileen knew he thought he'd gotten off light but Pup hadn't finished. "The chickens, the hog and the goats—keep them fed and where they belong. People in Summervale don't like loose animals. Jozef, keep the wood pile stocked. I hear there's a tree down over in the Mason's yard. See what you can do. Make sure there's enough wood for the fireplace and the stove."

"Yes sir."

They ate, heads bowed, no sound. Pup pushed out his chair. "That's it." He pointed toward Eileen. "She's in charge in the house. If I hear one word about any problems from you..." He pointed toward his two oldest sons.

"I'm going up to town," and he exited through the back door, the smell of his sweat and coal lingering in the air. They sat like newly hatched chicks for a few minutes. Joe finally spoke. "He didn't even ask! He didn't even ask about her."

Itz sneered, "Yea, that's our Pup. A real sweetheart."

"He's doing his best, Itz. Like we will." Eileen didn't know if she really believed that, but it seemed the best approach at this point. "He's tired and without her it's going to be tough. He's not as bad as you guys make him out to be. It's not an easy life."

"Yea, she's right. You watch what you say, boy." Andras turned his bulk toward his brother. "He's still our Pup. He's just trying to make the best of a bad situation. Eileen, are there any more potatoes in the pot?"

Joe suppressed a smile. *That's just what Pup would ask.*

"I can't imagine this house without Mum. I mean, she's always here. When do you think she'll come back?" Joe had his head in his hands, looking like Mum when she was tired or worried. He knew his question couldn't be answered.

"C'mon, let's get out of here." Andras finished chewing his last potato while he spoke. "There's a game down in the park and it's not too late to get in."

"Oh no you don't." Eileen stood up. She felt like she still had the gun in her hands, and the boys were flat on the ground in front of her. They would listen.

"You heard him. I'm in charge in this house and that doesn't mean I'm going to do all the work. First, you guys are going to help me clean up here."

Andras snorted. "The day I do dishes…" He pushed back his chair with a loud scrape and started to leave the room.

She finished the sentence for him. "will be today." He kept moving. She had to fire a shot to stop him. "Because if you don't, you will have him to deal with, not me. Keeping order in the house means helping with the housework, not just trying to be your brothers' big boss." She really couldn't believe her own voice. It had some new notes in it that she hadn't heard before, and she knew her brothers heard them too.

"Are you threatening me?" He tried to sound gruff to counter her but it came off as whiny.

"No. I'm stating a fact. Itz, you bring in what's left of the food and put it away. Joe, you bring the plates and scrape them off into the garbage. Andras, you wash the dishes."

To their stunned surprise she added, "I know you're not good at this but I expect you'll get better."

As she watched them drag themselves into the kitchen to begin their assigned chores, she thought, "This is the only good thing that's happened today."

During a sleepless night she realized that her father expected more than supper on the table. He wanted her to assume complete responsibility for her mother's job. The thought of it staggered her. It seemed like she was trying to run the length of a football field with her brothers on her back. They would of course be bellowing constantly.

She rolled over and over in the bed. Two boys sprawled on mats on the floor. Itz slept downstairs—he made the living room couch his bed, even though Mum didn't like it. She said he would wear out the couch and they would never be able to afford another. Eileen knew that Mum really feared him getting out of the house more easily. But when she heard her daughter's stories of the routine nighttime skirmishes, she knew the exchange of her beloved couch for nocturnal peace made sense. So Itz stayed downstairs.

149

Still, even two boys could not comfortably splay their growing bodies on mats strewn on the bedroom floor. Pup refused to buy more beds; they wouldn't have fit anyway. It just meant hours of sleeplessness for Eileen while they thrashed and kicked and grumbled and snored like a pride of lions. Just now, Joe's foot landed perilously close to Andras' ear. It could have escalated into a full scale bloody fight, like the ones so common downstairs in the daylight. Nobody wanted to wake Pup. Not many things made him angrier than losing sleep.

As if in answer to prayers none of them had ever learned to pray, Joe rolled over away from Andras, who grumbled and rumbled some more, but sleep pulled them back from the edge of violence.

Joe slept through the whole thing, like a baby. It hadn't been that long since he took his thumb out of his mouth while sleeping. Fortunately none of the other boys had discovered this.

The next night the meat was overcooked. Eileen had had to deal with a sick piglet and clean the chicken house (Itz did not consider that his responsibility), plus getting her regular work done. She did not apologize. When Pup grumbled about the meat, Eileen asked Joe to please pass the potatoes. It took a while for Joe to accomplish this. Pup tried again. "And the potatoes are cold."

"They are not cold..." Itz started an unusual attempt at crusading for his sister, but Pup's grimace silenced him.

She said nothing, just cut her potato so everyone could see the steam rising out of it. She knew instinctively that making eye contact with her father would be a mistake, so she kept her head down. Nobody moved. Even a quiet snicker now could have meant disaster.

150

The moment passed. A new space opened inside her, like the first time she put her head underwater or when she had to crawl along the edge of the roof to rescue a baby turkey lodged up there.

Eventually Pup commented less often on her cooking or cleaning or anything she did. Once she cooked exceptional chicken and dumplings—just the right size, just the right softness, just the right amount of salt—almost as good as Mum's, Joe said. Pup grunted something like, "Harrumph," but more guttural, more phlegm. A compliment. Eileen tensed a little. Then, Pup released a long, loud blast from his back end. She pressed her lips together, trying not to giggle. Shortly she heard the whisper of a snicker to her right, along with the slurping of the dumpling gravy and scraping of chairs as the boys got ready to run. Pup swallowed his last bit of dumplings, placed his spoon beside his bowl and stood. The room quieted.

"Ha szerencséd és bátor vagy, akkor megtalálod a helyes utat. Valaki, aki szeret téged. Gyermekek, akik tiszteletben tartják."

His eyes and mouth drooped, and he looked sad, not angry. Maybe he had had some good whisky that afternoon.

Pup turned on his heel and left with as much dignity as he could. Eileen felt sorry for him, knowing he had been mocked for the first time by his own children. He stood in the street for a moment, long enough for her to come out to the porch. He turned back to her.

"You don't know. No family of my own. No one to back me up."

151

Does he mean his dead parents? Or maybe because he had no brothers? No one to joke with or fight? She couldn't ask. Wouldn't.

He turned and headed up the street before she could register her surprise and sadness. Then turned and walked back into the tumult of her brothers' lives.

Inside, Itz fiddled with his knife, trying to balance it. He looked at Andras. "What did he say?" After a pause he added, "The Hungarian."

Pup had taught Andras Hungarian when he was small. Itz, a baby at the time, did not remember that, but Eileen did. Andras didn't answer Itz's question. Instead he started clearing the table without being reminded. Itz reached for the dumplings and Eileen slapped his hand.

"No more tonight. You've had enough and he'll need this for lunch tomorrow."

Itz backed off.

Andras didn't knock anything over or run into anybody, He usually did while clearing the dishes.

Joe said, "I guess that mystery will not be solved," but then Eileen told them this:

"He said, 'If you are lucky and brave you will find the right way. Someone who loves you. Children who respect you.'"

Even as she repeated his words she couldn't believe he said them. 'Someone who loves you?' Nobody talked about love in this family. What did he mean? And he hardly ever spoke in Hungarian. Itz grimaced—his face twisted up as

152

he tried to figure it out. They didn't even ask how their sister knew the Hungarian.

Pup had not taught it to her when he taught Andras, but he didn't realize that a tiny child could listen too. No dictionaries, stories without books, language without instruction. She inhaled the language like a dolphin devouring a school of fish. It became part of her automatically, without thought or effort. She knew enough to understand her parents' words at the dinner table. Mum had learned her Hungarian from Pup's mother, Marta. Eileen understood enough to know that they were not usually happy.

Joe brought the plates to the kitchen. He, of course, wanted to know how Eileen had ever learned the Hungarian word for 'love.' Surely Pup had never said it.

"From Mum, of course. She would say it to one of us, one of her babies every now and then. She would say that word. 'Szeretlek.'"

Joe stood in the doorway, flexing his arms and pulling his shoulders back. "I miss her."

She choked a little. "If you don't stop growing you're going to be a monster."

"I know. I could probably take Andras down, if I weren't scared to try."

She pressed her lips together, trying unsuccessfully to suppress her amusement.

"No, no. You could be twice his size and still not take him down. You're not mean enough. Now go play football or whatever you're going to do and get out of my way. I've got a few things to do." She swatted his behind with a dish towel as he exited.

The next morning at dawn the fire in the bedroom had dwindled to lukewarm ashes. Eileen shivered in her thin nightgown and almost stepped on Andras, asleep on the floor. Stocky, broad and tall, his torso long, tight with muscle, his shoulders wide and his legs thick and powerful. Built like a true Hungarian, a boy in a man's body. Like Mum said, in many ways he was still a baby. Unfortunately, way stronger. A few college coaches considered him, although he could only play sandlot so Pup wouldn't know. He wouldn't let them play for the high school team because if they got hurt it would mean extra bills they couldn't afford. Eileen didn't blame him. The money, like their dreams, never lasted long.

Once Itz had tried to play anyway. He practiced with the high school team right up until the first game, in the field behind the school. Joe told Eileen that five minutes before the game started, Pup walked up to the school, onto the field, right up to Coach Farkas. "Cierc doesn't play." Turned and walked back to the house. Never looked at Itz.

Coach shrugged helplessly. No arguing with Dominic Cierc. Itz left the bench.

'Time is wasting,' Mum would say. Eileen lit a fire so her brothers wouldn't rise to this icy stillness. She hurried into her clothes and crept out of the bedroom as soon as the coal caught in the tiny fireplace. She glanced at yesterday's flowers on the kitchen table and remembered there would be no school for her again today. She loved school—reading, history, science, anything but algebra. She just didn't get that. But no matter, she couldn't go anyway.

Also, no school meant no Lane. They had been together for two years. He finally noticed her after she'd been in love with him for a long time. He asked her to go for a walk after school, and she risked Pup's wrath (she should have been home helping Mum) to say yes. A sweet Irish boy, he had straight dark hair and blue eyes that seemed to gaze right into her heart. She knew Mum and Pup never talked to each other like she and Lane did.

Mum knew about him, even liked him, except she said things like, "Don't give yourself to him—you'll be sorry." Really, they just walked and talked. And kissed a little.

Eileen started thinking about losing Lane. Even if she could get to school she'd only be able to see him in small snatches, because she'd have to be home right after. Some other girl, prettier or smarter, would catch him, because she would be available. Lane loved her, but she understood how impatient boys were.

I'll just grow old in this house, taking care of this horrid family, working myself to the bone while my mother stays at Mrs. Boyle's, playing cards and eating scones.

Down in the kitchen she put the kettle on and stirred some oats into the big pot. They would be tumbling down the stairs soon, tussle haired and full of sleep. She sat down in her mother's chair and considered. *I could run away, but where? Winter's coming. And how could I take my books?*

She heard Pup's bed groan, and everybody starting to patter around. Some days she had to wake them, but if they were roused they got up pretty quickly. Except for Itz, he would be the grumpiest. How that boy hated to get out of bed.

She turned the kettle low, then hurried to the stairs to hush them coming down. Pup would sleep till noon, since he

155

worked the night shift. Mum said he never got enough sleep. Maybe that's why he got mean sometimes. Maybe he couldn't help it. Plus those boys would make anyone bad-tempered. Keeping them quiet so he didn't wake up like a hungry bear in the middle of winter must have made Mum crazy. Well, that and other things.

She waited for the pot to boil as the sky began to lighten. She wanted to live somewhere far away, read books all day long, and go out dancing every night. Instead she made breakfast.

Andras and Joe exited, rowdy as ever as soon as they finished wolfing down their oatmeal. Itz, who had arrived late, scraped the pot. When not a morsel remained, he stood up and turned toward her, grimacing. His thick eyebrows slanted toward the bridge of his nose.

"What?"

He shifted his weight onto one foot. "I had a dream about Mum."

As far as Eileen knew, that was closest Itz had ever come to self-revelation. She stopped washing dishes, dried her hands on her apron.

"Yea? What happened?"

"Not a lot. Anyway, I should get going. Already late."

She couldn't let him go, although she feared he would leave anyway.

Gently, like stroking a lamb, she persisted. "Itz, tell me about your dream."

He hesitated, facing the door and not her.

"Well, she wasn't married." He chuckled. "I don't know where we came from, but they don't tell you that in dreams."

"No, they don't." She smiled.

"She lived with Mrs. Boyle all the time." He pushed the words out.

"Hmm. Anything else?"

"She looked young. I could see her like she stood right in front of me. She was happy."

"Well, that's a nice dream." Eileen didn't know what else to say. The conversation was wandering toward something a little scary, something she could glimpse but wasn't sure she wanted to see.

Itz shook his head. "Living with Mrs. Boyle. And happy."

The screen door slammed behind him.

Eileen had just finished the yard chores when they got back home, rolling in on top of each other like a pack of wild dogs, throwing down their books and packs and heading for the kitchen. She had made some bread for dinner, to go with the thin potato soup, and they were already on it, Andras and Itz pulling off hunks of bread and cramming them into their mouths while Joe watched.

She stood in the kitchen door.

"That's your dinner, so you'd better take it easy. And save some for Pup, you know how he is about his food."

They put down the bread and headed outside.

Soon it seemed like she'd never known any other life. She turned into a kind of machine, or a pack horse, doing what she had to do automatically. The biggest challenges were the too-often empty pantry and the boys' usual fighting getting dangerous. A lot of times those two things went together. One night, after the bean soup and what remained of the bread, Pup slurped his down and grunted, "Needs more salt," and left the table and the house.

Andras said, "Needs more beans."

Itz jumped on it. "Why don't you go grow some then? Instead of romping around town with that no-count girlfriend of yours, showing everybody what a big guy you are."

Andras tried, she gave him credit for that. He kept spooning the excuse for soup into his mouth, but she saw his jaw tighten. Itz never could quit.

"Yea, must be sweet to have the girl of your dreams…and you know what I mean by dreams."

Andras bolted toward Itz and lifted him off his chair.

"Off the property," she yelled, just like Pup. "Take it off the property."

And they did, and farther than that because of what she'd told them when she had the gun. Half surprised they even remembered, she guessed that gun made a difference.

Eileen cleared the table while Joe soldiered out to make sure his big brothers didn't kill each other. Andras had left his tasks, not for the first time. Also, the boys were

supposed to wait until Eileen stood before they left the
table, but sometimes her energy for that simply vanished.
She started thinking about what could be scraped together
for breakfast.

14

JOE

The boys were in the back acre picking beans. It seemed
endless. Joe thought his mother grew beans to punish them.

Both the picking and the eating were tortuous, night after night for weeks on end. If they complained, and that included even making a face or a slight groan between bites, their father would simply say, "Tomorrow night again," continuing to stare at his food. The cycle continued endlessly.

Worse than the bean problem, Mum was still gone. Joe missed her as much as her chicken and dumplings. Again, she'd turned into someone else, Joe thought, someone lost, helpless. Joe wished he could understand what made her so unhappy, so distant, and then so plain crazy: talking gibberish, threatening Andras with a cleaver, then exiting with Mrs. Boyle. Everything seemed gray, like cold ashes in the fireplace. *What about Mrs. Boyle? What magic does she have that makes Mum well?*

Andras, in an unusual outburst of words, had said to him this afternoon, "It ain't right. Other Mums don't act this way. Is her life so much harder? And why does she almost always go with Mrs. Boyle? Why not somebody else sometime? Somethin' ain't right." He nodded to himself.

They turned away from the beans, finally picked, and headed out into the woods toward the shack they'd built years before. The work of young boys, not something they were any longer proud of, but it sheltered them from the sweltering sun. Joe had remembered to bring water.

Andras laid out his plan. Sweat rolled down their faces, but the idea of the Great Adventure eased the pain of the August heat. Joe wondered why they needed this secrecy, but he didn't ask. He had too many questions.

"Alright now, listen up." Itz came up behind Andras, mimicking his words and gestures. Joe knew not to pay attention to him or there would be trouble for everyone, so he kept his eyes on Andras.

"We deserve a break. All this craziness and Mum being gone who knows where. Plus doing women's' work. Enough's enough. We're going up to the old hunting camp on the mountain for a few days."

"No," Joe breathed. "That's fifteen miles at least, and steep.

"Ten at most." Itz smirked. "Don't exaggerate."

Joe had been to the hunting camp once with a neighbor, Jack McGowan. Jack hadn't married yet and unlike some other people, he liked the Cierc boys. He offered to take the three boys, but by that weekend Itz had the flu and Andras couldn't leave the house as punishment for a drunken brawl with Billy McGoogan. Jack and Joe only killed a few rabbits and a groundhog (mistakenly), but Jack treated him like an equal and his brothers not being along constituted a minor miracle. A great time. He still thought about it.

"And," Joe continued quickly, before Andras could interrupt, "even if we could get there what would we eat?"

Andras frowned out of the corner of his mouth. With exaggerated patience he replied, "I have our food, and it's good. No beans and no potato soup. And as for us getting there"—his chest swelled like he'd inhaled extra muscles—"we are going to borrow Krushksad's horses."

A small knife of fear pierced Joe's heart. The pain of it radiated over his body, made him weak and nauseous. Andras' face had transformed into a collection of shadows and his smile slid up one side of his face. It hung there like overripe fruit, holding his scary, evil plans.

161

This is wrong. Mum wouldn't be angry as much as ashamed. She taught us better. Joe stared at Andras, trying to summon the brother who sometimes helped him with his chores when he got behind, or stood between him and his father's rage. He couldn't find that Andras, but the memory gave him the strength to speak. Any sign of fear delighted Andras and pushed him further toward his true love, danger.

"Horse thieves get hung Andras. Nobody asks questions."

"You been watching too many of them Tom Nix movies, Joey. I got to quit sneaking you in there."

Joe had to find an ally in an unlikely place. He knew he couldn't change Andras' mind after he had been called 'Joey.' He turned to Itz.

"You knew about this?"

Itz's face showed nothing Joe could understand. "Sure," he said, casually.

Andras iced the cake. "You can always stay home."

"Won't Pup send somebody after us?"

Andras frowned. "Pup won't notice if the chores are done or not for a few days. Eileen thinks we're going to camp down by the river--she'll tell him if he asks. And she'll cover for us, just because she won't want to see him mad. You've got to keep it a secret. You've got to keep quiet or else stay home."

Joe felt himself breaking in two. He knew it was crazy, but he couldn't let Andras keep him out of it. "I won't stay home." He stood, his hands folded across his chest. He wanted to hide his fear of being left behind. Never big enough, strong enough, fast enough, he spent his days trying to keep up. Once when Pup mistakenly locked his key in the house, Andras pushed Joe through the slightly open basement window like a crab into its hole. A few minutes later he threw open the front door and grinned at them, head held high. His moment of triumph. Pup handed his dirty son his handkerchief and said, "Clean yourself up."

But Andras put his arm around Joe's shoulders and said, "Way to go buddy."

One of the few times he remembered his big brother praising him.

Joe stood in the bean field and squinted at his brothers. "I'll be fine.

"All the way through supper?" Itz asked, and Joe just nodded..

Andras scowled. "We can't leave him here. He'll squeal." So they left it at that.

Supper was agony. The beans were even worse than usual. You could see through the greasy potato soup. A spoon raised from the bowl left a thin slimy trail that resembled mucous. Some part of a potato apparently. Once Itz choked slightly and they froze, waiting for the thunder, but their father missed it and the moment had passed with no punishment.

Joe thought the house closed up without Mum. None of the aromas of retes or goulash, or her singing softly in the afternoon with Pup gone or asleep.

Nothing Joe could do about it. Mum would come back when she could. He didn't understand it, so he couldn't help. He sat, forcing down the beans and his sadness. When Itz asked for the salt he didn't hear the request.

Pup came out of himself for that second. "What the hell'sa matter with you, boy? Didn't you hear him ask for the salt?"

Joe ducked instinctively, but the blow fortunately didn't come. He suspected his thoughts were speaking out loud from the top of his head, yelling like Gulliver's tormentors. He reached for the salt and passed it to his sneering brother. Joe knew Itz didn't really need the salt, he had just asked so Joe would be caught and would give the secret away. Itz would gladly give up the whole adventure to have Andras' wrath fall on Joe instead of on him. But his ploy failed— Joe managed to keep his mouth shut and the meal continued.

Eileen stood after the last son lowered his fork. In some families this ritual might be time for conversation or prayer, but in theirs, nothing but a tortured silence. Pup nodded his head and Andras began to clear the table. The fading light softened the room a little, but not enough. The thin, worn curtains Mum made had been pretty once, but they could not be replaced. Any available fabric, even scraps, went to making and patching clothing for ever growing bodies.

Later, Joe hung around the kitchen. That wasn't usually a good idea, because Eileen would find a chore. He didn't take long to say what was on his mind.

"Eileen." He fidgeted with one of the few buttons left on his shirt. He puffed up with his own importance and she had to work hard not to laugh at him.

164

"We're going camping up in the hills."

She turned back to the bread on the table, kneading it slowly, both palms moving rhythmically through the dough. "So? You've done that before."

"Yea, but this time we're going really far. His face reddened. "Oh, but please don't tell nobody ("anybody," she reminded him). "Don't tell anybody but specially don't tell Andras because he made me promise not to tell and he'll kill me."

"Woah, slow down. You're going camping? So what? What's going on?"

Joe's face faded to white. "Andras said…"

"Andras says a lot and does almost nothing except when it comes to fighting and getting in trouble."

Joe spoke the truth. Andras would be worse than Pup if he found out Joe had blabbed. Her little brother appeared crestfallen, like he had when a bird he tried to save inevitably died. Eileen softened, as she always did with him.

"Joe, what I'm saying is for your own good. Whatever you're up to is a dumb idea. Because it's Andras' idea. Whatever it is, you're too smart (she almost said 'little' but caught herself in time) to get mixed up in it.

"We won't get caught. We won't. We'll have lots of fun and you're just jealous cause you're a girl."

"So why did you even tell me? You don't want to hear what I have to say. You want my blessing, but I can't give it to you. You will get what you deserve. Now leave me be."

She felt like a child again, but she couldn't stop it any more than she could ease her sadness when Mum went away.

"I can go anywhere I want anytime. I'd be a lot smarter about it than you and your big, dumb brothers and you can tell them I said so."

Joe moved toward the screen door quickly, then turned with his parting shot.

"No you can't because you have to do the work."

The sad, heavy truth of it weighed on her and she had nothing more to say. The animals needed attention. Joe skipped out the back door and she picked up the few scraps leftover from dinner and headed toward the pigsty.

The boys started to head out the back door toward the freedom of the evening, but Eileen's drill sergeant demand halted them. They skidded to a stop. Chores had to be done, they knew that. Still, the chance to escape pulled them like that mighty current toward the dam of Pup's anger, and they were momentarily oblivious to the danger. Eileen brought them to their senses and they came back to the house. Boosted by the night's possibilities, they finished their work so quickly that Eileen remarked, "What are you guys up to? You're usually slogging through this like box turtles."

"Just wantin' to get down to the river." Andras' answered curtly.

Itz cocked his head to one side and added, "Just like box turtles," and Eileen didn't push it. They often went down to the river without asking permission. Joe never understood it, just one of those things. They couldn't move from the kitchen table a second too early, but could spend the night out of the house without being asked a question.

They raced across the field behind the house. Joe turned back once. The kitchen light winked like a crazy old woman, drawing his eye and his heart toward its mean, loving, poverty-stricken self. He thought again about his mother, where her heart could be. Something pulled him away, toward adventure. Bye Mum. He hurried after his brothers.

In the woods, daylight dimmed but the heat held. The boys assembled near an old oak tree not far from the river.

'How do we do this without getting caught?" Joe asked. "Horses make noises, you know."

Andras, cocky as ever, took this as Joe's assent and continued, his voice deep.

He's puffing out his chest like some kind of bird trying to get a mate.

"It's easier at night. They're sleepy. As long as you know them and they're real gentle they don't get spooked. Piece of cake."

Joe thought for a minute. Andras had never been around horses much. Itz sat sucking on a piece of straw. "They know Joe best," he said.

True. Joe cleaned the horses' stable every week. Nobody else wanted the job and he loved the excuse to be nearer to the horses. They calmed him. Now, he realized his own fear, but he knew Andras would count it as another failure of nerve if he backed out. Besides, he wanted to get on board with this thing.

Andras sneered, watching Joe's hesitation. "You look scared. Yes or no? We're in this together. Everybody does what they do best."

There was no question who handled the horses best. Who handled them at all, in fact. Joe threw back his shoulders and announced, "Of course I'll get them. Nobody else could pull it off. Anyway, Krushksad doesn't deserve those horses."

Itz grimaced. "Slow down, boy. We're going camping for a few nights. And we're just borrowing the horses." Joe decided not to ask. He dreaded the answer to his next question. "We got two horses, three guys. How does that work?"

He already knew Andras' response.

"I'll ride one horse. Got to keep watch and I can't be bothered with one of you on my back."

Joe and Itz didn't want to be on a horse together, but they didn't want to be with Andras even more.

Given his new assignment of apprehending the horses, Joe felt some confidence. "I'll be in the back, I'm a better rider."

Itz's lower lip curled. "Like hell you will. I'm bigger and stronger and you know it. And if you want to be reminded, I'll be happy to oblige."

Joe tired of trying to swim away from the dam of his brothers' anger. The decisions had been made and as usual, he would go along with them. He stood up, dusted his pants, and grumbled, "Let's go."

Andras raised his flat palm toward Joe. "Woah, slow down, Cowboy. We got a few plans left to make."

"Really?" asked Joe, but sarcasm had always been lost on Andras. "So I sneak in with sugar cubes and tie a rope around their necks and lead them both out together. You guys should be way back in the woods. We don't want Daisy and Maisy to even smell you until I get them calmed down."

Andras managed half a smile. "You got it."

Still a kernel of doubt lodged in Joe's mind. "We are stealing..."

"Borrowing," insisted Andras.

"Okay, we are 'borrowing' two horses."

Andras' narrowing eyebrows reminded Joe of his intent to be part of the team. "Okay, okay, we'll be back so far in the woods they won't even smell..."

"our big brother." Itz finished the sentence with a smirk.

Andras ignored it. Joe was impressed with his ability to brush Itz off sometimes. "We've wasted enough time. We're going now."

Itz and Joe hesitated, then struggled into their backpacks. Joe knew Andras' pack contained whisky. Itz and Andras had formed the habit early; they certainly came by it honestly. Joe had never tried it. Itz said it burned your throat and made you dizzy. Joe had not yet figured the sense of self-inflicting pain just to be accepted.

The road led downhill toward Krushksad's sad little farm. It didn't have a silo or a red barn like the ones in books, just a brown shed losing its shape like an aging woman, more every year. Krushksad had begun to build a house for his family twenty years before, but never got further than the foundation, which ended up being their living quarters long after they had raised and released most of their children to the outside world. The flat-roofed, cement–walled house must be cold, Joe thought, even colder than his own house. The Krushksads had one daughter still at home, Dorothy, pretty and mean as a snake. No one admitted it, but Joe knew the brothers were all a little bit in love with her, himself included.

Krushksad raised cattle, but never could support his family that way. He and his sons ran a car repair business up on the hill behind the house, where old jalopies came to be rebuilt or to die. The boys stopped and hid in the weeds behind the barn. They could smell the cows.

"Wow," breathed Itz, gazing up the hill.

"What?"

"It's a 29 Chevy Coupe. In great shape too. Wonder what it's doing here with these other heaps of junk." Itz loved cars. The speed and the noise drew him, Joe knew, who couldn't really understand the interest.

Andras turned around. "Shut up, you two. We don't have time for sightseeing."

Itz nudged Joe. "Big word for Andras. 'Sightseeing.'" Itz whispered it and Joe couldn't help but snicker. Andras growled, "Don't take any more time than you need. Our asses are the ones out in the open."

Itz snorted. "Ah shit, Andras. You know whose ass is in danger and it ain't yours."

Joe headed toward the barn, snaking along on his belly in the waning light. He wanted to spend a little time with the horses, get them good and calm before he could bring them out. His brothers stood behind a fence in tall grass, about twenty feet from the barn.

Joe thought about how Itz could have pushed it further. But if Andras got mad, that would end it. He scratched a mosquito bite under the bib of his overalls. He hated wearing them. They were hand-me-downs from his brothers and they hovered above his ankles these days.

He continued to crawl out from the trees to the road, tortoise-like, up and down the ruts made by Krushksad's tractor.

Joe stopped. Krushksad had come out of the house and was peering down toward the barn. Toward him. The old man turned and headed toward his yard full of cars. If he turned around he would be able to see Joe. Still as a trapped animal, he didn't feel like he was breathing. Then he realized Krushksad had a flashlight.

Oh God, I'm trapped now. He began crawling backwards, his belly scraping the earth, till he reappeared at his brothers' hiding place. He crawled up behind them so they didn't know he was there at first.

Itz, on his belly, whispered. "The little shit is scared."

171

"Too scared," said Andras, who was crouched down a little ahead of his brother. "I should have gone myself."

Joe coughed, and both his brothers jumped.

"What?" Andras tried to lower his voice and hide his surprise.

"What..." Itz began.

"How did you get..." stammered Andras.

"Easy, I just went in reverse." Joe flecked a clump of dirt off of his shoe. "We'll just have to wait until he's in bed for sure. We were too early."

"You mean you're going again?"

"Go back out there?"

"Crawl on your belly again?"

The brothers were incredulous. It occurred to Joe that he must have wanted their approval more desperately than he realized.

Andras recovered first. "Way to go, Joe."

Joe shrugged, but couldn't hide his smile.

"Before too long Krushksad will be in there snorin' like the old Silver Bullet coming down the tracks. Ever hear that man snore?"

Itz nodded. "Yea, I did once. Me and Tim McPhee were over here helping him and his son Mike lift a car." Itz puffed up a little.

172

Joe knew it hadn't happened that way: the four of them, each on one wheel, lifting the car, straining. Really, Krushksad lifted one end while the boys kept the car steady.

"Anyway, when we finished with the car he invited us for dinner."

Again not true. Krushksad never invited anybody for dinner. Joe let it go.

"Afterwards we were messing around in the yard. Krushksad had gone to bed. We heard this sound and Tim said it sounded like a buffalo coming over the hillside and I asked him how would he know what buffalo sound like, and Lenny Krushksad said, "Ain't no buffalo. That's the old man snoring.""

"Me and Tim stayed real quiet because dumb Lenny didn't mean it to be funny, just a fact. You know him; he has a temper. So we just laughed all the way home." Andras stood staring at Krushksad's house through Itz's story. Joe realized that meant he just couldn't be bothered listening to such crap.

Itz spat perilously close to his older brother's feet. The boys loved to spit. They had learned it as toddlers watching their father. Spitting spoke its own language. If you spat straight down you were mad. If you spat straight ahead of where you were and made it into an arc, you were okay with the world. If you aimed for something like a tree or a rock and spit harder, you were saying, 'I don't give a rip. I'd rather spit than listen to you.' If you aimed at somebody's feet, you were asking for it. You were pissed at them.

Joe couldn't stand it. He knew if another fight started the night would be over. They needed to get those horses and get moving. As the air cooled, so did their fever for adventure. "Can you guys just remember the plan and quit acting like a couple of girls?"

"Woah, listen to the boy." Andras' face twisted into a typical sneer.

They waited a little while longer, crickets echoing their edginess.

Itz couldn't let it go. "Should have known Krushskad would come out. If somebody with half a brain had planned this thing, we'd be out of here by now."

Andras grabbed Itz's neck like a snake in pursuit of prey. He rumbled, "I'm gonna kill you."

Joe inhaled. *Now we will be found out for sure. No one gets killed without some noise.*

He stepped between his brothers. It hadn't become a full-fledged fight yet, just a wrestling match, which is the way they always started. "What is the matter with you guys?" he hissed. "This is the last thing we need. You're going to get us killed for sure. Cut this shit out now!" Joe never swore. He surprised himself as much as the two of them, and they froze, but they didn't stay frozen long.

Andras stood, addressing Joe but not looking at him. "Probably could get going back out there, if we're ever going to get this thing going."

Joe nodded his head and headed back toward the road. He turned back once, but couldn't see his brothers well in the dusk. He bellied his way into the barn and soundlessly led the horses out and back to his brothers.

15

JOE

They mounted without a word. Andras led the way on Daisy, who had a beautiful black coat and one bum leg. Krushksad got her cheap because of that. Everybody could see the slight limp. Krushksad had gotten a bad deal, but he'd never admit it. Joe knew the horse's limp would only get worse as she climbed the hill. He and Itz straddled the bigger, older brown mare, which moved like a trickle of water, steady but slow. It seemed especially so now, when they had lost so much time and every sound in the woods convinced them Krushksad had discovered his loss. Just as well though, since they rode bareback and had to work hard not to fall off. Itz had insisted on sitting in the back for some unknown reason, but that gave Joe the reins.

Darkness finally covered the earth, except ghostly shapes and shadows illuminated by a sliver of moon. Joe struggled to calm his shaking hands, not wanting to show fear,

175

especially not to Itz. Maybe that's why Itz sat in the back, to see if Joe would buckle.

"Whazzat?"

Joe turned the horse away from the noise.

"Probably a rattler," said Itz, although they both knew rattlers wouldn't be out this time of night, and there weren't many of them anyway.

"It's just a twig snapping for Chrissake," said Andras. "Let's get going."

He seemed to be trying to get himself going as much as his brothers. They had tired of the slow pace, not just with the horses but the whole journey. The black pony started to amble where he pleased, and Andras had made no move to stop him.

"Okay, so where is this place?"

Andras assured them he had found a campsite where they'd be hidden and safe, but Joe knew by now his brother's plans were not always smart or even complete. Still, he wanted Andras to be in charge. He'd been quiet for too long and they needed someone to lead, to appear confident. Now he seemed less sure of himself, and that was not good for any of them. It gave Itz nothing to react against, which diminished him and his energy, and it worried Joe, who could not yet assume the reins of power.

Surprisingly, Itz got things back on track. "Is it close, Andras? Can you see it?"

The brothers rarely used each other's names. It seemed to Joe to be a sign of respect.

Andras responded, "Up a ways. We'll tie up the horses near that tree there." He pointed to a large beech, barely visible, and Joe started to object that there wasn't a lot of space around it, but thought better of it. Andras didn't need any challenges now. The horses would probably be alright there.

Darkness surrounded them by the time they made it to the tree. Andras pulled a flashlight out of his pack and rode with one arm extended, pointing it into the woods. Joe glanced over at his brother. It was Pup's flashlight, he was sure. Andras didn't have the money to buy one. But stealing Pup's? Joe wanted to object, but he knew he was in too deep.

They reached the campsite and slid off the horses, except for Itz. He lost his balance dismounting, fell slowly to the ground with a sort of plop, and lay there face down like a trapped, angry possum.

The brothers laughed, long and loud. They laughed away the evening's tension and fear, their father's scorn and their mother's strangeness, their continuing need to defend themselves and their poor Hunky family against the tight Irish who surrounded them, who had cast their mother out because she had married down. They laughed away their own hunger and pain.

At some point Joe helped Itz release himself and then even he, red-faced and hot-tempered, fell back down on the ground with them and they roared.

After they unrolled the skinny sleeping rolls Andras provided and tied the horses up, they lay back down and gazed up through the trees into the night. Joe said, "This is the life. Do we really have good stuff to eat?"

Itz laughed. "Of course we do. What do you think camping is? Eating, sleeping outside, eating…"

"Peeing in the woods." Joe laughed.

"Yea, and other things too, when you get up the nerve." Andras grinned.

They snacked on bread, cheese and bacon sandwiches. *Where did Andras get bacon?* But it tasted so good, Joe didn't ask. Andras told them he'd packed even better food for tomorrow. "Did a damn good job getting the horses," said Itz.

"Yea, quite a guy," said Andras, and Joe couldn't tell if he meant it or not.

"Hey Joe, you want a little hooch before bedtime?" Andras' derision showed in his lopsided smile. Joe itched to try the stuff, but he had seen his father reeling in the backyard, cursing his children, proclaiming them the cause of his problems. More than once he had been the victim of short, quick blows delivered to the back of his head for any reason, accidental or not.

Andras wandered off. When he didn't return Joe knew he had opened the liquor bottle, and guessed it would be a wild night.

"Aren't you going with him?"

He had to ask the question although he had tried hard to hold it back. He really didn't want Itz to go.

"Probably went to pee. I'm surprised he didn't just stay here and see if he could put the fire out." Itz rubbed a bruise on his left arm. "He'll be back. He can't stand being without someone to boss."

Joe chuckled. He stirred the embers on the fire and added another log. "You're right. Nobody to boss means no Andras."

"Besides, I don't need that jerk to enjoy myself."

Joe didn't think he wanted to know what that meant. The night air had cooled. Joe stared into the fire, listening to crickets, fighting to keep his eyes open. Then he sagged like a sunflower on the other side of daylight.

Mum called to him from the kitchen where a large slice of retes awaited. She smiled and started out the door. Someone stood in the backyard. A tall, shadowy figure, maybe a woman but Joe couldn't be sure. The retes tasted sweet and sour simultaneously. He ate every bite.

The clink of a bottle awakened him. He stirred, opened his eyes, and sat up like a coiled wire unbound. He wondered again if he would ever be as tough as his brothers, drinking and fighting or just doing anything better than they did. Well, he had taken the horses out. He had a way with them, something that made him be there and nowhere else. The horses knew it and respected him. He had that. He stretched his arms over his head.

"Where is he?" His voice was sleepy yet already anxious.

"Dunno. Don't care either." Itz appeared sleepy too. But then Joe noticed he had a small flat bottle in his hand, and he understood it wasn't sleepiness.

They sat in silence for a while. Without Andras mixing things up there seemed to be little to talk about.

Itz gazed up at the treetops, took another swallow. "Tell me a story."

"What?"

"Tell me a story. I didn't bring a book and it's too dark to read anyway."

And depending on how much of that hooch you've had, you probably couldn't read the words anyway. But okay.

"A story about what?" Joe was sure he'd never told a story.

Itz surprised him again. "Tell me a story about Mum." Another gulp.

"Now I know you're drunk. You want me to tell you a story about Mum? I don't think there are any stories about Mum." He stared into the fire. "She's just Mum."

Itz persisted. "Nuh-uh. She saved a kid's life once. Fat kid, Norbert Pusztai. He's a grownup now. You know, Mr. Pusztai."

"She saved his life?"

Itz rolled his shoulders back, poked at the fire with a stick. "He fell outuva tree. No, wait. S's another time. A bear attacked him."

"A bear?" Joe doubted it, but let it go. No predicting Itz any time, but especially when he'd been drinking.

"Yea. He could have bled to death but Mum saved him."

"How did she do that?"

"She and her friend stuck leaves on his cuts and carried him all the way back to town."

"Really?"

Itz nodded. "Bleeding. And really fat."

Joe didn't respond. He stretched his own shoulders back, trying to imagine Mum as a girl, and the things she might do. *I can make up a story. A story about the real Mum, but maybe not real things she did. That's how you tell a story, right? It could be true and not true.*

Itz lay back on his bedroll and laced his fingers behind his head, imitating Pup. Joe wondered if he knew it.

"Mum ran away once," he began.

Itz sat up. He shook his bottle as if to see what was left. Joe again stifled the urge to laugh.

"She did not. Girls can't run away. They have to learn to cook and sew and stuff."

Joe sighed, his shoulders drooping. "Okay, if you don't believe me, I won't tell you anymore."

Itz's face shown in the firelight. He twisted up one side of his mouth. "No, I b'lieve you. Go ahead." He sat up on one arm, took another swallow from his bottle, then waved it toward his brother. "Want some?"

"Nah." Joe looked away, and hoped Itz had forgotten the story. He hadn't.

"What happened?"

"Uh. Her father made her chop the wood in the back yard from a tree he cut."

"Why?"

Joe thought that Itz was paying very close attention for a boy who'd been drinking. He dug deeper into his growing hole of fabrication. *Mum told me about having to carry wood. It not a great stretch for her to be chopping it.*

"Well, she did a bad thing."

"What? What bad thing?"

Itz's questions gave Joe little opportunity to conjure up answers. He stood up and threw another piece of wood on the fire, which afforded him needed time. "She...um...she hadn't milked the goat that morning because she slept late and had to rush to get to school."

Itz sat up again. "And he made her chop the wood just for that?"

Joe tried to sound like an authority by deepening his voice. He knew a little about goats, and he couldn't change his story now. "Leaving a goat un-milked is bad business. They get crazy because they hurt so much. And they bleat and moan and start making trouble. You know goats can make trouble."

"But not girl goats. They're gentle." Then Itz mercifully let it go.

He really wants to hear a story.

"So did that happen? Did they make trouble?"

"I don't know." Joe pulled at his neck. Telling stories seemed to require more than his ability to remember detail. "I think her ma milked the goat later in the day, when she realized what had happened."

"Who is Ma?"

"Her mother. They called her Ma instead of Mum."

"Oh right. I knew that."

Between Itz's questions and his declarations of prior knowledge, Joe began to see this story stretching into his future forever. He sighed.

"Anyway, that's not the important part of the story. She had to chop the wood and she thought she would cry."

"Did she?"

"Did she what?"

Itz frowned, his eyelids squeezing together. "Did she cry? Geez Joe, pay attention."

"No. She didn't cry."

"What? Girls always cry."

Joe's teeth edged out over his lower lip. He wanted this to be over. "Not Mum. Mum is different. Mum is tough. Anyway, she thought she could chop a lot of wood but not that much. Then her friend came by to see if she could play."

"Did Mum get mad?"

"Oh yea, so mad she thought she'd explode."

"Explode?"

Joe groaned. *Are stories always this much work?*

"You know. When you're really mad and you get tight and red and you feel like you have to punch something or you'll...explode."

"Oh yea. I been that mad a lot. Usually at Andras but sometimes other people."

Yea, most times Pup, really. But you're even scared to say that here because of the times he beat you black and blue. I remember the sound of the belt, or sometimes a stick, thumping your back. You never even made a noise, but I saw afterwards. I learned to stay out of his way.

"How old was she?"

Joe thought about this. "Um. Eleven." He didn't know.

Fortunately Itz didn't much care. "Almost as old as you," he replied. Another swig.

"Yep, right. And so her friend came over and when she found out what Mum had to do she got mad and said, "You should run away. And I'll go with you."

"And Mum? Did she go? Did she run away?"

Joe said Mum did run away, but she knew her parents would have been so worried she came home after three hours. And they weren't even mad because they were so glad to see her, they just hugged her and gave her dinner and made her promise never to do that again.

"Wow! Don't know parents as nice as that." Itz lay back down on his blanket and appeared to be drifting off. Joe watched his arms and legs relax, and his sharp features soften in the firelight. He seemed to be asleep until he murmured.

"What was her name?"

Joe flicked the fire with a stick, still trying to conjure up his mother as an eleven year old girl, being mad, running away from her parents.

"Her friend. The one who ran away with her."

"Oh, I don't know." *Did he really not understand I'd had made the whole thing up. Besides, I thought the storytelling was over.*

Itz shifted to his side, closer to the fire and rested his hands under his head. "Brid."

"Brid?" *How could Itz know the name of a person in a pretend story? Did he just make it up that fast?* "How do you know?"

Itz's voice grew sleepier, but still sure. "Mum told me. Brid. The best friend she ever had, she told me. So I bet she wanted to help Mum run away, too." His voice ebbed. "I thought you were going to tell me a story about Brid."

Joe replied, "Well, I don't know about that," but sleep had won another night's battle over Itz, the warrior. Joe sat quietly, wondering.

Brid?

He kept adding sticks to the fire, hearing crickets and a slight rustling of leaves. So peaceful. Just as his head started to nod, the woods exploded with loud, angry sounds—men's boots and, most terrifying, his father's voice.

Andras spiraled back into the camp, screaming, "Run, just run!" Joe trailed Itz by a few yards. They crashed through the woods with a strength they hadn't known they had, charged by fear. Before they had gone twenty feet up the hill, Joe stopped and pasted himself to the back of a large hemlock. Itz returned and they stood trembling together.

"What the hell are you doing? They're going to see us. We need to get out of here fast.

"We can see them but they can't see us. The light from their flashlights is blocking their view of us. They're more likely to hear us if you don't shut up. I have to find out what happens."

"Well, I'm going. You can stand here as long as you want, but I'm going." He stood there all puffed up but Joe didn't move. He knew Itz wouldn't go without him.

Itz and Joe hid behind the tree together. The reflection of the half-moon shone on the river. *The same river where Itz almost drowned. Only last week?*

Climbing a little further, they could see the campsite.

Dorothy Krushksad stood behind the men. *Not so pretty now, her face is dirty from her chores. She must have seen the horses ride away from the farm and told her father. Maybe she didn't know who we were when she ratted on us, maybe she did. In any case, damn her grimy face.*

186

Krushksad must have sent word through the valley that his horses had been taken and the men headed up the mountain, enraged that someone would steal from one of their own. Joe imagined them grumbling about being roused from their warm beds by some no count thieves, and about decaying morals. Never mind that men were out of work and children were hungry. A man still had a duty to act honorably, which had nothing to do with having too much to drink or slapping his wife around a little when she needed it. But horse thieving? Unacceptable.

So they charged up the dark mountain to render true justice on whatever loathsome creature had stooped to such an act. Joe could see their disappointment, probably because they only found kids. Simply a boyish prank, something like what they all had once enjoyed. Still, eager for justice, they fell on Andras, the boy/man who faced them smirking.

And there in the back Joe could see his father, eyes cast down, shoulders slumped. Not the towering titan of their home. *Drunk probably, and ashamed.*

Joe watched with a sickening heart as they wrapped a rope around Andras' hands and led him down the mountain. Andras snarled like a captured beast and tried to pull away from his guard, weaving through the brush and growling at anyone who came near.

Andras got close to Old McManus, spit at him and sent the old man tumbling into another thrill seeker and then a third until all three of them bumbled over each other toward a small muddy creek a little further down the hill. McManus managed to get stopped and saved by a large oak tree, but the other two weren't so lucky, rolling down the hill and into the river.

The flashlights shone on them as they crawled out, dripping, shivering and plastered with mud. Everyone except Andras had to stifle their amusement. He threw back his head in a gesture familiar to his brothers, who knew he was sneering. That subsided quickly. His father's attempts at sternness and anger were futile since the whisky had got the best of him. Pup stumbled downhill like his comrades, fighting the unwinnable battle against gravity, tripping over an ancient tree root. From their perch not too far up the hill, Itz and Joe snickered when Pup fell like an old tree himself. Then he lay face down and unmoving in the mud, and even Andras quieted.

Joe stared. His father unmoving, unthreatening, scared him as much as any of his threats or ferocity. In a few minutes someone came to his aid. Pup had struck his head on the sharp edge of a rock hidden in decaying leaves, the kind that rises up to fell old men who are where they don't belong. There were unpleasant sounding words the boys couldn't hear from their distance. Some of the men would have to carry him, no light weight, and they still had a long way to go.

Joe knew fear gripped Andras despite his show of fierceness. His rage had quieted and the woods had gone silent. Joe and Itz turned away and began running again, knowing they could not help anyone except themselves.

16

JOE

Joe ran, walked and stumbled after Itz for what seemed like hours, losing track of time and place. He didn't know where they were going, except away. Sometimes he could smell the pines, come close enough to an oak to know its immensity. And once they were close to the river, close enough that he could hear the current and wanted to strip and dive in. But he hoped Itz could lead him away from

189

trouble, away from responsibility. He could almost hear his conscience cracking in the darkness.

"We left him, Itz. We left him to take the heat. It's not fair."

Itz kept moving, facing forward. "Then go back" he gasped, his voice angry, strangled like a wild animal had been caught in his throat. "He told us to run—since when do we deny the mighty Andras?"

From behind, Joe heard only "The mighty Andras." The picture of Andras, bound by ropes, insured the straight, sure path of their retreat. His heart seemed to be sinking like waterlogged branches, and he felt shame, which he knew well. Later he would wonder over and over why he didn't go back and face the music, especially having no knowledge of what lay ahead, and not being a guy prone to taking risks.

With Itz now running ahead, away from Andras and toward a safety they could only hope for, Joe stopped doubting. Mum would always walk with her head down, he remembered, studying the ground, never the future. She told him it made a hard climb easier.

Itz seemed to read Joe's misgivings. "We had a plan," he told Joe. "Me and Andras. I'll tell you about it later, when we're not running. But trust me, we're doing exactly what we meant to do. Except…"

"Except I'm here instead of Andras."

"Right. And that's a good thing."

Joe decided to accept the compliment and let it go for now. He had no breath left for dialogue, although he managed to ask more questions.

"Which way we headed?"

Itz turned his head toward Joe, his face like that of a dog chasing rabbits. Grim determination. "South, mainly. We're headed toward the city."

"Toward Pittsburgh? Why?" Joe's words were coming in spurts now, punctuated by his panting.

Itz didn't answer. He allowed them a rest stop, finally, their hands on their knees, chests heaving, shivering like saplings.

Joe couldn't stop himself. "Where are we going? What do we think we're doing? "

Itz stood up straight, stretching his arms over his head, his ribs sticking out under his t-shirt. "Do you understand anything? Do you see what we're eating for dinner these days? Beans or thin soup. Do you notice there are no eggs on the table anymore? Because Mum is, er, was selling them to pay the bills. Pup says he's not working because of that old injury of his, but it's really because there's hardly any work. They can't even feed us much. Andras should be with us but he had to be the big hero so he's probably sitting in a jail cell. At least he'll get three squares."

Joe felt his heart drop. "I thought we were just running away...you know, from trouble. Are we just going to keep running our whole lives? Riding trains like those old hobos?

Itz grimaced. "I don't know what's going to happen. I just know we couldn't stay there. I mean, I thought you would. With me and Andras gone there might have been enough for you. But things worked out different." He paused. Joe frowned, attempting to wipe away a few stray tears without it being obvious.

Itz ignored it. "Joe. You know I'm smart. Trust me. I need you and you need me."

Joe hid his surprise like a bottle of liquor in the woodpile. He wanted words that would make him feel better, safer. He wanted to believe his brother's every word but he knew Itz could make things up at the drop of a hat. *Are we really that poor? Nobody else seems much richer, these days.*

Itz said, "I've got a plan. I knew where we were going as soon as we took our first running step away from that camp."

This information did not comfort Joe.

"I know we're going south, mainly." Itz emphasized 'mainly.'

"Yea, but where south?"

"I mean the real, down home South, where it's warm and things grow so fast you can pick vegetables out of a garden and the next morning the farmer wouldn't even know. Where trees bloom before we've even thought about putting our woolies away and finishing up the wood pile."

Itz started to run again, lightly, like a tight end. Joe almost expected him to produce the pigskin in his hands and sprint for daylight. He followed, because going back seemed less attractive, especially if he had to do it alone.

At some point in the middle of the night they slowed to a walk. Itz had stopped at the top of a slope, and Joe finally had the wind to reply to Itz's description of the South. "Vegetables grow overnight?" No answer. The trees had thinned out and they were beginning to see their outline in the early dawn.

"Look here, I'm going to tell you once and then you'd better decide and no more whining. I've been planning this for a long time—me, Andras and Eddie McClellan."

"Eddie McClellan? He's a criminal! He's actually been in jail!

"Just once, and just for breaking and entering. He didn't steal anything. Plus he's ridden the boxcars."

"The only reason he didn't steal anything is because he got caught. He's not only a thief—he's a stupid thief!"

"Yea, well I'd rather have a stupid thief, especially one that's big and strong, than a whiny wimp. And one who doesn't even know about riding the rails."

"You want to see strong? I could take you in five minutes." Joe surprised himself. He had grown, now just a hair shorter than Itz and a good ten pounds heavier. He just might be able to take him.

The trees had thinned out and they were beginning to see their outline in the early dawn. Itz didn't get mad or anything. He just smiled and Joe felt more like a little kid than a tough guy. "Don't interrupt me again until I finish this. Listen to my plan—then you can decide."

Joe knew he had made the decision when they left the camp. Every step away probably doubled the punishment he would receive if he went home, so that possibility became less and less attractive.

"Did you plan this out—the route and timing?"

Itz scratched behind his ear. "Well, sort of. I told you. Me and Eddie were going to do it. Then me and Andras. We planned it for weeks."

"Going to do what? Get on those two sad horses and gallop away in the middle of the night? Leave me there to take the heat? Jeez. Anyway, you and Andras would have killed each other before you even got to this godforsaken city."

Itz tripped on a tree root but regained his balance quickly. "I know. I'm sorry. I should have planned this with you. You're as smart as any kid I know. You just don't care about school stuff. You're gonna be something someday with a beautiful wife and great kids and a real nice house."

Joe didn't speak. He'd never even thought about how his life would turn out. Itz surprised him with his predictions.

His brother squinted into the rising sun, and it seemed, into the future. "Unlike me." His eyes and mouth drooped, either because of the increasing heat or whatever he was thinking, Joe wasn't' sure. Itz's sadness felt like wet concrete. You couldn't touch it or you might get stuck.

"I'll probably spend my life running away."

A protest rose up in Joe's throat but he couldn't voice it.

Itz spoke again, even more quietly. "But you're right. Andras and I would have killed each other. And we weren't going to take the horses. Never would have done that to you. At least I wouldn't have. We were just going to sneak out one night and not come back. In fact, we did, and that's when I took the money off the top of the cabinet where Mum hid it. I only took 10 cents. But we started fighting before we were two blocks from the house. We were right in the middle of it, fists flying as usual, when Andras started laughing." Itz shook his head. "Chuckling. Pretty unusual, huh?"

"Chuckling about what?"

Itz shook his head, and gave a short chortle of his own. "About how stupid the whole thing was. Even Andras knew it. We would never have pulled it off."

But we are going to. Itz and me can do this together.

Joe nodded, his eyebrows knitting together as he waited. It didn't take long for Itz to continue.

"Either trust me or go home. You're in this or out."

Joe sagged. "We're, uh, not going to be home by Saturday, are we?"

Itz snickered. "This ain't no picnic, boy. This is the real thing. We got to do the hard stuff here. If you think we're playing, you better turn around and go home."

"I'm in." *There, I've said it. I'm in. I decided.* "But I'll probably ask you some more questions. Sort of." And he would continue to question himself. *Am I really in? Could I get back home by myself?*

"In Pittsburgh, we're going to hop a train going south. The Crescent Limited heads to Washington DC. Then we're on our way. It's easy. I've been practicing on the local. You just run alongside when they're taking off from the station, catch hold of handles, and hop up. Everybody's doing it now, so it's harder to get caught."

"How are we going to get to Pittsburgh? Where are we going to sleep?" Joe began to hate having to ask all these questions. He unconsciously tucked in his body to hide against the increasing light. They stayed close to the trees when trees appeared, although there seemed to be no pursuit.

"Right here, for now. I figure we've gone about ten miles. We should hide and rest because—it's practically daylight." Itz shivered and tried unsuccessfully to pull his sleeves down further. "Wish we'd of brought more blankets." He paused, studying the lightning sky. "But we didn't have much time to think. Those guys came up over the hill like bandits and were on us before we knew it." Itz had this new way of quickly throwing his head back and to the side. Joe knew he'd learned it from his friend Eddie and thought it made him come across as tough.

This sounds a little like a western movie. There is no one around anywhere—who is going to see us if we rest a while? No one will know us. No one will care. Joe still had a hundred questions but kept his mouth shut and listened. Sleep sounded now like the best possible gift he could be given. He wanted to sink down into the soft earth and sleep for two days, and dream of his mother's goulash and nut rolls.

Both of them were starting to feel the lack of sleep. One minute they made sense and the next they were three year olds jabbering nonsense. At one point Itz said, "We're starting to sound like the old lady! Pretty soon we'll be talking in letters!" He mimicked her face and started gurgling: "'URP!' Ha! Get it? 'U-R-P!'"

He slapped Joe on the back a few times. Joe tried not to laugh but he couldn't fight it. It felt like he'd been tackled and his glee pushed out of him.

 Despite the time of year, the damp early morning air chilled them. They shivered like men in need of a drink, then slept like men who have had too many. Joe listened to Itz moan and talk. He'd heard it before, back in the bedroom before his brother moved downstairs to sleep on the couch.

The sunlight strayed in and out from the clouds long enough to occasionally rouse them from sleep. Once Joe glanced over and saw his brother's eyes open. "What do you dream about?"

"Oh, girls, lots of girls, and riches beyond belief, and nice clothes and sunshine. Good whisky and good football. What else could a guy want?"

It sounded hollow to Joe, no joy on Itz's face, his tone flat and dry like a pastry Eileen had left in the oven too long. His confidence drizzled from him like oil from a pan, a small spear of dread shivered down his spine.

Itz spoke again. "I dream I'm alone outside and it's dark, and I try to run away from the cold and the dark but it keeps getting colder and darker." Itz exhaled. "Once I dreamed I met a man who said he could make me warm, and I wouldn't have to be alone for a long time."

Joe said nothing. At twelve he didn't know much about dreams or love. He reached over and placed his hand on

Itz's shoulder. It felt awkward but Itz allowed it, so he kept it there for a minute.

They woke from their restless sleep as the sun set. Joe's first question started ringing before he stood upright. *What about food?* Fortunately, his sleepiness made questions only bounce in his head and not escape to further irritate Itz. They plodded carefully on without talking. Exhaustion ended disagreements quickly.

Then a crick appeared, about twenty feet across, the water showing infrequent reflections of light. No telling how deep. Beyond it a long, sloping hill, a serious climb, threatened.

"I wish it were deep enough to swim in," Joe offered, knowing Itz felt the same way.

"We can at least get wet, and drink some too. But we can't take too much time. We've got a long way to go."

They tiptoed in, then splashed a little, forcing themselves not to hoot and holler like they would have under any other circumstances. Then they panted their way up the hill and continued, on and on. Around midnight they encountered Route 28, the road that ran through their hometown down into Pittsburgh. It hugged the river close, curving with it through every bend and fork and affording enough light for them to see and not be seen.

They reached the edge of a small, sad town called Kitteridge, with some houses, a few buildings and a gas station.

"10 cents a gallon." Itz chuckled. "We could afford that if we had a car."

"Yea, that's a small detail." Joe slumped against the side of the gas station. "Do you have any money?"

"Um, a little," replied Itz. "Remember that 10 cents I took?"

"Yea, but Mum never noticed?"

Itz frowned. "Mum hasn't been there, remember Joe? Anyway, it will get us some food till we get work."

Joe straightened. Enough about the money. He only knew the ache of his feet, the blisters and his body and soul begging for rest. He felt older than Krushksad's horses. They didn't talk for a while and only had a single purpose—to keep moving and put more and more distance between themselves and the mistakes they had made.

They stopped to rest and Itz leaned against a car parked in a back alley of the town. Neither of them had ever been here, not even heard of it, which made it seem like they were really getting far from home. They stood in front of a pawnshop, people's cast off, much loved belongings crowding a window lit by a single bulb.

"Why did we have to take the horses? We didn't need horses. We climbed that hill before—maybe not to camp, but we could have carried enough of the stuff. "

Itz spat and rubbed his hands. "Why do we do anything? Because Andras said we should. Stupid."

For a minute, Joe thought Itz meant him.

Itz spat again. "Definitely one of his stupidest ideas ever. I feel pretty stupid for not realizing how stupid." He squinted into the distance. "Why do we always do what Andras says?"

"Because he'll beat the crap out of us if we don't." Joe puffed up his arms and shoulders and frowned in a threatening, typically Andras way. "You idiots, pick it up." Joe spouted one of Andras' favorites. He snickered.

"I'm gonna beat you till you can't see the light." Itz was into it now.

Joe puffed himself up even further, furled his eyebrows and scowled. "I'm gonna kill you."

This had them in stitches, gulping for breath. They didn't even know what made it so funny. It just felt good.

When they finally settled down, Itz said, "Wonder what he's doing now."

"Getting beat till he can't see the light," and they howled again despite it being probably true and not so funny.

Itz pointed across the street, over the top of the hardware store, where a faint light crept over the rooftops of the little gray town. "We better get moving. We've got a train to catch."

They had to jump off the roadside into a ditch when a car rumbled past, not a lot faster than they were walking. Joe missed a heartbeat. He dropped to his knees and crawled until Itz snickered.

"He didn't see us, and besides what are you going to do? Crawl to Pittsburgh? Do you know the way to Pittsburgh?"

Joe scrambled to his feet. They moved further away from the road and closer to the woods, where the pine needles offered a sweet scent and more shelter.

"Do you know the way, Itz?"

"Now I know how crazy you made Andras when you asked him those questions. Don't you trust me?"

"Course I trust you, it's just that…"

"That what?" Itz flicked stones with his toes as he met them on the road.

"It's just that I want to know. I'm always being taken along, I always go along." Joe talked more to himself than to his brother, but Itz listened.

"Then I'll tell you what. Go out and make yourself some plans—it's a free country."

I will. Someday I will.

17

GRACE

Grace sat staring out into the summer heat, wondering about her children. Eileen would be feeding the chickens, or getting dinner. There was no fairness to it. The girl should be out with Lane, or gossiping with her friends. Things Grace had never done because Brid had taken every bit of her attention. She didn't regret that, but the thought of Eileen losing her youth to her mother's choices and their results crushed her. What was she doing here? She should be taking care of things, releasing Eileen to the delightful and scary world of adolescence.

And the boys. What sort of trouble were they in now? No more escapades at the river, she hoped. Maybe they were just playing football or hiking in the woods. They would come home hungry. She hoped Eileen had enough to feed them.

Grace almost succeeded in not thinking about Dominic. But there he was, his sad and angry self, trying unsuccessfully to remedy his perceived losses in life. She had not thought about that much—too busy fending him off and holding bodies and souls together. But now, as she gazed at the roses in Brid's garden, she shifted in her seat. What had been so bad about his life? His parents were good to him, he always had plenty to eat (and drink), he had had lots of girlfriends, was good at sports and his friends adored him. There was only one thing in his life that must be unsatisfactory.

Her.

No. It wasn't her. If anything she had been good for him. She kept his house clean, made his meals, bore and raised his children. Plenty of men's wives didn't want them after the children were born, and plenty of men were happy to find younger women in the bars or on the street. She would not accept responsibility for his unhappiness.

But she must for her own.

After all, she still had Brid in her life. Her children, while admittedly rambunctious, were basically good kids. Though there wasn't always a lot to eat, she was able to stretch things thanks to the long ago instructions of Marta.

Marta. Even the memory of her was a cause for gratitude.

One afternoon, she sat with her mother drinking tea and saying little. Ma believed firmly in the curative powers of tea. Grace had to admit she felt a little better today, noticing the sun shining through the window.

I need to get along," Ma declared. "Time to put the man's supper on the table."

Supper on the table at Ma's house. Just the two of them, maybe an occasional grandchild. One of Claire's children, not mine. And Da. Did he ever even think about me? Communication with her father had been minimal over the years.

Before she left, Ma hesitated at the door. Grace sat quietly. Ma sighed deeply and addressed Brid, who was sitting across the room.

"Thank you," she whispered as she opened the door. "Thank you." And she was gone.

Her words were like the first scent of bread rising in the oven. Grace could feel the warmth of her even after her exit.

Brid squeezed Grace's arm as the door closed. "She's a good woman, your ma. She is."

Grace allowed herself a slight smile, rose and moved toward the kitchen, considered cooking dinner for Brid. She might make chicken and dumplings, her family's favorite. Maybe she could begin to be of use again.

18

EILEEN

Eileen watched out the window as the crowd of men propelled Andras down the street. Snarling and throwing back his shoulders, he tried to wrestle himself away from them. Or, she wondered, was it just another Andras show? Pup slouched in his chair, his head bandaged, and said nothing.

"He's a horse thief! Jail's the only place for the likes of him!" The men's strident, cheerful voices threatened and condemned.

Her heart melted for Andras, just this once. But she wondered. She had learned in school about the U.S. Constitution. Weren't people innocent until proven guilty? The men seemed to have no doubt. Some thought he didn't even deserve a court hearing. Still, it took place a few days later. Then they actually imprisoned him in the city jail, to await his trial.

She visited him with sandwiches and tea, carrying her anger like a writhing cat. Still, she spoke to him calmly, asking how he felt, whether he needed anything. He stared out through the jail cell's bars and did not reply. When he put his feet up on the tiny stool in front of his cot and his hands locked behind his head, her curtain of detachment fell away.

"Andras, why would you do such a thing? You endangered your brothers and now they're gone, God knows where..." She hesitated at the sight of his dirty face and clothes, his hollow eyes. *Didn't he feel any regret? Not even a little shame?*

The damp cell took its toll. Two days after his coughing began, the phlegm rising from his throat in waves, his accusers carried him home on a stretcher and slid him onto the bed in the upstairs bedroom.

The judge dropped the horse thieving charge, much to Krushksad's chagrin. Maybe he had decided that pneumonia constituted a worse punishment than a jail sentence. The truth of it was no one wanted to be around Andras, pneumonia being a big killer.

He had never been sick. While the rest of them suffered through childhood illnesses and once Itz even edged close to death from whooping cough, Andras played and teased them, oblivious of their danger and pain. But now he lay on the small bed, his big feet sticking out from the bottom of the blanket, coughing almost constantly, his eyes glazed and runny, his skin hot and moist. For the first time ever he needed his sister to fight for him, and she determined to do that, not knowing exactly why. Maybe to battle the great thief who slipped into bodies and stole lives, young and old, strong and weak. She learned about a new medicine called sulfa, more effective than anything else. It cost dearly, so she did what she knew Mum would do and sold two of the best hens to pay for it.

She spent hours marching up and down the stairs from the kitchen to his bedroom, bringing ice and cold cloths to lower his fever, water and chicken soup. Pushing, pulling, grunting, she somehow managed to replace his grimy sheets with clean ones. One morning, while she sat by the bed, Andras made a sound, a slight, hoarse whisper..

"What did you say Andras?"

"Mum."

"She's still at Mrs. Boyle's. Remember, she went away again."

He didn't reply for a while, and opened his eyes when he finally said the word. His voice was so soft, too soft for Andras. "Love."

She wanted to ask him to repeat it, to be sure that's what he had said. As if he knew her thinking and her fear, he repeated, "Love."

She knew what that meant and what he too dreaded. Not that Andras would ever say. She continue to sit, not moving any part of her. Andras looked deep into her eyes.

"Only love ever."

She couldn't stop her heart beating so loudly. Her hands shook. He had turned his head to the side and closed his eyes. She knew if she ever mentioned this moment, he would deny it. Delirium, she wanted to believe, but didn't.

One more word, as she left the room.

"Thank you."

Eileen rarely cried but she couldn't squeeze back the tears that rolled down her cheeks.

That afternoon she spooned soup into his mouth, forced down the medicine. His face reflected the gray morning and his eyes, dark brown since birth, appeared gray as well. He seemed so old, older than Pup even. But he took the soup, to her satisfaction.

"Itz and Joe are little runts."

Eileen agreed. Compared to Andras, they were. Besides, she had no desire to cross him now. His next words however, stunned her for the second time that day.

"But they're smarter than me."

"People have different kinds of smart, Andras." She could feel herself beginning to tighten, a long familiar defensive reaction against him.

He shook his head. "My smart is in my muscles."

She decided safety lay in not responding.

"I'm not dumb. I know stuff. Just sometimes it gets all mixed up in my head and I forget what I know. That makes me mad. Especially when Itz…"

"I know, I know Andras." She patted his leg. Unease and compassion sparred in this new territory. Compassion prevailed. "You are not dumb. You are a leader and leaders have a lot on their minds."

He turned toward the leaden light coming through the window, said nothing more.

She sat, testing her own patience, eventually knowing her restlessness had overcome any other emotion. Taking the empty bowl from his hands, she kissed his cheek and hurried out.

A few mornings later she entered the room carrying a bowl of turkey broth, hoping she could get some of it down his throat. To her amazement, he sat straight up in bed and reached for the bowl.

Eileen stiffened. "Well, I see you're feeling better."

"I'm fine. I just need some real food, instead of the crap you've been feeding me."

She opened her mouth, then closed it again, set the broth down gently on the table beside him and smiled pleasantly. "I'm so glad to see you're feeling much better. Now you'll be able to take care of yourself again while I get back to more important things."

She heard something like a gasp as she left the room, and as she descended the stairs he growled, "Hey, wait a minute!"

But she didn't wait a minute. It didn't take long for Andras to return to his old oppressive self, strutting around the house giving orders. Without Itz and Joe he didn't have much effect, as Eileen had learned to ignore him completely.

Still, people said it was amazing how quickly he recovered. Eileen only regretted that the illness had not changed his spirit.

After Andras had recovered, Eileen had time to think about what Mum would have done. Cared for him, no doubt. But would she have tolerated his rudeness? Eileen doubted it. But then she wondered what she really knew of Mum, still gone, still with Mrs. Boyle. Itz once hinted at something Eileen had questioned in her own mind. Why was Mrs. Boyle so special? She certainly liked Mum, and could be a lot of fun. But Mum seemed so different when she came around. Happier, more alive. How did a person make you feel that way? Of course Lane made her feel that way, but only Lane. But that wasn't the same. She and Lane were in love. Committed to one another. It couldn't be that way with two women.

Could it?

Anyway, Mum deserved to be happy.

Eileen felt uncomfortable thinking about it, and decided adults had their mysteries. No figuring them out. She'd leave it at that.

19

The city scowled down on them, noisy, dirty and threatening. They stood across the river from the huge buildings, and it scared Joe more than Andras ever had. Early morning, but Itz said they didn't need to sleep during the day anymore. Here in the metropolis they would not even be noticed. Black soot cast off by the giant mills looming over the south side blanketed buildings and streets. The streetlights were on and necessary. Even peoples' broad faces and backs, handed down from generations of laborers, were sooty and sad. Or angry.

In the first hour Joe thought for certain he would die. He couldn't breathe, couldn't see, and his mouth tasted like burnt biscuits. They might have attracted some attention if the city had not been so dirty. A few quick splashes in cold mountain streams and no soap had not erased the last twenty four hours of sweat and grime. And they were hungry. They had been hungry many times before, when Mum or Eileen put bowls of lukewarm, watery soup in front of them and called it supper. February, March, when the last of their garden's produce had filled empty stomachs and was gone. They watched other kids open lunch boxes full of bread and meat and even fruit in the wintertime, and

211

wondered where people got apples and pears at that time of year. Once Joe snuck into the Walsh's back orchard to make sure their trees weren't bearing fruit in February. Eventually he discovered the truth. In the winter, fruit for some people came from some faraway places like Georgia.

But this hunger differed from empty lunch boxes. No kind of supper to come home to.

Where were they going now, he wondered, coming back to the present with a bit of a jolt, and would it be any better? Itz said Georgia would be always sunny with plenty to eat. And, according to his brother, there would be jobs for teenage boys. *No sense doubting it, I've already made my bed.*

"Hey, watch out you little punk, you almost knocked me down." A short, squat, bald guy with beady eyes and a dirty shirt scowled at Joe and stalked away. Joe said, "Guess he's pretty upset, huh?"

"Why, because you bumped into him? Nah, don't worry about that. People do it all the time. Guys like that don't start fights, they just snarl a lot. We're safe, little brother."

But how do you know who are the fighters and who aren't?

For the second time in five minutes someone had referred to him as little. It started to feel like sandpaper rubbing on his gut.

A lot of men were wearing suits and ties. "There must be lots of dead…" He stopped when he realized how dumb that sounded. In Summervale men only wore their suits to funerals. But here it seemed they wore them every day. Joe felt relieved he'd caught himself.

Itz located a street vendor selling potato pancakes. Joe's stomach seemed as big and empty as a warehouse. The smell of the pancakes made his knees weak.

"We shouldn't eat," said Itz. "It's only been twelve hours since we ate," but he didn't even convince himself.

"Well, that's easy for me since I don't have any money and I don't think he's giving them away." Joe knew for certain he could smell the butter and taste the salt in his mouth.

"They're only a penny…" Itz stood staring at the food.

"A penny is a lot of money when you only have ten cents." Joe's voice still squeaked sometimes when he got excited. Itz said he sounded like a squirrel with a cold.

He'll do whatever he's decided to do, come hell or high water. Sure enough, Itz made a beeline for the vendor and bought…something. Joe wasn't sure what. Itz handed one to him—a kind of a long roll containing a reddish cylinder-shaped piece of, was it meat?

"It's a hot dog," Itz declared. "They're supposed to be really good."

How does he know these things?

The scent of it tantalized him like the river on a summer day. He had to struggle to keep from drooling.

Itz took a bite and said it tasted like 'food of the gods.' Joe didn't know what that meant, didn't care. He bit into the thing. He would have swallowed it whole except the first nibble burned his tongue. His gnawing belly made this the best food he'd ever put into his mouth, better even than

Mum's chicken and dumplings. Seemed traitorous, but he didn't care.

They walked along Sixth Avenue for a long time. Joe tried fighting the onslaught of images and smells, so he could concentrate on what they were doing. It was a lost cause. His eyes and thoughts flew everywhere, as one inviting sight or sound toppled over another. Noticing the street signs, he realized that Sixth and Seventh Avenue intersected. "What the heck?"

Itz had what Joe called his "teacher look" on. "The city's built on a triangle, because of the rivers. Did you listen in school?"

Itz got good grades in school. Joe bristled, then decided to ignore the remark.

Itz stopped on the sidewalk. An old lady with a babushka and an old gray winter coat bumped into him from behind.

"Watch where you're going, sonny! This is a city, not some farm. Ya gotta pay attention here."

Joe realized that their clothing gave them away: worn, homemade shirts, ill-fitting pants, always too short for boys who grew like sunflowers despite their lack of nutrition.

The old lady hurried on past and disappeared into GC Murphy's, maybe to buy chicken for that night's dinner. Joe and Itz had never in their lives eaten chicken raised any further away than their own backyards.

Mum could be cooking chicken and dumplings right now, if she's come back. Are we mad at her? Is that why we're running away?" Trying to understand felt like trying to cut wood with a hammer instead of a saw.

"The 'Crescent' comes through at 10:05," Itz said through his last mouthful, gazing up at a huge clock on the side of a very tall building across the street. Joe counted up eight stories high—another thing he'd never seen before. The bottom floor of the building, gray like the rest of the city, constructed mostly of glass rooms, revealed fake people inside them wearing fancy clothes. Joe had seen a picture of a wax museum once, and it had frightened him until Andras had explained what the corpse-like figures were made of.

"Wonder where Andras is now?" He continued to gaze up.

"That is one beautiful clock, and I don't know, but we got somewhere we got to be."

"It's 8:30, if that beautiful clock is accurate." Itz continued to keep his 'plan' to himself, while Joe gritted his teeth in frustration.

"C'mon. I want to see something." Itz started up a hill just outside the railroad station. Fortified by the potato breakfast, they climbed for twenty minutes till they reached the top. They left behind the tall, crowded buildings, replaced by drab shacks much like the ones back home. They could see Pittsburgh's other side, formed by the wandering Monongahela River. It joined the Allegheny at what Pittsburghers called The Point. Eons ago the two rivers pushed the land into a triangle and formed the Ohio River, bigger, wider and darker as it flowed away toward the Mississippi. Together they defined the city.

Itz shielded his eyes and pointed across the river. "There they are."

There they were, the steel mills the boys had always heard about. They stretched along the river, low, grey and eternally somber. The buildings themselves seemed incapable of producing this tough metal which took men's limbs or lives, often Hungarianlives, in the process. But the soaring smokestacks shot their fiery breath into a perpetually overcast sky and signaled danger, even death within.

"Pup told me men die in those places." Joe felt a shiver up his neck.

"They had this big strike once, for better pay, better working conditions. Men died."

How did Itz always know this stuff? "Fights?"

Itz nodded. "Frick's men and the Hunkies. They'd come straight off the boat into the mills." He sighed. "Must have been some fights."

Joe heard the longing in Itz's voice. "You think you would have wanted to be here?"

"Hell yea. I would have given those cops a thing or two to think about. "

"They would have had clubs, Itz. They would have smashed your head open before you even saw them."

Itz grinned. "That's why you'll never be a fighter. You're right; they can smash your head in. The odds are against you—that's what makes it fun." He paused, considering the mills one more time. "Well, I've seen what I came to see. Wouldn't want to work there." He stayed still though, staring and shading his eyes. "Won't."

He shifted his stance. "We got a train to catch."

216

Back down to the city. The train station loomed just north of the business district, away from the suits and street vendors, so they dashed back down the hill they'd just come up.

He knew right away he'd entered a different world: diesel fumes, a dusty, oily train yard, men in overalls and work boots, and people lounging around. Hobos. *This seems a little crazy, but I made a promise. I said I was in.*

No time for more talk, but Joe wondered if the train didn't stop other places, smaller towns. He had to stop these questions, he knew. He just didn't know how.

The #48 to Washington DC, the 'Capitol Limited,' began pulling out of Track #7 when they started to run. Sweat ran down Joe's backbone, caused as much by fear as exertion.

They ran harder and faster than they'd ever run in any of their pickup football games, the ones Pup didn't know about. The train roared along beside them, picking up speed and noise like a storm gathering leaves and debris. Itz seemed miles ahead. Joe tried calling out to him but dust and fear choked him and no sound came out. Later in life he would remember the noise, the sound of it reverberating in his chest. The greasy oily smell had disappeared. He fixed his eyes on the ground.

Itz disappeared into a boxcar just ahead of him and Joe began to panic. If he couldn't get to that car he'd be alone in this city. He had to make it. He ran harder, faster, believing he would miss the platform, his doubt seeming to slow him down. But he didn't miss. Somehow he managed to dive up onto the boxcar floor at the last possible second. Raising his head and peering through the sudden darkness of the car, he could hear Itz still panting.

217

"Glad you made it."

Joe didn't yet have the breath for a response. He was sure Itz would have jumped back off the train if he hadn't made it, because that's what brothers do.

He stretched out on his belly on the smooth, flat floor. No safety yet, though. The floor slanted toward the open door. He began to slide backward toward the speeding earth. Itz yelled his name from the opposite corner of the car.

Out of nowhere, two strong hands caught him and pulled him to safety.

"Yinz aht to be home with yer mum." The speaker, shrouded in darkness, could not be seen.

"Wow." Joe swallowed hard and squinted. Sunlight caught their corner of the car, revealing an enormous man, bigger than any he'd ever seen—much bigger than Pup, with dark hair and eyebrows that moved like fat caterpillars. The man stared at him. His beard reached his belly. Joe wanted to touch it.

"Yinz are going ta be real quiet, hear? And when I say so yer going ta jump off here lickety-split." He clicked his fingers in Joe's face.

"Where could we go? I..."

"Not my problem. This is my car—everybody knows that. I'm letting you stay because I didn't want you to get caught. Believe it or not, I was a boy once m'self."

The silence in the dim light, made it seem to Joe he could hear the wheels in his brother's brain turning. Itz would think of something. "What's the next station?" he asked.

218

"Washingon. D.C." the big man replied. "About eight hours."

"You ain't gonna throw us out before then, are you?"

Joe had thought saying 'ain't' would make him seem tough. It didn't. It made him feel foolish.

Another long pause. Joe wished Itz would say something. He kept trying to get his brother's attention, but Itz perfected his ability to ignore anyone or anything long ago. After what seemed like days, Itz stepped, or rather scooted--the moving car made walking impossible--toward the middle of the car, close to the giant.

"Mister," he spoke with a tremulous voice Joe had never heard before. "Our Pup threw us out because we didn't have enough for everybody to eat. Our older brother is in jail—he's a horse thief. Our Mum drinks all the time. We had to get away."

Joe practically choked. In just a few minutes his brother had invented that sandwich of lies with only a little truth in the middle. The big man stared at Itz. Then grabbed his beard and pulled on it so hard Joe thought he would yank it off. He started to laugh so the boys did too. Then the man stopped abruptly, leaving them hanging on the cliff of their own hysteria. They watched him, sobering. He kept pulling his beard.

"You're lying." he said, but not with anger, just amusement.

Joe couldn't let it go, not the part about Mum anyway. He knew Itz would kill him, but he didn't care. Itz could be the boss until he hurt someone Joe loved. Until he hurt Mum.

Joe knew it didn't matter to his bearded savior; still he had to set the record straight. He scooted closer.

"The only thing Mum drinks is water." He coughed a little. "That's so her kids can drink the milk. Goat's milk." He probably didn't need to say this much, but he couldn't stop himself.

He said things he'd only begun to realize.

"She's a good person. Works real hard, with us and in the garden and the chickens and pigs and she even sews at night to make extra money."

Itz put his hands up, facing Joe. "Stop. He doesn't need to know this."

"No. Let him go on. We got time."

Joe brightened. "And she's still pretty. I mean, other women are worn out. You know, gray and wrinkled. Not Mum. Just a little, I mean. I think she does it by what's inside her. It's her spirit. Her fight."

The man regarded each of them for a long time. His thick eyebrows furrowed, actually touching each other. Joe thought of a garter snake sliding through the grass, never displaying its intent. He stroked his beard gently, chuckled and peered at Itz.

"Two pretty different stories." He wiped some sweat from his forehead, then reached a huge hand toward Joe's shoulder.

"You, boy, are a truth teller. That's a good and a bad thing. Be careful. You ain't going to recognize a liar upfront. You might have to get hurt first. I think you are your Mum's boy, and by that I don't mean a pussy. Far from it. World could use..."

Joe felt his face flush. The man shook his head and bent toward Itz. "It ain't news to you that you are a storyteller when you need to be. That's good and bad too, cause you'll know right away when you're up against one. There's a bunch of them out there. Might save your life, your brother's too."

He stared hard at Itz. "You sure are pretty though." Itz inched back, and the man snorted. "I'm just messin' with you boy. I don't go that way...I like women, soft and round. Now, let's get down to business."

The boys stiffened, not knowing what he meant by 'business'. "You're going to jump out at the Union Station in Washington and run to the very next train on the track. The Crescent Limited."

Joe felt fear again. It seemed to be turning into his constant companion. "Why? And why are all these trains 'limited?' Don't sound very good to me."

The man sighed. "You sure ask a lot of questions." He shifted his legs, slapped them a little. "This train don't go to Atlanta. But the Crescent does. What else you gonna do? That's where the train goes. See, we don't get to decide where they go, or what they're called. And you're lucky, 'cause this train will pull in right across the yard from the Crescent. So in DC you jump from this car and when you jump, keep running fast. Get off the tracks quick, if you value your life. The Bulls are bad there. Keep watching for them."

"The Bulls?" Joe felt a twinge in his spine.

"Jesus, you don't know who the Bulls are? The company cops who guard the trains, and they ain't human. They'll kill you with their sticks. Seen lots of guys get killed."

"Oh God." Even Itz's reckless bravery fell away now.

"Yea, but the workers will help you, crazy as that sounds. They'll tell you what you need to know. You got to judge them though, and talk polite. 'Yessir. No sir.' Like that."

They sped along toward what Joe believed was their doom. It seemed like forever when they finally dropped off the train in Washington, which turned out to be a little easier than clawing their way on. They saw only one Bull, sleeping soundly in the pre-dawn light, propped up against a dilapidated shed. Maybe the giant had exaggerated. There didn't appear to be any workers to help them, so the boys tiptoed past the sleeping man. When he rolled over and snorted in his sleep, Joe shuddered. They began to run again.

20

JOE

Atlanta, Georgia. The train pulled into the station on Sunday morning and the sleepy southern town seemed as stricken by the heat as the boys were. Sweat rolled down their faces and dust and grime stuck to their bodies like a new layer of skin. Itz said they smelled like the foul limburger cheese Pup brought home and ate just to torture them.

No Bulls here, none they could see anyway.

"Maybe it's just too hot for them."

"Or maybe it's because we just got off the train and aren't showing any intention of trying to get back on. What would they arrest us for – walking in a train yard?

"Who knows? That guy made it sound like they'd arrest for fun. Anyway, these mosquitoes are worse than Bulls. There must be a thousand of them for every person in this town." Joe whined.

"Ah, quit yer griping. Leave them alone. You're just making it worse."

Joe wished Itz didn't always have an answer.

They walked along Peachtree Street, gazing at closed shop windows. Only a few other people roamed about.

Itz had been uncharacteristically grumpy the last hour or so. Joe didn't know exactly why, and knew that he wouldn't find out. Itz kept things in, but he could snap, fists flying, if his mood worsened. Joe didn't want to be dragging him out of a fight in a strange city with who knew what kinds of boys or men.

A thin man wearing a brown hat and suit with sweat stains under his arms approached them. He had a long nose and a worried brow but he extended his hand. The boys shrank back, having learned long ago to beware of strangers, especially friendly ones.

"Name's Billy Thick. Um guessin' y'all ain't from round heah."

They had to have him repeat what he said. He didn't smell much better than they did.

"I think I can help y'all out. Y'all a little hungry? I know a place, it's called 'The Boys' Christian Association.'

Itz moved back. "Oh. No. We'll just be moving along. Thanks but no thanks."

The man chuckled, even though Joe hadn't heard him say anything funny. "Bacon and eggs, biscuits. Big fat ones."

Joe felt his stomach growling.

"Boys." Here Billy tipped his hat back. "We don't preach. These are tough times. Just tryin' to help people."

Joe understood that. *Ministers and priests wear long black robes, so this guy's not a preacher. Can we trust him? Sure am hungry.*

Their hunger led them through town behind Billy. Small wooden buildings that could be brought down with one match.

Billy stopped suddenly, pushed back his hat, shaded his eyes and pointed across the street. "Well, here we are, boys."

They faced yet another nondescript building wilting as much as they were under the heat. It reminded Joe of the decaying body of a squirrel he'd once found in the woods.

"Ready for a man-sized breakfast? Bacon, eggs, grits, biscuits, pancakes, sausage, milk, juice, coffee. Whatever you want. Come on."

He started across the street. The boys stepped off the curb and followed him. On the way, Billy told them about a field being cleared about ten miles outside of town. "Yep, they're going to build a prison there, so it's a pretty big space. Need lots of men with scythes. You know how to use a scythe?"

"Sure," said Itz. "Of course." Joe had never heard of a scythe, he would just have to figure it out.

225

The promised breakfast turned out to be a dry roll and some beef jerky.

"Guess they ran out of eggs," their brown suited savior declared, and disappeared to the back of the building.

It took them little time to devour the meager fare, but they stayed at the table. It felt good to sit. Then Billy yelled from the doorway to the back room. "Truck's loading boys, you want to work, you need to go out there and get on it." Itz shrugged. "Let's go. What else do we do?"

That doesn't seem like much of a reason. What happened to his plan?

Joe didn't ask because he didn't have any good options.

A dusty old pickup with a dozen men, old, young, black, white, everyone slouched or squirming for a better seat. Joe asked an older man tucked into a corner of the truck where they were headed.

"Mostly east. About fifteen miles."

"Where does that take us?"

The man grimaced. "The middle of nowhere."

The truck carried them to a field about an hour outside the city. They stood in a slovenly huddle behind the truck.

"One dollar, paid at the end of the day, if you finish your work," the boss man said. He rested his hands on a huge belly, and Joe couldn't help but stare. *No surprise he got that fat when nobody has enough to eat.*

"If you don't finish, you're gone. Get out and get back on the train, cause there ain't no other work around here."

Itz spoke up. "How do we know if we finished our work?"

"You don't know, whippersnapper. I know."

They sweated in the blazing sun all afternoon, but no dollars surfaced at quitting time. "Didn't work a whole day," muttered the boss. "If you do right tomorrow, you'll get a dollar and a half at the end of the day."

Tired, broken men, desperate for work, did not protest.

 The boys' 'beds' were in a barn with the other men, covered with moldy, hole ridden blankets. They lay there in the waning light, shivering in the cool, wet air. Joe nudged Itz.

"You awake?"

"Now I am.' Itz grumbled.

"What about Mum?"

"What about her?"

"What do you think she's thinking? Do you think she's worried?"

Itz sat up on one elbow. "If you remember, little brother, the last time we saw Mum she was marching around the house talking some alphabet language. Half out of her gourd."

"But she's better now, I bet. I bet she's home. Maybe worrying about us."

"I know one thing. She goes off sometimes and she's not giving us a thought. If she's better she's got other things to deal with. And maybe…"

"Maybe what?" Joe wanted something to hold onto.

"Maybe she just likes staying with Mrs. Boyle better than with us."

One of the men growled, "Shut up you two. Now."

Joe lay back and put his hands behind his head. Tired as he felt, he couldn't sleep. *Maybe she likes staying with Mrs. Boyle better. Maybe she doesn't even care about us.*

"Hell can't be as hot as this," Joe grunted and lifted his scythe again, swinging the blade through the tall grass. Even in the early morning, sweat rolled off their faces in rivulets as they worked. They saw a man carried out on a stretcher after he surprised a timber rattler lying peacefully underneath his blade. The men stopped for a minute and stared as the victim howled in pain. Two of them picked him up and carried him off to the boss's hut.

Joe feared snakes almost as much as his father's wrath. A tall, angular man with burnt skin worked near them. He shifted back his ratty hat. "Hmm. Not many of them up this way. Hadn't seen one in some time."

"Is he going to die?" Joe asked.

The man stood up and rubbed his back. "Who knows? Ain't none of our business anyway. We're just the workers. Got no souls. Ain't supposed to wonder about things."

Itz said, "Get back to work. The man said 'Get back to work,' so that's what we do."

Joe lifted the scythe and swung it toward the ground. It caught the morning sun, then plummeted and stuck in the red soil.

"Never hire city boys," A grizzled, toothless old black man stood studying Joe. He put his hand on Joe's right arm and brought the tool down close to the ground." Yer gonna cut off yer foot instead of the weeds. Just back and forth easy, and step forward at the end of each swing. That's it. Don't stop. You make a rhythm. It'll help you."

"Thanks. I've never done this before."

"No kidding." The man shook his head a little, but Joe felt his kindness.

The morning passed more slowly than a school day.

Finally, Itz said, "Here comes The Man."

A thin, wiry guy carrying a rifle turned out to be 'the man,' the boss's foreman. Joe didn't know why he needed a gun, but it did seem to make him bigger. Did he think they were going to try and steal the weeds? The assistant spoke one word, "Lunch," then turned on his heel.

"Enough food to keep us alive and working," complained Itz, stirring some kind of porridge-like stuff in his bowl. "Just like home." He winced.

"No, not just like home," Joe remembered the retes, although he realized Mum hadn't made it in a long while.

"What are these green leaves?" Joe asked the man beside him.

"Greens." He put a hand on Joe's shoulder. "You never ate greens? They good for you."

Joe started, "They taste like…"

"Shut up." Itz took a spoonful of the greens, made a sour face. "It's what we got."

Another six hours sweating and swinging the blades, then they had dinner, exactly the same fare as lunch. They lay down again along with the other men. Joe smelled sweat and urine, listened to snores, some loud as freight trains, some soft and purring.

By the third day in the field, and still no pay, Joe had had all he could take. Day and night he dreamt of food --- chicken and dumplings, goulash, even Mum's thin potato soup. And the desserts—pastries, cookies, once even a cake. Joe felt an ache, not just in his belly. He missed other things about her—her singing the old Irish songs, which always made her a little happier. Once, at home with a stomach upset, he let her teach him 'Molly McGuire' and 'The Hills of Connemara.' Joe liked to sing, he liked music. His brothers were at school and so couldn't tease him, pointing out mistakes and belittling his attempt. But he couldn't find a song in his heart now.

"We gotta get out of here," he declared to Itz.

Itz just kept swinging the scythe. He seemed to have lost his fight, which worried Joe almost as much as the snakes. And he'd almost quit talking. Joe, on the other hand, felt himself getting stronger. He wondered if he could take Andras now. Probably not. His brother seemed like ancient history, but he knew Andras would have gotten them out of here. Now he would have to do that—Itz had lost his swagger.

230

Itz emitted a strange high laugh. "There's nowhere to go, whippersnapper. You heard the man, there's no other work."

"The man lies. He's lied about how much we get paid, when we get paid. Everything he's told us is lies. The men say get out if you can. We'll walk. They say some of the farmers' wives will give you food, maybe even let you eat on their back porch. We'll ask around in town."

They were walking to the field, carefully threading their way through patches of uncut grass. Itz spit, but not much and not too far—not like the spitting contests they used to have in Summervale, but spitting nonetheless.

"They need us to stay, no matter what he says. At least until they get this field cleared."

"Yea, so how are they going to keep us here?"

Itz's mouth turned down as his eyes went up. "Have you been paid? Do you want to be paid?"

Joe felt himself starting to boil. "Jesus Christ Itz, what is going on with you? You tell me this whole plan. You've got it figured out. Then we get here and you're just giving up. Are you the same guy that dared Pup to come after him? Doesn't seem like it."

Joe stared at his brother. Itz mumbled, "I didn't think it would be like this."

"Like what? Hard? Well hell yeah it's hard. But you can't just quit."

231

He felt himself cool down a little, and realized this whole situation seemed odd. Backwards or something. He had never given orders before. But he kept doing it. He had to.

"We need to get out of here. You're good at running away. We just have to do it again. And no, I haven't been paid, but I thought about that. You're going to steal our pay. Well, not steal really, because it's ours."

Itz, standing there like an old man, like old McManus, mumbled. "I'm tired, Joe, but I don't want to end up getting beaten up by these thugs. Give it a few more days. The job will end and then we move on."

"Yea, we'll move on with these guys like a bunch of ants hunting for crumbs. Feeding the queen, ending up with nothing. Do you really think they're going to pay us? Cause I don't. You could get the money and we could get out of here. Do something instead of just crawling along. I'll help you. We'll go at night. It will be easier to get away and a little cooler. I'll do whatever you say. Anything."

Itz stared out into the pines. A tight lipped smile spread slowly across his face. "Well now, that kind of offer is hard to refuse."

After dinner, Joe and Itz sat with their backs against a huge hickory tree. Joe whittled a short stick in between scratching while Itz talked.

"I saw The Man yakking with a white haired guy in a fancy suit. Then he went toward the house where he stays with a sack against his belly. You know what was in it, right?"

"Our money."

"Right.

"Can't believe he took that money out in front of everybody."

"He figured we'd be too tired to be watching him. Besides, he's arrogant and stupid."

Joe didn't answer. At least he knew what stupid meant.

"He put the sack in a small metal box under the porch."

"Why?"

"Two reasons. He doesn't want it in his room in case somebody tries to steal it and he gets himself in the middle of something. Coward. And two, he figures nobody except him is skinny enough to get under that porch."

"Except you."

"Except me." Itz sat up straighter, stretched his arms out over his head.

He's a little more like himself. At least I hope so. "What do I do?"

"Two things. Find us some kind of cutter to get the lock on the box open. And then you just have to watch out for him."

"What?" Joe felt fear beginning to freeze his body again.

"We've got to get the box open. We could just take the whole thing but I know your sad honorable self would not agree to that. Then you need to keep your eyes on the door of that house every second. If it opens even a tiny crack, you run. Like the biggest, fastest linebacker ever is chasing

233

you. We need to make sure he doesn't kill both of us. One of us needs to get back home and tell the story."

"No. I couldn't leave you here."

"You said anything, little brother. You said you'd do anything.' Itz stared at him, his face hard but with this triumphant expression on his face.

Damn. He had.

"I can get the box open. Old Man McManus taught me a trick with a thin piece of metal."

Itz gave him that sideways Cierc smile."Mmm-hmm. And where are you going to get a thin piece of metal?"

Joe extracted the very thing from his back pocket. "I've actually got a few of them." He lay the small shiny pieces on the grass in front of them.

"So you were planning for us to steal money from a lock box?"

Joe grinned at the irony of it, wished he could have thought of this earlier. "I found them beside the tracks." He held up one of the pieces, the smallest one with one sharp end. "Figured it might come in handy."

Itz's eyes were wide with something close to admiration, Joe thought. He swallowed and spit, for lack of any other appropriate reaction. He held the cool metal in his palm, the only cool thing he had felt in days. Sweat still slid into his eyes despite a tiny evening breeze. He curved his hands around the metal and knew he could do this.

By dark, the men lay in an exhausted sleep on the floor of the barn. Joe and Itz eased the door open and crept out. Isolated clouds afforded some cover from the small bit of moonlight.

Itz had come back to life, his body tight with purpose and plan.

"We'll give it our best shot." He disappeared before Joe had a chance to reply. The clouds made most of their surroundings hard to see. Joe took a deep breath in. He thought he could hear Itz crawling the hundred or so feet toward the house, swishing against tall grass just before he slid underneath it. But there were no other sounds, no screaming boss, no stamping feet, so Joe figured he imagined it. Fear could do strange things, he had learned.

Itz returned in less time, it seemed, than it took for Joe to breathe out. He took the box and set to work. He had to ease the piece of metal down to where the lock caught, and break the seal. McManus could do it in less than a minute. Joe hadn't told his brother that he'd never actually done it, but Itz sat, watching intently. Joe's work defeated his fear. He believed they were going to get out, and get what they deserved.

It took three tries to fit the thin metal piece around the lock and down into the hole that held it. Itz heard the click and had the box open in an instant. He grabbed the pile of bills. "We could…"

"No. There are eight sleeping men in there, who are older and more beaten than us. They deserve some of this money."

Itz had been counting. "Eight men, plus us, three days at $1 a day. That's what he promised us, right?" He didn't wait for an answer. "There isn't even enough for that. There's $18 in here. So, Mr. Goodright, how much do we take?"

A pause. "No time to think, Joe. You got to decide."

"Okay. We take our share."

Itz grabbed six dollars out of the box. "Let's go."

Joe hesitated, his eyes on the sleeping men.

"We gotta go, Joe. Now.

21

GRACE

Eileen's help sometimes kept Grace balanced, but there were times nothing did and she would reach the breaking point once more. Her family referred to her losing her wits and almost her soul as 'going away.' Without her mother and Brid, another return from that shadowy world that held her captive might have been impossible. Dreams of mountains falling onto her house, rivers flooding the town, terrified children screaming came nightly, and the days

236

were no better. Anxiety pushed down on her until she could barely rise from a chair. The world's troubles were her responsibility, and she drifted through each day, helpless.

She found herself at Brid's house, poorly again. Grace's mother came to Brid's almost every day with soup or soda bread and words of encouragement, a lioness returning to her injured cub. She confessed to Grace that she had changed her mind about many things over the years, particularly about Brid, whose marriage to John Boyle defined her, at least in Nora's mind, as a normal woman. Grace gazed at her mother, almost seeming interested.

"Brid takes such good care of you when you... well, when you need it. Poor dear. I never expected you...You were always such a fighter, so sure of yourself as a child. Perhaps we could pray the rosary together. Would that help?"

Grace stared at the floor. *No. The rosary will not help. The truth might.* Ma sighed.

Brid didn't change, fluttering around through the cleaning and cooking. She and Ma struck up an unlikely friendship. Ma even went by Grace's house sometimes, to help Eileen. What woman can resist her granddaughter? Grace knew the girl loved her nana, her undivided attention, her Irish brogue, her hugs. Ma would tell Grace about her visits. In any other situation, it would have gratified Grace immensely. Mostly she sat gazing ahead like a drifter on a park bench.

Brid never stopped trying. "Come on! Get up! Don't just sit there! It's a beautiful day and we're not going to waste it sitting in here."

Grace sighed. "It's too hot."

Brid grinned and held out her hands. "Just into the yard," she urged. "I have something wonderful to show you."

Grace had not been outside in four days. Sunlight would be a shock. She sighed but knew she could not resist Brid, who practically dragged her around the yard, then skidded to a stop like a robin about to seize a worm. Just around the corner into the back yard, she pointed to a dogwood tree at the edge of the property. "Look! See those beautiful red leaves/"

Grace saw two or three of them hanging from a lower branch.

Brid slipped her arm under Grace's. "The dogwoods are always first. You know what this means, don't you?"

"No, I don't."

"Yes you do! It means fall is almost here. Cool evenings again. Beautiful leaves and pumpkins. It will bring you peace Grace. And you will rise again."

Grace considered Brid's lovely, freckled face, full of hope, and wanted to be well if for no other reason than for her. She smiled sadly. "Maybe."

22

JOE

They crept across the field, staying low to the ground and thanking the clouds. Once they heard a sound behind them in the tall, uncut grass. Joe felt Itz's body stiffen with his own--they were that close together in the darkness. He thought he would rather take his chances with a bobcat or a coyote than the foreman. The animal hustled off after a few minutes. The boys made it to the road as the moon peeked out, then they started to run.

There were no trees along the roadside. Fortunately there were also no cars and only a sliver of moon. The night was quiet as a dead man's breath. Their feet started to hit the ground in a now familiar rhythmical pattern. They ran at a steady pace, sweating heavily.

Why don't we have some kind of tongue thing, or paw thing, like animals? Joe tried panting, but it didn't cool him off.

He wished he had the great powers of 'The Shadow' as they ran along the dirt road back toward the city. Then he noticed Itz's ashen face. "Let's stop a minute."

Itz nodded and they lowered themselves into the ditch beside the road.

"We're not going to make it." Itz had that faraway look again. His hands were shaking.

"Of course we are. We've got this far, haven't we? Haven't been caught yet."

"You don't know what you're doing. You're too young. And besides you're...you're Joe. The guy who can never decide."

"Yea, well, you gave up soon as you realized Billy Thick didn't lead us to Breakfast Heaven. You – Mr. "I'll Try Anything, Mr. Brave, Mr. Risk. Yea, right." Joe grimaced and immediately wished he could take back what he said. Itz drooped like an old man. He didn't argue, surprising

Joe. Instead he murmured, "Don't know, just don't feel so good."

Joe stood. He said what he'd been thinking the last two days. "It's time to go home, Itz. It's time to face Pup and see about Mum." He reached his hand down to his brother.

"Let's go."

Itz hesitated, took Joe's hand and pulled himself to his feet.

An hour later, the rains came, blowing straight across their chests as they slogged through the swampy side of the road. Itz irritated Joe the whole way. "Why are we going this way? Atlanta is west. Don't we want to get back to Atlanta? We're going east."

Joe sighed, not sure he liked being in charge. "We're going east because that's where we catch the train. I heard guys talking about it back in the field. They said, "There's a station in Stone Mountain, it's closer than anything else. That's how we get back to Atlanta."

It took the better part of a day to reach the train station, and the rain didn't stop. They could only get a glimpse of the mountain, a boulder bigger than they could have imagined. The small train yard in Stone Mountain meant hiding from the Bull would be a challenge. They waited, shivering in the damp. Joe just hoped they wouldn't drop to the ground like dying leaves in the fall. He managed to pull Itz onto a car where the old grizzled men and gaunt boys sought a little refuge and a ride to where life might be better. Water poured down through rusted holes in the roof. The boys slid off the train in Atlanta around sunrise and found their way to a group of men hovering close to the tracks. The rain had let up and dozens of wet and dirty

241

hobos wandered around trying to figure out their next move.

An older man with a mustache and the remains of a soldier's uniform led them to what he generously called his 'tent,' a ragged blanket propped up with a stick, not protecting him from the rain.

He talked in a streak. "It's pretty close to the fire, that's when there is a fire if you know what I mean. Name's Jimmy." He stuck out his hand. "Veteran of the Great War yes sir, 19 and 17, the year I signed up. Tough times my boys. Trenches, cold, guys getting their legs blown off. And that damn flu, killing more guys than the enemy."

"Ah, we were just wondering if we could get some food, maybe a place to lay down tonight."

A different voice, high pitched, interrupted. "Come with me. I'll find a place for ya." The voice belonged to a slender kid slouching toward them with a cigarette dangling from his mouth. He had a newsboy cap positioned on his head so that the shadow of it made it almost impossible to see his face. His oversized, faded shirt still showed a sign of fashion: big pockets in the front, wide sleeves reaching below his wrists.

"C'mon with me." He turned his body to the right and started to head away.

Joe nudged Itz in the ribs. "Let's go. We gotta get away from the soldier. He'll want to tell us war stories, and we'll never get food or sleep."

Was Itz hanging his head a little? Itz?

"Whatever you say."

"Whatever I say? Since when?"

"Since about yesterday."

Joe thought about this as they followed the boy into the darkness.

A few minutes later, coming to an abrupt stop, taking a long drag from his cigarette and blowing out the smoke, he said, "Name's Cody. Who are you?"

Joe imagined they were about the same age. "I'm Joe, he's Itz."

"Itz? What kinda name is that? Never mind. Let's go get some grub." They followed him to the center of the camp, where a sad man stirred grits in a big pot.

"I guess we're not in Mum's kitchen," Joe whispered to Itz.

"Guess not."

The soup at least warmed them; sloshing around in thei bellies as they trailed Cody to a small pile of blankets and each grabbed one.

The moon lit up the center of the restrainungle, what hobos called their resting place near the train yard. Some of the drained men already slept. Joe and Itz's new friend peered out into the darkness and in one quick motion removed his cap.

Hair fell down in all directions. Joe felt a shock. Cody, a girl. A pretty girl, with bright blue eyes and red lips and now that Joe studied her, a chest that obviously didn't belong to a boy. He covered his own embarrassment by convincing himself that she had hidden that too.

243

But Cody didn't pay any attention to Joe. She had her hand on Itz's shoulder, explaining how being a boy made life on the road easier and how she had a head start by being given a boy's name. Itz nodded, staring at the dying fire. He didn't seem to be enjoying the attention.

"That doesn't make sense. If it were me...Why isn't he..."

He lay down on his blanket with his back turned away from them and slept, dreaming of girls the whole night long.

He and Itz woke before dawn, no longer able to find any comfort on the cold hard ground. Joe had locked his question inside himself like the dam containing the river back home. Finally, he couldn't keep it in any longer.

"So, how did things go last night?"

Itz didn't answer for a while. When Joe's thoughts had moved on however, Itz spoke up.

"Things didn't go."

"Didn't go? What does that mean?"

"It means nothing happened."

"Then you either got rocks in your head or you're dead. She liked you."

Again no response. Joe sat up and pulled his ratty blanket over him. Itz didn't sound like himself, maybe some younger version of his voice. None of the steady deepness that Joe so envied now.

"Just didn't feel anything."

244

"And what does that mean?"

"It just means that. Now leave me alone so I can wake up."

They didn't speak of it again.

Joe lay there, missing Mum, and not just her cooking. He almost ached for her soft brogue and her eyes, how they danced sometimes when she forgot about her life for a moment. The river, Eileen, even Andras filled his thoughts. Joe wondered for the hundredth time what happened to him. He had told them to run, had taken the heat for them. He still couldn't fit that into his picture of Andras. Joe dreamed of Andras being pulled toward the dam, helpless, silent. No one to save him.

23

EILEEN

A sliver of evening light showed through the clouds as Eileen came into the back yard. Then like a dream, Lane appeared. She smiled for the first time in days.

"Why, hello! You didn't catch me at my best here." Her wrinkled apron had flour and coffee stains on it. There was no improving it, but it gave her something to do with her hands besides having them flutter around like hummingbirds.

"Just came to say hello. Haven't seen you around." He cleared his throat and made circles in the dirt with his foot.

"Lane, I'm sure you've heard what's happened here. I can't see you because my mom...this work..."

She gestured toward the house, the garden, the chickens, shrugged her shoulders and forced back tears. Mum had taught her that only weak women cry.

"I know Love. I've lots of work to do too, remember?"

That irritated her a little, but she said nothing.

"I heard about your mum being sick. I'm sorry."

Well, at least the grapevine's only gone that far. Sick, not crazy.

"Lane, there is no time for walks after school, no time for school even. And I don't know when it will be over."

Lane put his arm around her shoulders and Eileen led the way to the porch. "Five minutes Eileen? Can it survive without you for five minutes?"

246

The only time she cried even a little was whenever somebody was nice to her. She pulled out her handkerchief and pretended to blow her nose while she was really wiping tiny tears.

He sat back on the swing, puts his hands behind his head. They were quiet for a while. She listened to the crickets.

Lane leaned forward. "I want to live in a little house on the edge of town, back near the woods and…I want to live there with you."

Did he just propose? I'm fifteen. Usually I would be going out to dances.

"Stop, Lane." She jumped to her feet. "Stop!"

"It's shameful of you—talking like that to a girl before you dump her for the next one. You know there is no chance of that ever happening. Just how do you propose making this dream come true?"

I really want him to have an answer.

"This whole family is depending on me. I…"

"This whole family is depending on you because you let them, Love."

"Stop calling me 'Love,' you sound like some…"

"Irishman?"

He stood up and hitched his pants. "But you do let them."

It isn't fair how men are almost always above you.

She rose and put her hands on her hips, and said, "There is no choice. I'm the only one who can do this. Besides..." She glanced out into the yard, to the trees that needed pruning, to the fruit that needed picking, the weeds, the peeling fence. "Besides, everyone is helping out."

She studied the porch floor slats, some curling up on the outside, one broken, one completely missing. She felt him move in closer. His big, rough hands turned her face toward him.

"Eileen, c'mon. Where are these brothers of yours who are helping out? Off running around the country or playing football or getting into fights or steal...Well, you know. Getting into trouble. They don't need you—they get in and out of their brawls just fine."

Her heart pounded. "Don't talk about my brothers like that. I know what they are, and all the things they've done. They're still my brothers."

"You're right. Sorry."

After that, she felt so tired she wanted to lie down right on this porch. *If I could just sleep, and not have to work all the time. And if I lived with you, Lane, would my life change that much? I would take care of you instead of everyone here. And then I would have babies and take care of them. It wouldn't really change.*

He kissed her swiftly on the lips and then he was gone.

Should I go feed the pigs or just go with him?

And then there was Mum, home again. She looked healthy, at least healthier. And she had come home, finally. She was leaving Mrs. Boyle, something Eileen had not been sure she would ever do again.

She returned pale but less tired and calmer than the last time Eileen had seen her. Standing silent in the back doorway with Mrs. Boyle, her eyes moved around the kitchen. Eileen felt invisible. At last Mum spoke.

"Eileen, my girl." Her fingers twisted the sides of her skirt.

"I'm not your girl, I'm your replacement."

A long pause, and the saddest look she'd ever seen on her mother's face. And she had seen a lot of sad faces.

Then Eileen imagined a fledging the first time it flies, how much stronger it is and how it leaves the nest with hardly a thought. She didn't speak, just took her mother's hand and led her into the kitchen. Mrs. Boyle said her goodbyes, hugged Mum for a long time and exited, teary eyed.

Mum asked where the boys were, and if the chickens had been fed. She lifted the flour crock from the shelf, preparing to make bread. Eileen watched her for a long time, now understanding what a hard life her mother had led. How little happiness. And yet she kept returning to them, doing her best to make their lives bearable, sometimes even a little fun.

I guess she deserves a little pleasure, even love, no matter where it comes from.

24

GRACE

Grace knew that her ma's wish for a life with Brid remained a fantasy, one that could only happen in a much better world. Grace loved her children and had duties. She resolved to take more care of herself, to recognize the good in her life: her children, her garden and flowers, Mrs. Nyilas, her mother, and Brid. Dominic bothered her less and never hurt her anymore, mainly because of his weakened state. However, not angering him remained a trick she never fully mastered.

She had returned to an emptier house. The boys had had another adventure, this time culminating in Andras' arrest and the disappearance of Itz and Joe. Eileen explained the situation the day after Grace came home. Time for talk had not come until then, given all the work and Grace's need to readjust.

They sat on the back porch swing, their toes touching the floor as they slowly swung back and forth. The late afternoon had cooled, mercifully.

"They decided to go camping up in the hills, and stole Mr. Krushksad's horses to get there. They got caught, so Joe and Itz ran off. They've been gone a week, no word. They arrested Andras and put him in jail."

Eileen held her head high, but didn't feel confident. She started toward the kitchen. Her mother also stood, straightened and folded her arms.

"Just a minute, young lady."

Eileen turned back, her fists clenched at her sides. "I can't believe you tripped out of the house not able to speak a single word less than two weeks ago, and now you think you can be in charge again.

Her mother ignore the remark. "Did you know anything about this?"

Eileen had never been able to lie to Mum. Grace watched little beads of sweat form at her daughter's hairline. She knew the truth before Eileen spoke.

"Just a little bit that Joe told me. He thinks his brothers' ideas are crazy but he always desperately wants to go with them. I warned him, but you know Joe."

Her daughter's attempt to forge an alliance amused Grace, but she kept a straight face.

"But you didn't say anything to Andras or his brothers."

Eileen straightened, folded her arms.

"No I didn't. No. I needed to do the dishes, clean the bathrooms and one of the goats had climbed onto the shed roof. Those boys are worthless when you were gone. Gone, doing who knows what, and I had to do everything"

The words pierced Grace's heart and left it racing. Tears began to roll down her daughter's face. Grace could not soften, not yet.

"But where are they? Where?"

"I don't know. Nobody does. I've just been doing my best here. You're their mother."

Grace's body tightened like someone had her in a vice grip. Two of her children were gone, were in danger, and she could think of nothing to do.

Did I even think about how I left my family? What has my recovery cost them? I have lived a lie. I love Brid and anyone who finds out would condemn me, even my children. They could never understand. Would they hate me?

No matter what, now she needed to deal with her daughter. She moved toward Eileen and held her. "Oh Eileen. It has been so hard for you and I'm so sorry."

Eileen stiffened. She had not finished. "They let Andras out of jail because he got sick. Really sick. Pneumonia. I nursed him back to health, feeding and cleaning him." Her face soured.

Eileen resisted the hug, then collapsed into her mother's embrace. After a bit she pulled back.

Grace swallowed hard. "Tomorrow I want you to go out with your friends and have some fun." She hesitated, her eyes glued on her daughter's face. "I love you."

Eileen stood up straight, looking down at her mother. "I love you too." Eileen swallowed, looked away into the yard. "Whatever you do."

Her lovely face softened and she started back into the house, leaving her mother warmed and dumbstruck at the same time.

Did she know? Or what did she know, and what could she make of it?

Grace felt the familiar fear creeping into her belly. What if? She watched Eileen disappear, back to her books, and took solace from her last words. "Whatever you do, I love you too."

What more could she ask? She accepted her daughter's gift. Warmth filled her and her trembling body relaxed.

One evening a few weeks later, Grace again sat on the porch for a long time, watching the sun set, even though chores and her husband's demands awaited. When she came into the house, she found him sitting in the living room, reading the paper as usual in his chair by the window.

Dominic's eye did not leave his paper. "How is he?"

Grace knew through almost twenty years of tears and regret that he did not look at her but through her, finding the best route to whatever he wanted or needed. All of that mattered much less to her now.

"Eileen says he's fine. Out causing trouble again."

If she didn't know Dominic she would have been amazed. Her husband did not even realize that Andras had been out of bed for two days. He snorted and placed his hand tenderly behind his neck shifting his position in the chair. The old injury, his 'accident' with the mule. He had returned to work in the mine reluctantly, after two years of complaining and demanding, two years of hungry children, and the landlord at the door. At least a little money came in these days but who knew how long it would last? Grace heard rumors that her husband couldn't pull his weight at work and that he had shown up with liquor on his breath more than once. Dangerous stuff, down in the mine.

Eileen burst back in and pranced to her father's side. She knelt down beside his chair, smiling. His face brightened as he put his hand on her shoulder. Moving toward the kitchen Grace heard Eileen say, "How are you today, Pup? Feeling okay?"

Grace didn't quite understand the recent connection between her husband and daughter, but knew it had begun when she "went away." She was glad for it though. Anything that made things easier.

"About the same," he answered. "You know. The pain doesn't go away. I just have to push through it." Grace began preparing dinner. Clattering pots, she covered her amusement at Dominic's words, knowing her glee would not be taken kindly. "Push through the pain?" He had pushed liquor into his gaping mouth and he'd certainly pushed her, but never had he pushed through pain.

Enough of that. Her determination had been to make the best of things. Eileen and her father's friendship, if she could call it that, could only be a good thing. Grace would have never believed it, given his disregard of his daughter since her birth, but Eileen learned something on her own, something Grace could not teach her. Once Dominic perceived strength and perseverance in a person, even a girl, his attitude changed. Eileen had somehow figured this out. Marta had those qualities and he had respected her more than anyone. Grace knew that strength would serve her daughter well. She turned back to the two headless chickens lying on the kitchen table, plucked and dressed for chicken and dumplings tonight. Joe would especially love this. But Joe and Itz were lost somewhere. Her heart skipped a beat.

25

JOE

A whole day waiting for the train back to Atlanta. Word had it there had been a wreck coming out of the city, a collision at the junction. Nobody killed or hurt unless you counted a hobo, which nobody did. But the tracks were tangled like tree limbs after a storm. It would take at least a day to get everything going again. The brothers sauntered around the camp. The rain had stopped but mud and muck still prevailed, covering everyone's clothes and thoughts. Cody had disappeared. Joe figured that was for the better.

As darkness fell again, Itz lay down on his blanket and fell asleep like a man with no sins. Joe tried to sleep for a futile hour. Restless with hunger, heat and dirt driving at him like two penny nails into wood, he stood and stretched.

Itz sat up. "What are you doing? Doing begins with D! Get it? D. Andras begins with A! Andras is a pig! Pig begins with P!" DAP! DAP!

He grinned at Joe. "Well, you woke me up with all your moving around over there. I figured instead of killing you I'd introduce a little humor."

Itz stood and slapped Joe on the back a few times. Joe tried not to laugh, but having even some part of the old Itz back pushed him into it. Itz imitated Mum almost perfectly.

Itz reached into his pocket and pulled out a small bottle. "What have we here? Wee—hee!"

257

Joe considered the bottle. "I have two questions. One, where did you get that? And two, how did you recover so quick? You were dragging like a sad dog's tail yesterday."

"I've been sleeping for the better part of two days, brother. Besides, being sick is boring. I'm done with it. And answer to question number one, none of your business! You want some?"

Joe stared at the bottle.

"This 'heah' is your first ticket to heaven, little brother. Pure, unadulterated all American moonshine. Gift of our southern brothers, otherwise known as White Lightning, Bootleg, Firewater, Hooch. It's going to make you happy, real happy."

"Yeah, well if it's as bad as that fake southern accent, I don't think so. I'm not going to touch it. All we need to do is get plastered here. Somebody will be on us in a minute. Uh uh. Not me. We're in the middle of a camp full of desperate men. You never know what could happen."

But why not now? This might be the best time. What if I never try it? How would I know if I like it or not? I don't want to end up like old McManus. Still, I could try it just once, then I'd know.

"We have to be really quiet, so nobody knows. Besides, I hate loud drunks."

"Like Pup, you mean."

"Mmm. Well, I'm not going to be any kind of drunk."

"For your whole life? You got to at least try it. At least once."

Itz unscrewed the top of the jar, took a swig and made a sound like "Ahh" only with some gravel in it. He held the jar out. "Just try it."

Joe snatched the jar and swallowed a mouthful before his brain could tell him to think about it some more. His last thought before the liquor went down: *How bad can it be?*

Bad. The night splintered. His throat felt like some large, hairy claw had reached down and grabbed it hard. It drew up his insides and shook him with the force of a tornado.

The storm abated quickly and mercifully. Joe tried to place the jar on the soft ground, but Itz stopped him.

"Good job, Jozef! You have the makings...But, don't put it down yet. How do you feel?"

Joe had to admit he didn't feel too bad. The claw had disappeared and his insides relaxed.

"Okay," he mumbled.

"Good. So what you need to do now is take one more sip. That will settle you down and you can have a nice nap."

Itz sounded a little too much like Mum convincing her children to "play nice with each other," but Joe didn't care. He wanted that second drink even more than food or a ride home. He tipped the bottle back again. This time he understood the name "Fire Water." It burned slowly down the soft inside of his throat, which smoldered, still hot but more like embers. His brain quieted some more.

"This is sorta good."

"Yea." Itz took the jar and swallowed again.

They sat close in the humid darkness, handing the jar back and forth. Once Joe almost missed Itz's outstretched hand.

"Damn! Be careful. This is all we got."

Joe sniggered. "Seems like iz plenny to me. Anyway, yer getting me drunker 'n a skunk and telling me to be careful? Ha. Thas a good one."

"Take one more Joe," Itz muttered. "I think that's all you'll need."

Joe obliged willingly, more than once, more than he needed. Each time the liquor oozed down his throat he felt a little better. Happy even. Finally, he returned the jar to Itz and sighed. "Keep it." But Itz kept passing it back. One more turned into three more.

He lay back down on the pine straw, made a pillow with his hands and closed his eyes.

The trees above him wobbled like pick up sticks, certain to fall. But they didn't fall; they just kept going round and round. His stomach trembled. Itz jostled his arm.

"Sit up. You don't want to go to sleep yet."

"But you tole me I could."

"Never mind what I told you. You drank way more than I expected and you're a little rough. Sit up. You just need to let the hooch settle. And since we can't walk around, we'll just…talk."

Itz wants to talk? Even in his compromised state Joe could not imagine this. Kind of like Andras giving you a pat on the back, or Eileen smiling.

Joe struggled to a sitting position. "Whaddle we talk about?"

"Talking…well, I'm afraid I'm out of my element here."

"Whazzat mean?"

Itz smiled. "Never mind."

"Ya know, sometimes you look jus like Mum."

"Mum is a woman, you drunken fool."

"No! I mean like a man Mum."

"You are loaded."

"Prolly."

The boys faded back down to the pine straw. Itz turned away from Joe.

"Itz?"

"Yea?"

"What about Mum?"

A moment's silence. "What do you mean what about Mum?"

"Ya know, how she goes away sometimes."

"Yea."

"Well, why? Other guys' mums don't."

"I guess she needs a break from Pup."

Joe stared up through the trees into the waning light. His happy feeling had faded. "No, thas not it. She gets crazy."

"Okay, so what do you think, oh wise one?"

"Dunno. S'why I asked you."

"Go to sleep. We gotta get up in a few hours." Itz rolled over onto his side. Joe tried to sleep but he could only fidget and turn. The pine straw bit at his neck and arms. *Had it gotten hotter?*

"Itz?"

"For the last time, go to…"

"Jus one more thing. I gotta tell you this one more thing. Then I'll go to sleep. I will."

Itz didn't reply, but Joe could tell he hadn't nodded off yet, so he plunged in. "Once I stayed home sick from school."

"Fascinating."

"Yea, but I got up to pee an saw Miz Boyle at the bottom of the stairs."

"Even more fascinating."

"Yea, but she and Mum were there kissin'."

Joe waited in the darkness. His happy feeling had vanished.

"Yea." *It didn't sound like the yea he usually heard from Itz. It sounded like maybe Itz understood what he was saying.*

262

But then he answered." Women are always kissing everybody. It's just what they do. Lipstick and big sweaty boobs smothering you. I hate it."

"Not that kind of kissin' Itz. I watched for about five minutes and it din't end. Then I had to go back to bed. Din't feel very good."

Itz didn't move but his voice changed, more quavery. Joe heard him take a deep breath before he spoke again.

"I don't know Joe. I've thought about it too but I don't know what it is or what it could be. Women don't..." He stopped there, leaving Joe with more questions.

So he had seem some things too? Women don't what? Does he know something else?"

Joe didn't know what he expected, but it wasn't this. He felt himself skating toward a huge hole in a frozen pond. He didn't know anything, and realized he wanted no more.

"Right," he replied. "Let's get some sleep."

They didn't get much.

The clammy air seemed to mix with the liquor. It oozed out of Joe's forehead, armpits, and the back of his neck. A cool breeze would help a lot. He hadn't meant to make Itz mad or sad or whatever he was. He just needed to tell somebody that secret. He thought Itz could explain it, but Itz didn't know

either.

All he knew was he wouldn't forget that kiss.

The next morning, they sat by the railroad tracks. Itz rubbed his forehead.

"It's still fifteen miles to Atlanta. We can walk that far. Do you really want to sit here and wait for those tracks to be fixed? It could take weeks, who knows?"

"You're right. And we are stronger now. I feel like we could walk fifty miles." Joe grinned and showed his muscles, trying to ignore his throbbing head.

Itz frowned. "Don't use up your energy. It's still a pretty long way."

"Maybe we can get a ride. Nobody's hunting for us now, I don't think."

The road had not lost any of its heat, or the numbing boredom of the journey, which made it longer. After a half hour they heard the rumble of a car: a Model A Ford heading toward them. The driver wore a black hat. A younger man whose blond curly hair fell out from under a brown derby, squinted at them as the car slowed to a halt. Joe's heart sank. In spite of his statement that no one could still be after them, he believed it altogether possible. This could even be the foreman.

The driver got out and strolled toward them, his thumbs hitched around his overall straps. A tall man with rough hands and, Joe thought, a kind face. Joe breathed out. Definitely not the foreman.

"You boys okay?"

The sound of his voice lifted an unusual feeling out of Joe's chest. Hope? Still on guard, he stood straight, trying to affect some confidence. "Oh, yessir, we're fine."

The man smiled. "Maybe you could use something to eat?"

Joe started backing off. "Oh no, oh no," he repeated like a bullfrog on a midnight pond.

Itz's response surprised him. "We've been taking chances this whole trip. Some have worked and some haven't. Might as well try another one."

The man smiled. "Ready for some dinner?" He stuck out his hand. "Name's Mr. Cain."

"Does a bear sh…" Itz started to say, then stopped.

They found themselves in a sizable room with twenty wooden tables, eight chairs at each, lined up in perfect order. The distinct and delightful smell of cooking came from one corner. Two large fans whined in two corners of the room, not doing much more in the steamy afternoon than pushing hot air around.

Not Mum's cooking, still enough to make Joe feel faint.

Itz groaned. "God it smells good. Is this real or just somebody else trying to trick us into whatever they want us to do?"

"I'm going to believe it for ten minutes. If we don't get some food by then, I'm headed for the door."

"Sounds like a good plan."

Mr. Cain stood with them, just inside the door, smiling broadly.

"Do you think he can be this happy all the time?" Joe whispered.

"Are you a minister?" Itz scowled at their benefactor.

Joe rubbed his hands together. *Great question Itz, it worked really well the last time.* He just wanted to eat. *Save the questions.*

Mr. Cain nodded slowly. "Kind of. This is my church," he said, raising his arms and hands from his sides.

"We better get the hell out of here right away," Itz said, turning towards the door.

Joe wiped the back of his hand across his mouth. The smell of the food had him drooling.

Mr. Cain shifted his weight. "Yea, no more time for talk— you boys need to eat."

Joe thought no sight had ever been sweeter—no campfire, no football field, not even any girl he had ever admired. Fried chicken and fish, corn and green beans and some vegetables he'd never seen before, biscuits and potato salad, more vegetables: squash and pickled peppers (he thought). He just wanted to get to that table, and stuff all that food into his mouth at the same time. It seemed he'd been hungry his whole life. His feet started forward involuntarily.

"Whoa," said Mr. Cain, pulling him back.

"Oh god, please don't torture us." Joe's stomach moaned. He felt he would soon collapse, just fold in two halves like cardboard. Then someone would put him on a shelf and he would stay there forever, hungry.

"No, no," said Mr. Cain. "Just listen to me one minute. Don't go over there and stuff every bit of food you can into your bellies. You want to do that of course. But if you do you'll make yourselves sick, and believe me that kind of sick is no fun. Okay? Can you do that?"

The boys replied, "Sure," in unison. They would have agreed to anything. Mr. Cain directed them toward the food line. They lost no time heading that way.

"And don't eat the fried food yet. It'll be there tomorrow," Mr. Cain called out after them. About thirty men and boys had lined up ahead of them but the line moved quickly. Itz slapped Joe's hand as he reached for a fried chicken leg.

"No fried food yet."

Well, Itz the Boss seems to be feeling a little better. Guess he'll be ready to be in charge again soon. He didn't say anything though. He could smell the food, almost taste it already. Everyone sat and ate, ragged men and boys with downturned faces. The only sounds were chewing, the clank of silverware, and the occasional belch from a finally satisfied belly.

Mr. Cain came by as they were finishing up. "I wanted to explain, set your minds at ease." He lowered himself down into the chair across from them. "I'm not going to try and convert you." He fiddled with the small salt and pepper shakers, moving them around and around each other, tipping their silver tops together.

"I have a son," he said, and the small bottles stopped. "About your age. Loves to play baseball. That's all he wanted to do, play baseball."

Joe felt uneasy, even with a full belly.

267

Mr. Cain winced. "One day I got mad at him for not doing his chores. Told him he couldn't play baseball again. Ever."

Itz said, "Pup told me I couldn't play football again ever." Joe sat up straighter. Itz didn't usually say personal stuff like that.

"Is that why you ran away?"

"Not exactly, but one reason."

Mr. Cain waited.

"I guess we were tired of him always telling us what to do, not letting us decide. And…" Itz scowled. "And being mean."

Joe added, "And our mum, well, she's just different. She goes off sometimes."

Itz scowled. "Nothing wrong with Mum. It's Pup, the reason we left."

"And because we were in trouble."

Mr. Cain chose not to pursue their stories. "My boy ran off a year ago. I don't know if he's dead in a ditch or working some slave job and eating slop."

Mr. Cain stared at the back of his hand and picked at a little scab on one of them. Joe knew that trick. Anything to keep from looking people in the eye.

Wonder if Mum is that sad?

"When my daddy's mechanic business failed he still had this building, and nobody wanted to buy it. When my boy left I had to do something besides try to find him and comfort his mother."

Mr. Cain continued. "So I do this to keep myself from going crazy and…" He hooked his thumbs into his overalls and watched men and boys, whose hunger had been staved off one more time, file out of the door into the unforgiving sun.

"And I have this hope that one day he'll just walk through that door."

Joe felt Itz's foot begin to tap, tap, tap on the wooden floor. Mr. Cain put his hand into his pocket and said, "And when I see him I'll go right up to him but I won't hug him right away. Instead, I'll just give him this."

The baseball, thrown and batted maybe a thousand times, nestled in the man's hand.

"I'll just give him this."

Mr. Cain stared at the ball for a minute, then put it back in his pocket. "Now you two go see that lady over there. That's Mrs. Cain; she'll find something for you to do. I think by the day after tomorrow you'll be ready to go."

"Go where?" Joe trembled. *The scythe glinting in the morning sun, the sour, dank odor of the barn at night. God, no.*

"Go home, of course. Until you're old enough to leave home instead of running away, that's where you belong. I believe there's a reason you're there. Maybe your mama needs you."

Joe and Itz stared at each other. Mum, need them? What would she need from them?

But maybe. Maybe she needed us just because she loves us.

"Okay, get to work boys. I'll see you later."

Their savior rose and started to walk away.

Joe felt a little shaky but he had to say it. "Mr. Cain?"

The man turned back toward them. "Yea?"

"I hope he comes home."

"Thanks. I do too."

They'd only been gone a week, but it seemed like a whole lot more. Their days on the road stretched back like a railroad track and home seemed an eternity away. Time to head that way. Mrs. Cain had packed as much food as they could carry, but they had to hide it. There were too many hungry mouths on the trains. Men would fight for meat and potatoes. Even just for potatoes.

It took them the better part of two days to arrive back in Pittsburgh. Mr. Cain had given each of them a dime before they left Georgia, in case of emergency he said. They had spent all their 'stolen' earnings, but Itz said to save the dimes. Joe didn't question that.

26

GRACE

Grace sat with her mother sat on the porch of her childhood home. Ma said her older sister, Catherine, had taken sick. The sisters had rarely seen each other over the years, communicating by letter and occasionally, telephone.

"Could ya be getting down there to see her?" Grace recognized the catch in Ma's voice. Her sad eyes evidenced a woman who had recently lost her husband.

Da had died the month before, in his shop, alone. Claire found him when she stopped to say hello. The shop sat empty, silent. There was so little business for a blacksmith these days. Da could have retired but insisted he had nothing else to keep him busy. He lay there, still warm, but unquestionably gone. Claire sat with him for a long time, then went to find her mother.

He died with no final word to Grace, no forgiveness, no understanding. Grief pierced her like a lance, and for days she wandered in a thicket of memories and regrets. The time when she was small and he had lifted her onto the horse, she simultaneously terrified and thrilled. And then making the pronouncement that condemned her to this life, agreeing and walking away from her when her mother insisted she married Dominic Cierc. After Da's death she had to put her sadness away and busied herself with life's demands again.

Ma recognized her daughter's grief, different and yet the same, if only because she drifted in the same space. She wanted a way to connect Grace to someone who might love her with no demands.

Grace felt a small leap in her chest. Yes! She could do that. The timing could not be better. She'd had a call from a man named Cain earlier that morning. He said her sons, Joe and Itz, would leave Atlanta tomorrow and arrive back in Pittsburgh the following day. Now she had to plan. She would take the train and spend the night with Aunt Catherine, see if she needed help. The next day she would find her boys. Her sons' "adventure" presented new challenges. Andras had regaled her with his story, no doubt exaggerating his heroism. He had little to say about his brothers, except that they had disappeared.

Grace's sharp blue eyes and silent, kind requests constituted the only pressure Andras had ever believed or accommodated. He informed her they probably headed down the river to Pittsburgh with plans to hop trains south, maybe Georgia. Grace didn't know how much she could believe, but decided to simply accept the information and use it as best she could. Finding her way into and around the big city constituted her challenge.

She checked the train schedule first, then walked up to Pittsburgh Street; her scarf tied tightly, head down against the wind. The hill always reminded her of the day Marta died, tugging at her heart, yielding a few small teardrops. How long ago? More than eighteen years? No, more. Andras hadn't been born yet. Still a young bride, younger than Eileen. Just yesterday she and Brid chased each other around the woods. This morning when she slipped her arm through her coat sleeve, the hand that appeared at the cuff looked like her mother's, not her own.

Never mind. Still strong, with enough energy for two. A good thing, since my husband has no energy at all.

Grace breathed a sigh of relief--no other person in the railroad station except Mr. Jenkins, the stationmaster. He knew her of course. Everybody knew everybody in Summervale. A friend of her father's, he had never been friendly to Grace. His attitude did not deter her. She needed to find her boys.

A bulky man with huge hands and feet and thick, wiry eyebrows, Mr. Jenkins rose from his chair behind the counter and frowned down at her. His eyelids drooped so that only half his sad gray eyes could be seen.

Grace cleared her throat. "One ticket to Pittsburgh, please." Mr. Jenkins remained motionless. "For tomorrow, the 10 o'clock train."

"Nope. No train at ten."

She had checked. "No? Then what time is the train?"

He glanced at his watch, which only perplexed her more. *Watches don't have train schedules on them, do they? Even a station master's watch?*

He waited another long moment, slapped his palms down on the counter, startling her. She could see bits of breakfast still in his teeth. "What would you be going to Pittsburgh for? Does your husband know?"

Irritation overcame fear. "Why would you care if my husband knows or doesn't know? You have not passed one word with him in your whole life."

She repeated the question, firmly. "What time is the train? I have my fare, you have no right not to sell me a ticket."

She would not have thought such thick, stiff eyebrows could raise, but they did, forming two diagonal lines meeting just above his nose. Perhaps he rarely received a challenge. Or he remembered he worked as a public servant and even Grace should expect courtesy. Or she had simply shocked him into submission.

"10:06."

Oh for Pete's sake.

The old man handed her a ticket and $1.37 in change, remarking with a smirk, "Not even enough for a meal down in the city. Better have some other plans."

"I do," she replied with more confidence than she felt. Other than a few eggs and bread from home and a bit of emergency money, she had little. She turned and opened the door without another word.

A thump like the sound of rising bread being punched down came from behind her. She dropped her things and ran back to Mr. Jenkins, forcing herself to be calm. He had landed in the chair and slumped there gray faced, pulling his left arm toward his chest.

"Is it your arm?"

"Yes. No. Maybe. Feels like it's moving up my arm. Hurts here." He winced and opened his hand over his chest and then his ample belly, grabbing her hand with his free one.

Oh Lord, he's having a heart attack. Her nursing skills were not up to heart attacks but she couldn't just desert him.

"I'll call for help."

"No! Don't leave me."

"I'm only going to the telephone, Mr. Jenkins. Right over here. You need to get to the hospital."

He released her hand. She hurried to the phone and dialed Dr. Torok, who said he'd get an ambulance there quick as he could. The station clock, insisting on the passage of time, ticked, ticked, ticked while they waited. It would take at least a half hour to arrive from the hospital seven miles upriver in Tarrytown. Grace imagined turtles crossing a dirt road. Back home, dinner, Dominic, the children and their needs. She hadn't planned to be gone this long. Her mother always said too much planning tempts God to intervene. Grace only knew her strategy had gone awry. Speaking words of comfort to Mr. Jenkins pushed away her despair.

Finally the ear splitting siren sound and medical attendants bolting into the station allowed her to leave Mr. Jenkins. With a quick "Good Luck," she flew out the back door and toward home. Reaching Pittsburgh Street, she forced her steps to slow. Running would attract attention, ladies didn't run in Summervale. She stood panting in her kitchen before anyone else arrived.

Late that night, Dominic again sat in his chair, a small brown whisky bottle on the floor beside him. He reached down, lifted it to his mouth just as Grace appeared and faced him. She had resolved to show no sign of trepidation. "I'm going to Pittsburgh tomorrow. Andras says he and Itz planned to head there first, then head south. So that's where I'm going to start searching for the boys."

Dominic lowered the whisky bottle slowly to the floor, didn't reply. Grace noticed he had not replaced the top. He used to hide his bottles in corners or under furniture.

Grace had decided not to mention Mr. Cain. Dominic's deteriorating mental state had only enhanced his gloomy imagination; who knew what he might have thought.

A low, guttural grunt. "The boys? Ya know, I've always thought those crack ups dint help your brain." Another move to the whisky bottle, but this time he misjudged the location and knocked the bottle onto the floor. Both of them stared as the amber liquid snaked through the rug. Grace didn't run for a rag and soap like she once would have.

"Damn!"

Dominic needed another drink. Gone were the days when she would try to prevent it. Now she just wanted him numb and nonreactive. She walked back through the kitchen and down the cellar steps, pulling a bottle from a high shelf, in the midst of her jars of preserves. Returning to the living room and uncorking the bottle, she handed it to him.

"I'm leaving at 9:30. Eileen will take care of dinner. She's done that before."

"Yeah, she has."

"I'm also going to visit Aunt Catherine. Ma says she isn't well. I'll be back Sunday night." She turned away before he could say another word. Just before mounting the stairs, she turned back at him. The bottle stood like a little soldier at his side.

"What about me? Who's going to take care of me?"

"You'll be fine, Dominic. You can take care of yourself." Here another glare as he wiped his chin with the back of his hand.

"And time," she thought to herself, leaving Dominic to his pathetic pastime, "I took care of myself."

Up in her bedroom she finished packing. Then she undressed, sighing with gratitude that Dominic slept alone and rarely came to the tiny room she called her own. After she finished her sewing and the children were asleep, she would rest for a few moments with a warm, damp cloth over her sore eyes. Then a little time for herself. Time to think, to imagine, to remember. But Brid could not be the focus of her attention tonight.

"Good morning! And welcome to the Colfax Street Station! What can I do for you, young lady?" The substitute station master could not have been more unlike Mr. Jenkins. Short, white-haired, plump with teeth that dominated her face.

"Actually nothing. I have my ticket," Grace replied, retrieving it from her purse, giving a proud little wave with it. "Just came to wait for my train."

"Of course you did! I should have known. Silly me!"

Why should she have known? Here the woman issued something that sounded like a cross between a sneeze and "tee-hee!" Grace felt a small cringe travel up her spine. The lady fiddled with some papers on the counter, checked her watch and gave Grace an abashed glance.

"Oh! Forgive me; I'm such a scatterbrain."

Then you're not the best person for this job.

"I am just replacing Mr. Jenkins for a few days, you know, until he's feeling better. You've heard, haven't you? Oh, of course, everybody has heard."

Grace hadn't heard what had happened after she left the station, but knew the information would be forthcoming without a word from her.

"They thought he had a heart attack, you know. So frightening. But it turned out to be just a wee bit of the wrong kind of food for an Irishman. You know." Obviously it didn't matter whether Grace knew or not. The lady grimaced slightly and only momentarily.

"So his 'heart attack' turned out to be indigestion?"

"Chicken paprikash. He craves that dish even though it's Hungarian. I guess I didn't do too well with the spices this time. And he is getting older. Can't digest like he used to, you know?"

Grace didn't want to know.

"And I guess you might wonder why a lady would be doing this job, even for a few days."

Grace waited.

"Well, I guess you know who I am? Mrs. Jenkins, of course! So I know this job as well as he does, practically!" Another giggle, this time with a grin partially hidden behind her palm.

Grace glanced nervously toward the station clock. "My train is at 10…"

"Ten-oh-six," Mrs. Jenkins corrected. Just going on ten now, so you have plenty of time." So I must take a moment to ask, why in the world are you going to Pittsburgh? Such an awful, dirty place!"

Searching for the attitude and resolve she had used with Mr. Jenkins, Grace tapped her fingers on the counter and again said nothing. Mrs. Jenkins stared her down.

"I'm going to visit my aunt. She isn't well."

"And did I hear something about two of your sons?" Her beam had almost straightened into a sneer. "Something about them in that city themselves just a week or so ago."

Grace began moving toward the back of the station without reply. A loud sigh, then "Well!" from the counter.

The delightfully quiet waiting area in the back included a wooden bench, just for her. Sitting, she checked her ticket for the tenth time at least, then her purse. A wallet with a comb, a pencil, a few bandages and a gift from Mrs. Nyilas: a small, wooden-framed mirror.

The train screeched into the station, louder than the mill's noon whistle. Huge iron wheels slowed down like a child suddenly tired of the race. Grace clutched her small suitcase and mounted the steps into the first car, wondering how in the world anyone could throw himself onto a moving platform car this high. *Anyone, like my sons. Oh Lord.*

Her search for an empty seat failed. The closest possibility held a woman with a large blue hat and a small book, so

Grace assumed she would continue to read and not be a bother. That turned out not to be the case.

No sooner had she arranged herself and her belongings under her seat, and just as the engine began to noisily return to life, the blue hat turned toward her. At first, just the grin. Then Grace whispered one word, full of joy, aggravation and disbelief.

"Brid."

She felt her spine stiffen. "What? How…" Staying with Brid out in the woods or when her mother visited seemed safe enough. But traveling together tempted fate. People would know.

As she had so often done, Brid read her thoughts. "It's one woman traveling alone that would make people wonder," she mused. "Two women, that's just smart and safe."

"But how did you know my plan to go to Pittsburgh?"

"I'll tell you why I'm on this train with you in a few minutes. For now, can you just say you're glad to see me?" Brid straightened her shoulders, grinning.

Brid had always loved secrets. She reveled in their plots and hidden meetings while Grace stewed.

She sighed. *I am thrilled to see you, but I'm not ready to say that now.* "What is your urgent business in Pittsburgh anyway? I didn't ask you to come with me, and this is not the only train going to Pittsburgh today." Grace's voice rose just above a whisper and she glanced around to see if anyone had heard her.

Brid's eyes narrowed. "No, you didn't ask me to come. But you didn't ask me when you and your children came to my house all these times."

Grace turned to the window, her body stiffening like laundry hung out to dry.

"Oh, oh God Grace. I didn't mean that. Of course you couldn't ask then. I'm sorry, I just...it's been so hard for you."

Grace saw Eileen's imploring face and heard again her angry words: "I've had to do everything." Had she hurt everyone she loved? Brid hiding her pain all this time, Eileen exhausted, Andras always angry and his two brothers gone. She felt an emptiness in her chest, like she had borne this love and these children wrongly, and now she could not change that.

She gazed at the face she knew as well as her own. The steady, mechanical rumbling of the train's wheels seemed to soothe them, allowing them to speak more freely.

"Those times I came to you, I couldn't take care of my children. I wanted to, but sometimes I couldn't move. I wonder what I've done to them."

Brid raised a finger to Grace's lips. "I know. I didn't mean what I said. It's just the way things were. But when you would leave me, there was nothing else. A few accidental meetings here and there. I sit up there in that cold, empty house, imagining I'll become the town's crazy old lady if I haven't already."

"No Brid, you couldn't."

"You've never languished in a mausoleum, love. You wouldn't believe the things that go through your mind. Once some boys came onto my property. Pranksters, no real harm. Someone had probably dared them to be brave enough to come to the door and knock."

Something my sons might have done.

"So one boy finally did knock. They were all hooting and shouting enough to wake the dead. My dogs set off a howl and they took to their heels."

Grace found the story amusing. The image of boys running away from their test of bravery. Brid, however, stayed solemn.

"Later I cried. Not in fear—I have my dogs and my gun. I just don't want to be the crazy lady of Summervale."

For once Brid's voice faltered. Grace strained even more to understand her.

"All these years, dreaming and hoping it would work out somehow produced nothing but heartbreak for me. You have your children, your responsibilities. Me? Only memories and fading hope. "

"And would you trade with me, Brid?" She shouldn't respond this way, but couldn't stop herself. "Would you give your quiet nights for my unruly children and drunkard of a husband?" Grace's neck muscles tightened.

"He came to my house once. I couldn't believe it—there he stood, or teetered really, at my door. I don't know if he even remembers what he shouted at me that night.

"He doesn't remember, I'm sure. He doesn't really hurt me anymore. Too old and the drink has taken its toll. There's not much left of him."

"But I remember. He told me if I ever came near you again, he would kill you."

Grace did not speak.

"I didn't know if he would really do it. Anyway I missed you so much, just wanted to see you. I didn't even have to touch you."

Grace took Brid's hand and stroked it like she once caressed her babies' heads. She didn't care then who saw or what they thought. She loved this woman and hated her pain.

"Oh Brid, I'm so sorry. Why have we had to suffer so much?"

Brid whispered, "Nobody really has a choice. And we've had a lot of joy too. You get whatever you get, and you live with it. You and I know that as well as anyone."

"Now, do you want to know why I'm on this train?"

Grace didn't need to say anything. *She's dying to tell me.* She nodded.

"Your ma."

"My ma?"

"Of course your ma. Who else? She didn't really want you to go to the city yourself, so she asked me to go with you." Silence descended finally, like the first, soft snow. Grace settled back into her seat, in the company of the woman she had loved for so long, a rare feeling of calm and safety permeating her body and soul.

After a few moments, Brid spoke again . "You're not going to believe it."

"Not believe what?"

"I'm going to join a circus."

Grace's mouth opened wide. A few hairs had come loose from her carefully placed pins. "You are not."

"I am! I'm going to be the cook!"

"You, the cook?" This surprised Grace even more than Brid's joining the circus. Brid had never had any affection for the kitchen.

"Grace, who fed your children all those times you stayed with me? I learned to cook and served John Boyle for years." She paused. "He was good to me, you know. Kind, and not hard to nurse. Never complained, even at the end."

"There are so many gaps in what we know about each other. John Boyle turned out to be a blessing, didn't he?"

"Yes."

Silence fell for a few minutes as the women sat considering.

"Things work out, you know?" Grace felt Brid relax, a rarity.

Grace gave a little chuckle. "You've been saying that for almost twenty years, Brid."

"I still believe it, Love. I'd almost given up but here we are together again.

27

GRACE

The train chugged into Penn Station. Grace and Brid grabbed their bags and descended the few steps to the platform. Grace ducked her head to the side and shaded her eyes. She had never seen so many people--rivers of them flowing everywhere.

Brid's eyebrows curled upwards, a tinge of a smile on her face. "Why are you shading your eyes Grace? The sun never shines in Pittsburgh. Too much smoke and soot, way more than Summervale, even."

"I'm not worried about the sun. I just don't want anyone to see us."

Brid howled with delight. "You mean you're afraid someone might recognize us? Are you a famous movie star? The only people who might have recognized us just got off that train, and obviously no one did."

"How do you know that?"

"Because they would have made some smart remark or given us a look. They always let you know." She used her handkerchief to pat her damp forehead. "There are over 600,000 people in this city Grace. We are lost in the crowd. And so what if we did meet someone? We are two respectable ladies on a mission of mercy."

Brid searched up and down Penn Avenue as if expecting someone.

"We?" The surprises and emotion of the last hour had robbed Grace of any thought of the future and she had forgotten her carefully made plans. "I am going to visit Aunt Catherine. She isn't well. I think I told you that."

Brid finally moved her gaze from the crowds down to Grace. "Where is Aunt Catherine? I'm having no luck finding her."

"Oh for Pete's sake, Brid. I told you. She's not coming here. She isn't well. And anyway, you haven't seen her since we were fourteen. You wouldn't know her."

"I would."

Grace just looked at her. *Same as ever.*

"Okay, okay. Silliness. We've been awfully serious today."

"I'm pretty sure you could never be serious for a whole day." Grace couldn't help chuckling, feeling her sulkiness disappear. "Anyway, you can't come to Aunt Catherine's."

"Why ever not?"

"Because...because..."

"Grace, my love, nobody knows us here. What's more, nobody cares about us. I have spent some time in this city."

Would there be no end to her adventures, Grace wondered?

"If you have an address, I can get us there." Brid continued her search up and down the street. "Uh-huh. Do you know where she lives?"

"I have the address."

Grace swallowed her pride. "I would love for you to walk with me. Really. Because I certainly have no idea how to get there. But you can't..." Grace hesitated, coloring a little.

"Can't what? Sleep there? Of course not. Aunt Catherine is a widow who lives alone. Not a wealthy woman?"

"No... she's not," Grace replied slowly.

"Have you ever stayed overnight in her house?"

Another no.

"Because it's obviously too small. Where were you going to sleep? On the living room floor?"

Grace's hands fluttered. "I don't know. Maybe on the sofa."

287

Brid led Grace across to Liberty Avenue, heading toward the river. Grace considered the name. 'Liberty." What a lovely name for a street.

"On the sofa," Brid repeated, with what sounded like a little scorn to Grace.

She stopped suddenly, and the man behind them knocked into her back. "Sorry, Madam. Sorry." He hurried away.

"Chinese?" Grace looked quizzically at Brid.

Brid peered. "You've never seen a Chinese person before?"

"Only in a book."

"Oh, Grace, we need to get you out to see the world! Anyway, the sofa does not sound comfortable to me, and you'd be putting Aunt Catherine out. All the trouble of a visitor, when she doesn't feel well at all. She'd want to take care of you—you know these Irish ladies."

"Brid McQuaid Boyle, I may not know a lot about the world, but I do know you. All these questions are not really about Aunt Catherine's house. They are your way of getting around to telling me whatever hare-brained scheme you've come up with."

A pause.

"Well, what is it?"

"I…I have a place for us to stay. A nice place, in a hotel. The William Penn Hotel, in fact."

Grace's eyes widened. "The William Penn! Even I've heard of that! It must be expensive. Brid. Very expensive."

"Not that expensive. And lots of famous people stay there. Katherine Hepburn. Bette Davis. Clark Gable. Fred Astaire and Ginger Rogers!"

Grace searched for a sight of the river. It would bring her back to herself. The self who would never dare to stay in such a fancy place.

"I can't do it, Brid."

"Why ever not?"

"I don't know. It's just not me. Besides, I have to get an early start tomorrow, finding the boys."

Brid murmured something Grace couldn't hear. "What did you say?"

"I said we'll talk about that later. But as we walk along to your aunt's, please be thinking about the William Penn Hotel and how you deserve a fun and fancy night. You told Dominic only that you'd be back Sunday night."

"But I…"

"Shhh. You've told me all the reasons not to do this. Try to think of some reasons to do it. Just try Grace. Can you do that?"

Grace nodded like an unwilling dance partner.

They stepped onto the Ninth Street Bridge. By the midpoint, Grace's thoughts had flown from fancy hotels to her consternation at how high above the water they were.

"Grace!"

Grace lurched forward." Oh, you scared me."

"I said your name three times! You have to pay attention in the city."

"I am paying attention, there's just so much to pay attention to. Huge buildings, this awful smell and fog, and all these people."

Brid opened her mouth.

"And," Grace continued, "this bridge! It's so high above the water it seems you would fall forever."

Brid linked her arm with Grace's. Grace immediately pulled back.

"Oh Grace, will you stop? Nobody cares about us. Besides, it's perfectly acceptable for two ladies to walk this way. Now, tell me your aunt's address and I'll find our way."

"How?" Grace continued. The river enticed her, but she did listen for an answer.

"I've told you, I know my way around."

Grace contemplated the great, gray city, then brought her gaze back to Brid.

"Well, sort of."

They arrived at Aunt Catherine's, a distance of less than three miles, three hours later, thanks to several wrong turns and at least one set of bad directions given by a nice old Polish fellow whom they could barely understand. Brid took advantage of the long walk to try and convince Grace that her plans for their evening and night were not only safe, but the greatest possible adventure.

Grace finally relented—how could she not? A luxurious hotel, could it even have a real tub where she could stretch her legs out all the way? Fresh towels? Soft soap, not lye, and a bed with a downy pillow, maybe two. She and Brid could talk all night, maybe even... Who could guess? It had been so long.

Aunt Catherine's tiny house stood behind a huge Victorian mansion on Mallory Street. She greeted them herself at the door, surprising Grace, who expected her to be bedridden. A smaller version of Ma, she still had a hint of red in her gray hair, dancing blue eyes and freckled skin on her pale hands and face.

After Grace made introductions, they were led down a short hallway to the living room. Oddly, Catherine seemed to be in the best of health, offering them tea which she insisted on preparing and serving herself. They could view the kitchen, the size of a broom closet, and the dining room, actually a space with enough room for a table and four chairs, from where they sat. There followed congenial conversation, the kind that women could have in rare free hours. It began with Catherine's inquiry about Ma and Da, then Grace's children and finally questions addressed to Brid, ending with Catherine's expression of sympathy.

"Oh, I'm so sorry, dear. Losing one's husband at such an early age. Any children?" Brid studied her hands. Grace had never broached that subject, although she couldn't quite imagine Brid as a mother, a calming influence in a house full of boisterous children.

Finally, a break in the conversation allowed Grace to ask, "Aunt Catherine, you seem well. Are you?"

"Fit as a fiddle, dear!" She slapped her knee, something Ma would never do.

"But Ma said…"

"Oh, your Ma would believe anything, but I think she knows my health has always been superb. I needed an excuse to get you down here. Hadn't seen you in years, got to thinking. Won't be around forever, even if I'm hale and hearty now! The truth is I wanted to see you, get to know you more. And I must say you've turned out fine! What a beautiful woman! Don't you agree, Brid?"

Brid brightened, nodded. "So beautiful."

Catherine leaned forward. "I think your mother had another reason. She wanted you to know me more, and feared you wouldn't leave your family, even for a few days."

Grace knew Brid found Aunt Catherine's ploy entertaining.

Grace's aunt nodded. "I knew your ma wouldn't come! She hasn't returned since she married your da. Always did hate the city. Wanted me to move up there with her. But Jimmy had work here, and we had built a life. 'No more moves,' he said. Wouldn't have worked anyway."

After a moment of uncomfortable silence, the first she'd felt since arriving here, Grace uttered the one word on everyone's mind. "Da."

Her aunt's eyebrows lifted. Appearing to be only slightly surprised, she replied, "Ah, so she sent you to me to learn the story. Well, I guess that's fair. From the horse's mouth and all."

"She just said to come. That you were not well."

"That's what she told you. You know, I adored her, just a girl, seven years old when I left. Afterward, even when they came here, we had little contact, and only in the beginning. I know Nora well enough to know she sent you here to listen to my story."

They waited while Catherine sipped her tea, slowly, returned the wafer thin cup to its saucer like a mother putting her baby to sleep. She wiped her mouth with the lace napkin, smoothed her hair and rearranged her sweater collar. Grace noticed a painting showing a woman perched on the end of a fallen log, like she belonged there. Oh, to belong, to be truly at home somewhere, Grace thought. She turned toward Brid, who winked at her. Still, uncertainty.

Catherine cleared her throat lightly, and regained her guests' attention. A woman with an air of amused authority, she sat straight as a young pine despite her age, which Grace knew to be at least sixty-five. Sitting forward a bit, she began to talk.

"I left my beautiful country at sixteen. With tears in my eyes, believe me. Ireland is a bit of heaven." Catherine sounded like Ma, the brogue still thick after all these years. "We lived on a lake called Lough Neagh in County Antrim. Huge, as far as you could see. And blue, blue like your eyes, Grace. Blue like your mother's eyes. It is now in Northern Ireland. You might have heard of the Troubles back in the early twenties—that's when it became a separate country. Ah, but the troubles aren't over, I'm afraid. That's what Jimmy always said."

She paused, then took up her teacup again. "I'm afraid this story is wandering like a minstrel. Please excuse me. So many memories."

Grace and Brid nodded in unison. "It's not a problem at all, Aunt Catherine."

"I never got to return. Always thought I would." She coughed, then regained her firm voice. "Our tiny town, Ballymean, sat on a small hill overlooking the lake. Beautiful sunsets, boat rides in the moonlight. Everyone knew everyone and they knew about me and Jimmy Fallon. They made no secret of their opinion of us."

She picked up the picture sitting on the end table beside her: a fine-looking young man with curly dark hair and light blue eyes.

"Black Irish," sighed Catherine. "Handsome as any Irishman who ever walked God's green earth. We met by accident, literally. A girlfriend and I were rowing on the lake and a wind came up and upset our boat. Lucky for us, Jimmy came to the rescue. He'd been fishing for eels…"

"Eels!" Grace squelched a shriek.

Aunt Catherine grimaced. "Oh yes. Lots of people made their living eel fishing in the lake. Still do as far as I know."

"And you were in that lake?" Even Brid showed a little unease.

"Yes. We tried not to think about it." Clearly Catherine wanted to move on with her story. "I still don't know if I believe in love at first sight, but we were definitely interested, even with me half–drowning, hair all disheveled."

She paused, recalling the scene. Grace saw only eels, crawling everywhere, and worked to erase that from her mind.

"We were so young. Jimmy came from Randalstown, not far away. He asked me to a picnic."

Grace glanced at Brid through slightly lowered lids. *A picnic, imagine that.*

Aunt Catherine, lost in her own distant memories, didn't notice. "Jimmy's family went to the Protestant church. We were Catholic. I knew my parents wouldn't accept him, but I didn't care. I told my parents, only said 'we'd' be going, and they assumed I meant my girlfriends. Jimmy and I stayed at the picnic for a bit, then wandered off."

Grace heard a small gasp from Brid. Wandering off, the beginning.

"We talked and sat close (here she paused and Grace wondered exactly what that meant). On that very day, we fell in love."

"But Jimmy came from the wrong kind of family. Not that we had much of anything to brag about, but my parents could not accept him because they were Protestants. In those days they called such a marriage between two people a 'mixed marriage.' Religion made so much of a difference then, more of a difference than love."

Grace thought her aunt's furrowed brow and pursed lips made her seem more angry than sad.

"So they kept you apart?" Brid's spread her open palms out and toward Catherine. Eyebrows raised, eyes shifted to the left, Grace's aunt surprised them with a chuckle.

"Oh, they tried. Lectures and punishments. Not being allowed to leave the house. All of that. Guess what? It didn't work. Jimmy and I could not, would not be separated. We snuck out and met each other in hidden places down at the lake. Kissed and such (here a slight blush) in our stolen moments. He asked me to marry him two months after we met. And I said yes. Didn't hesitate for a moment. We went to the registrar's office in Randalstown that Saturday, expecting our families would have to accept us once we were married. They didn't. Ranting and sulking in both houses."

Grace fidgeted, wanting to hear her aunt's story but realizing it would be a long one. "My father tried to get the marriage annulled but he had no grounds. At that time we were of age to make a contract."

"You were so brave," breathed Grace.

Catherine chuckled. "Just young and in love. Nothing could stop us. We stayed with Jimmy's soldier brother for a few days, then decided to move to America."

"Just like that?" Brid perched in her chair like a red bird on a tree branch.

"Just like that. Millions of people were leaving Ireland again. Thirty years or so after the famine and still no jobs."

The famine. Ma had told Grace stories that her Ma told her. Hunger so deep down it felt like someone had taken a shovel and dug a hole. Worse than now. Helplessness, terror even, and despair.

Catherine continued. "My mother said she wanted only for us to be safe. Safe meant not hungry. What I did broke her rules for how to guarantee that."

She lifted the teacup again. Grace had never seen anyone take so long to drink a cup of tea. Catherine quickly wiped a tear with one finger. Then she folded her hands in her lap.

"My da, on the other hand, didn't care about anything except how he stood in the town. So we left. I went to say goodbye. I remember Nora—your mother—standing at the door crying and straining to get to me. I think she knew what kind of goodbye we were saying. Our Ma held her back, waving and crying. I waved one more time, then turned and ran until I couldn't run anymore. We didn't see each other for five years."

A momentary lull, then she brightened. Grace, who had an itch in the middle of her back, considered that Aunt Catherine paused almost as much as she talked.

"The boat from Ireland carried anyone who could pay and climb aboard. And that meant crowds of people. Hundreds. Jimmy's brother gave us money for the passage and our new life. Said he'd always wanted to go to America, but always thought "next month." Then he married, had kids. His chance had gone, but he wanted us to have ours."

Grace commented on the goodness of such a man.

"A good man. Yes, a very good man," Catherine agreed. "Our lives would have been so different without him. Anyway, that boat ride nearly did us in. Clouds and rain almost every day. People sick, even dying, everywhere. One night, a horrible storm that almost sent us all to the sea. We clung to each other, wondered if we had done the right thing. It took two months, but on the first sunny day we arrived at the harbor in New York and saw the great statue. 'Give me your tired, your poor,' it said. It filled us up. We made our way to Pittsburgh by train. I had a cousin here, on my mother's side. He found Jimmy work in the mill, and I signed on as a maid up in the big house, right up there."

She pointed out the window to the mansion they had passed.

"We tried for years to have children, but never could and never knew why. During dark nights I would wonder if we were being punished, but I pushed those thoughts away. That's probably what my da would have said." A small grin appeared, surprisingly.

"Probably just as well. I might have had to beat them, if they'd have behaved the way these kids do today." She pointed her finger like a stern schoolmarm, and Grace felt for a moment like an errant child.

Catherine settled again, and continued. "We worked and made friends, went to dances. I began to forget about Ireland, except every now and then. My employers, the Adleys, liked me. They should have, I worked hard, including practically raising their children. Kept them in line, too.'

"But you didn't kill them," Brid chuckled.

"No, that I did not. And eventually the Adleys sold us this house. Almost gave it to us, really. And we stayed here, so in love always, until Jimmy died three years ago."

"How old? So sad for you to lose him."

"Fifty seven. A heart attack. Just like that." She snapped her fingers, and Grace jumped. Aunt Catherine had a knack for the unexpected.

"Yes, sad. But I had him for forty one years. It seemed like a day. It goes so quickly, dears, you've got to seize all the love you can."

"What about Ma?" Grace asked her aunt quietly. "When did you first see her, and how?"

"I heard through my cousin that they'd come to America in 1899, I think. Five more years went by, no contact. I tried to find them, no luck. Finally my mother sent me their address. Imagine my sad surprise in knowing they'd been living right up the river, in Summervale, all that time! That first visit challenged us all. Your mother had become a young woman and barely knew me. Still, we were so happy to see each other. Hugs and tears."

A pause. "Except for Da, of course."

"Of course." Catherine softened. "But as you know, I did visit a few times over the years. Usually during the day, so your father would be working. And that meant that you and Claire were in school."

"Ma probably didn't want me there because she feared I'd burst out with something about you at dinner."

Catherine considered her teacup. "No dear, it wasn't you. Your da and I never got along."

"Why?" *Although she guessed she already knew.*

"Because I had rebelled. Hadn't gone by the rules. Your da believed in going by the rules."

I surely know that.

"You know how people will argue about the littlest thing when there's something big between them? When we were young, we did that. Education. Religion. Whether it might rain. Anything."

Brid sat quietly, for once. The story belonged to Catherine and Grace.

"We tried, for a while. Even your Da tried, I think.' Catherine sighed. "It just became too painful, too pointless. I could see Nora straining, trying to keep the peace, wanting us so much just to enjoy her cooking and a pleasant evening. It didn't happen."

"But all your visits stopped, at some point. After I was married. I remember one wonderful afternoon, with you and Ma and Marta.

Catherine placed both hands over her face for a moment. "It just became harder to come. We didn't have much money then, and I had my job here. Then Jimmy started to feel poorly."

Grace's tea was cold in her cup, but Catherine bent again toward the table and picked hers up again. "Families," she murmured. "Too much sorrow. Too little understanding. We always hope the next generation will do better. And of course, we never know."

A silence fell. The afternoon began to dwindle. Grace realized her aunt had fallen asleep when Catherine's head tipped forward and a soft snore rose gently into the room. It only lasted a moment. She woke herself up, opened her eyes wide and sat up straight.

"Well! How about a walk around the big house? The Adley boy still lives there, and he keeps up the gardens. They are lovely.

Grace jumped out of her chair. "Yes! Let's go."

"I hope I haven't bored you." Catherine wiped her lips, although Grace couldn't see why—she hadn't even eaten anything.

Brid opened her arms wide, then clasped her hands. "Not at all. Your story could not have been more...enlightening. And Grace has always been active. Not good at sitting, you know? In fact, I think this is the longest I have ever seen her sit still! You are to be congratulated!"

They emerged from the house.

Brid is a born politician. She could charm a witch to kindness.

The gardens boasted peonies, hollyhocks, foxglove, hostas and many more flowers that Grace didn't recognize.

"Aunt Catherine, I wish we had known each other better. It seems you could understand, when Ma didn't."

"And some things can't be said when we are young, my dear. But you and I are cut from the same cloth, as they say. I know you've had a hard life. But this friend of yours, this Brid, makes you shine like the first light of day. Spend the time you can with her. Life is too short for anything else."

What does that mean? What I hope it does? Surely Aunt Catherine does not, could not know. A moment wondering. *I will take it as I believe she means it, and leave it at that.*

301

Then the goodbyes. Brid stood at the end of the pathway as Grace took an extra minute with her aunt. Catherine embraced her, smiling, then withdrew a small envelope from her pocket and slipped it into Grace's bag.

"Oh no..." Grace started to object, sure she knew what the envelope held. Catherine reached one small finger up to her niece's mouth and whispered. "It's not what you think, dear. It's something far more precious. And it gives me pleasure." After they parted, her aunt turned around again.

"Grace!"

"Yes?" She could see Brid growing impatient.

"Tell your ma I'm feeling much better!" Grace could still hear her laughter as they started down the street toward town.

"Just a minute, Brid." She stopped and pulled Catherine's envelope from her purse, her hands shaking a little. Inside were two pictures. One showed Catherine and Jimmy in front of their house, smiling. It could not have been more than four or five years old. Catherine had written, "Love endures" on the back, along with their names. A young woman and a girl, maybe a teenager, smiled out of the second photo. They had their arms around each other. On the back Catherine had written again, "Love endures," along with "Catherine and Nora." Grace's eyes were brimming as she showed the pictures to Brid.

"What a gift to you." Brid draped her arms around Grace's shoulders. "The best one she could give."

Grace nodded, replaced the pictures in the envelope, and they continued. She whispered her thanks under her breath.

28

GRACE

They ambled through the streets, Grace gasping at the height of the buildings. Brid told her the newly completed

Gulf Building towered forty-four stories over the city, but that didn't mean as much as simply staring up at it, feeling its height and power. Her astonishment didn't diminish the discomfort of the gray, sooty air, however. Despite their coughing, Grace and Brid focused on the promise and adventure of the day, and the joy of each other's company.

"Look at that!" exclaimed Brid.

A white-bearded old man manned his food cart on a street corner, calling "Fresh and hot!" in a thick accent. A young boy next to the cart drew attention by juggling three brightly colored balls. They flew into the air above his head, then landed back into his palms with amazing precision. Passersby stopped to watch the show and inevitably succumbed to the scent of the homemade delights.

Grace couldn't remember the Hungarian name for them, but they were so familiar. Direlyes? Something like that. She breathed in the aromas—sausage, cheese, tomatoes, onions. Years ago, Marta taught her the art of rolling the dough flat and cutting into squares, filling them and folding the dough. They simmered in the frying pan to a golden brown while the taste buds suffered desire, then anguish.

"Direlyes," she murmured. "I haven't made them in so long."

"The Polish call them pierogies," Brid whispered in her ear.

Grace knew Brid wanted to announce their intimacy with the unnecessary whisper. She moved back a step, and replied calmly. "I know! And I want one!" Perhaps there were a few stray coins in the bottom of her purse. Brid gently placed her hand on Grace's shoulder.

"Please. Today is my treat, remember?"

Shame crept through Grace like a low fever, and she waited, a dull, obedient soldier while Brid made the purchase. "Thank you," she mumbled, with as much enthusiasm as a child given cod liver oil. They stood silently. The pierogies were good, but not quite as tasty as she expected. Maybe just a little more butter.

"Grace?" Receiving no answer, Brid repeated. "Grace O'Dowd. What is going on?"

Grace hadn't heard her maiden name in so long it snapped her out of her self-pity.

"It's just that I...I don't have money. You have money and can pay for whatever we need or want. It makes me feel like a child."

Brid's held Grace's face in her hand. "Listen. It's not really my money. It's all luck, don't you see? I happened to marry someone who had money. God knows I didn't choose him, any more than you chose Dominic. If we love each other, the money belongs to both of us. Here, I'll give you half. That way we won't have to think about it."

Brid transferred a roll of cash to Grace's purse, then turned and hurried ahead into GC Murphy's Five and Ten. Grace had to run not to lose her, then her attention strayed at the sight of the gleaming wooden floors. Fortunately she found Brid quickly, standing at the cheese counter, gazing lovingly at huge hunks of provolone, cheddar and Dubliner cheese.

Grace's brows softened. "My ma grew up in County Antrim. Always insisted on the superior quality of their cheese. Da, a Limerick man, disagreed of course. Their aged cheddar couldn't be beat. The argument was never settled. Of course, we didn't see those cheeses in Summervale."

But Brid didn't buy Irish cheese. Instead she asked for a quarter pound of provolone, and broke off a piece for Grace.

"I never! It bites your tongue!"

Brid nodded. "Take another bite. It gets better."

In fact it did. They continued through the store, where Grace bought a scarf for Eileen. Grace didn't know what she could bring home for her eldest son. The other two... She felt anxiety returning like a whiny child, and tried to comfort it, remembering her promise to let go of it for today.

There's nothing I can do except hope it will be alright.

Brid pulled her out into the street where the crowds and colors pushed her fears away. They wandered up Fifth Avenue, in and out of shops. Grace found the crowds less intimidating and not appealing. *You have to work harder here just to get your groceries. People aren't too friendly, probably because most of them don't know each other.* Many of them didn't react to her greeting.

Still, there were shops and beautiful things, and so many kinds of food she'd never seen. She finally purchased an Italian salami for Andras, knowing that the spicy meat would please him.

All of the sights and sounds did not compare to the joy of feeling Brid's hand brush against her own. They walked and talked and laughed together, and no one gave them a second glance. Back home that would be different.

Brid darted in and out of stores like a squirrel hunting nuts. She had to show it all to Grace, who exclaimed "Oh Mercy!" more than once.

Brid being Brid. How lovely she is. How alive.

The afternoon faded as the sun began to lower over the already darkening city. Grace's feet cried for a place to rest.

Brid touched her elbow, directing her to the right. Grace turned, her attention immediately captured by a huge green fairyland with immense oaks and fountains and benches where people sat, apparently with nothing better to do. Right here in the middle of the city! And the most elegant and stately building she had ever seen loomed in the middle of it, like a queen on her throne. Brid coaxed her up marble steps and through the front entrance. "The William Penn Hotel" announced a lighted sign above the entrance. Inside, Grace immediately shielded her eyes against the brightness of gold, which assaulted her from every angle: the walls, the chandeliers, rugs and doorways. It shone like a castle in a fairy tale. Keenly aware of her faded blue dress and plain, sturdy black shoes, she felt she should bow to someone, but she saw no living creature except Brid.

"Do you think we ought to head downstairs to the servant's quarters?" Brid whispered.

"I think so." Grace imagined serving dishes and dust rags, not so different from her life at home. Except the children.

"Oh c'mon, I'm kidding. Let's go and check in."

As they approached the desk a woman emerged from a hallway to their right. Obviously the queen. Her shimmering blue gown fell in folds to the floor. Sleeveless and gathered at the waist, it seemed to allow her to float. Her dark hair, cut and curled just below her ears, set off her brown eyes. Her jewelry gleamed in the lights. *Did she come with the hotel?* She passed them with a swish that reminded Grace of wind through the trees.

Brid leaned toward Grace and said, "You are more beautiful than she is."

Grace looked down toward the rich, floral carpet.

"Yes, more beautiful. To me."

Grace's eyes filled and Brid said again, "To me."

The process of 'checking in,' as Brid called it, shocked Grace again. "Brid, we can't do this," she mouthed when the clerk turned away to get their key. "It's too expensive!" She couldn't help gasping. "Three dollars!" More than Dominic made for a whole day's work. Brid nonchalantly handed the money over and turned back to Grace.

Brid spoke in a quiet voice, but firmly. "We can and we will, because we deserve it. We have all this money and what are we going to spend it on?" She whispered. "Because I love you and you love me." She took Grace's hand.

The grand hotel drew her in. She imagined herself an elegant lady dressed in a shimmering gown, traipsing through the palace, admiring eyes upon her. That this would actually happen seemed impossible.

"I can't quite believe it yet."

"Believe it. Here we are." Leading them to a room with two identical shining gold doors, meeting in the middle. A man stood there, waiting for something. Brid stopped. The doors slid open. "Is this our room?" Grace stared at the small room with mirrors and multicolored fabric on the walls. A uniformed man sat on a stool near the front, smiling broadly at the two women.

Brid's forehead wrinkled so for a minute she looked a bit like Aunt Catherine. Then she grinned. "Ha! No, silly. This is the elevator. It's going to take us up to our room. We're on the fifteenth floor! It will be a great view."

Grace backed away, frowning. "I'm not going in there," she insisted. "I don't care how pretty it is."

Images of the coal mine disaster flashed through her mind—men dragging dead bodies up in the crude the elevators, out onto the frozen ground. She began to shake. Brid grasped her shoulders.

"Grace. I know what you're thinking. This is not a coal mine, as you can see. It's totally different. I've been on hotel elevators plenty of times and they are safe. They're different from the mines. Trust me.'

How many times have I heard that before? Grace squared her shoulders, resisting like a young child being steered to bed.

Brid sighed. "Do you really want to mount fifteen flights of stairs after all the walking we've done today?"

Grace's feet, on the edge of cramping, made the decision for her. She peered into the elevator and back at Brid. A long silence and then she replied, "Okay. I'll go in." With a pounding heart, she led the way like a young army private determined to exhibit his bravery. She pressed her lips together as the door closed. Her feet seemed to lift a bit as the numbers crawled toward fifteen. She felt the sweat on her upper lip.

The doors opened and there they were, in a high-ceilinged hallway gleaming only slightly less than the lower level. Close to the end of the passage, they stopped at the last room on the hall, #1530. Brid slid the key into the lock and opened the door. Grace immediately crossed the room and peered out the window down to the gleaming ribbon of the Allegheny River. A barge hauling a mountain of coal rested on the far bank. The buildings that had seemed so huge this afternoon were now miniature, like dollhouses.

Grace felt dreamy again. Gazing around at the room, she felt like she had been swallowed by beauty and could barely breathe. Then she heard Brid's voice, which seemed to come from far away.

"This way, my dear. I am drawing a bath."

An old joke between them. When they were girls, one would say, "I have drawn your bath," and hold up a drawing of a tub filled with water. They had no idea why this always amused them. Pleasure came so easily then.

"A bath," Grace breathed. The idea of it felt like her mother's embrace, warm and simple. Depositing her meager belongings on the bed, she headed toward the bathroom. Steam rose from the doorway, relaxing her. Love rose in her heart, for Brid, her children, her mother. The steam of love, she reflected. And forgiveness.

In the bathroom, beginning to unbutton her dress, she felt Brid's presence behind her like a warm breeze. Her heart thumped for a moment. *Warm breezes mean easier*

310

weather, chasing the cold at least for the moment. "Let me," Brid whispered, and Grace let her.

She sank down into the tub all the way to her shoulders, and shuddered at the sensation that moved through her. Brid began to bathe her—back, arms, stomach, legs, feet. Slowly. Grace had never known the delight of a foot wash. Brid cupped water in her hands and rinsed Grace's body, then helped her kneel and brought the cloth to her hips. Grace wondered if she should protest but couldn't. Like that first kiss so long ago on the mountainside, this moment spoke only of goodness and delight. She succumbed.

After Brid dried her, Grace put on a floor length white robe that hung on the bathroom door, and walked back out into the room. Brid sat motionless, regarding her in a way that, even to Grace, meant admiration. Brid led her to the bed that seemed as soft as the down of a chick and kissed her. Exhausted, they both surrendered to sleep.

Grace dreamed that Itz lay on the ground, groaning, writhing in pain, a bone piercing his leg, blood everywhere. But she couldn't see his face. She reached for him and he disappeared. Bolting up, she cried, "Where is he? Where did he go?"

Brid's face looked kind, but the light in her eyes had dimmed. "Oh, my love. Just a bad dream. You are here in this beautiful place and we are together and finally alone."

Grace relaxed back into the pillows. Two pillows, even fluffier than the miraculous bed.

"Are you hungry?"

"Yes."

"Then come, my lazy girl." Brid pulled Grace, who came reluctantly out of the bed. "We'll eat in style, in the 'salle a manger.'"

"What?"

"The 'salle a manger.' It's a fancy word for the dining room. French. We might as well be fancy this once."

"I can't go down there." Grace noticed a beautiful clock on the wall, ticking away their precious time. "I have nothing to wear in such a place. I'll look like I'm going out to collect the eggs."

Brid rose and moved across the room. Grace loved to watch her in motion, full of energy and yet so fluid. Brid withdrew a dress from her suitcase. Such a dress, light wool with simple lines and folds draping down toward the floor. And a matching short jacket, the same color. Sapphire blue, her mother called it. The color of Grace's eyes.

"Oooh," she breathed, then caught herself. "You bought that for me, Brid? It must have cost more than my house."

"Maybe it did. I don't care. I would spend all my money on you if I could. Here, put it on."

The dress caressed her. She felt a light pull at her middle, like Brid's hands around her waist. She straightened her shoulders. It was frightening, this feeling. Then Brid produced two pairs of sandals, white slingbacks with heels (heels!). Brid had donned a purple silk gown with a pearl necklace, and Grace turned to her as they left the room. For the first time in her life, Grace felt beautiful.

29

GRACE

The dining room mirrored the elegance of the hotel. A smaller chandelier hung in the middle, and a huge floral painting dominated one entire wall. Spotless white tablecloths and a vase of white roses adorned every table. Brid ordered their meal, but Grace heard little of that. It seemed almost all of her senses were captivated by the woman she loved. "Oysters Rockefeller, filet of beef with sweet potato puree." The food choices went on as she sat watching, her hunger not so much for food, as for Brid's touch.

"Just eat some of each," Brid advised when the food arrived. "Otherwise you'll hurt yourself.

Grace emerged from her reverie with some effort. She managed to eat, enjoyed it even. The food, creamy, sweet and salty all at once, warmed and delighted her. *There must be words I don't know to describe it.* Then, raspberry ices and coffee arrived. She couldn't resist. Despite all of it, she felt Brid beckoning, felt herself being drawn. Her arms wanted only to reach. With effort she held them down.

Afterward Brid suggested they amble around the hotel, "to let the food settle."

So they proceeded back out to the street, lit now with electric lights. People scurried here and there in pursuit of their needs or pleasures. Grace and Brid soon tired of the crowds however, and when Brid hinted they might be more comfortable back in their room, just the two of them, Grace agreed.

As they undressed, Grace glanced over at Brid, and more than once she saw Brid glancing back. Dropping her dress, wriggling out of the girdle, she wanted yet feared the outcome of all this anxious fumbling. *How beautiful she is.* Brid had only her slip and underthings left to remove. Grace's words caught in her throat, but she summoned them. Two simple words.

"Brid. Stop."

Brid stopped, her eyes wide with delighted surprise. Grace crossed the room, sensing everything, the coolness from the window, the soft rich essence of the carpet, the steamy memory of her bath, the smell of soaps and perfumes. Then, the powerful draw of Brid. Grace reached her after what seemed like decades (in fact it had been) and removed the rest of her clothing. Draping her arms across Brid's shoulders, she kissed her full on the lips, past the lips, deep into her mouth. Grace felt compelled by some inner force, something she had not felt before. She lowered her mouth to Brid's breast and kissed her there, held and tasted her.

Brid moaned, her naked body shivering with desire. In a moment, Grace's clothes had also fallen to the floor. The two women stood at long last, gazing at each other with no hurry and no shame.

Then, no more standing. They fell onto the bed, their joy erasing years of doubt, sadness and longing. Caresses, kisses everywhere. Their love dictated every intimacy, every gift they gave each other. They were together, and whole.

One night.

The next morning, Brid and Grace stood in the railroad terminal, still as utility poles with a current running between them. They did not touch.

"I had hoped," Brid began, tears floating on her eyes like water at the top of a full glass. Grace had never seen her cry. "I had hoped but never believed."

"Our first and last night together has been exquisite, Grace. More than I imagined. I will hold it closest to my heart." She turned to go.

"Wait, Brid. You can't do that. It's not fair; you can't just turn and leave without giving me a chance. You've always done that. Just left."

"If I don't walk away I will be rooted to this spot forever."

"Then walk away knowing that I love you more than life, and will see you again and again. Except...not like last night. I can't do that and live in Summervale. I can't do that and raise my children."

Grace watched one solitary tear descend Brid's face. "You love me more than anything except your children."

"I love my children, Brid. But more than that I am responsible for them. My love for you is different, deeper. I too will cherish the memory of last night. What a blessing that we had it, and that I don't feel shame about it."

Brid replied, "Because sinning is the absence of grace, and in every sense of the word, grace endured in that room last night. It provided shelter for everything we did and are."

Brid took Grace's hand. "You will see me again. We will come and go. Someday we will be able to be together. Old ladies, knitting on the porch." A brief twinkle in her eye, then she sobered. She released Grace's hand. "I need to go."

No! Never!

But then Grace felt a release in her body and soul as she knew the truth of her lover's words. They had tasted happiness, more joy would come. She knew that as well as she knew her name.

"Yes Brid, go. I love you."

The swiftness of Brid's departure swallowed her reply. Grace whispered the words to herself.

Always. Always.

30

GRACE

As they approached the Pittsburgh terminal, noisy and smoky just like it had been a lifetime ago, last week, Joe grinned. "The last time," he grinned. "The last jump, the last roll on the hard ground."

"At least for now," Itz jumped from the car, hollering back, "I might need to do it again..." If there was more, Joe didn't hear it, because Itz had already leapt to the platform. He followed, knowing he never wanted to do it again.

They sat for a while at the depot, eating the rest of Mrs. Cain's fare and watching the crowds.

"God, it's still a long way home."

"There's a train, but I'm guessing you don't have the fare, and trying to hop a train again in this busy terminal...well, even brave boys like you might think twice."

The brothers gazed up toward the source of the world's most familiar voice. The sun obscured the view of her, and for that reason only Joe said, "Have you ever been totally sure of something and not believed it at all?"

Itz didn't answer. Instead he stood up and uttered one word. "Mum."

"What are you doing here?" Joe and his mother spoke the same words simultaneously.

She didn't reply, simply took both of her sons in her arms and held them close. Neither objected.

Joe pulled away first. "We wanted to come home. We've been, well, riding the rails as they say."

Mum grimaced. "As they say. You'll need a better explanation than that for your father."

She's more beautiful than ever. Shinier or something. Happy? He searched for the right word. *Joyful.*

A man sauntered past too slowly. He stared at Mum, up and down and Joe felt his stomach tighten. "You're too lovely to be stuck with them young know-nothings, honey."

Itz started to fold his fists but Mum's stern face stopped him. "These young know-nothings are my sons, you fool, and they know a lot more than you do. Now leave us alone, we're having a family reunion here."

The man slouched away as Joe and Itz stood open-mouthed. Mum never talked like that, to anyone. Joe raised his eyebrows. Itz nodded.

"What are you doing here, Mum?"

"I came down to visit my Aunt Catherine, my mother's sister. She hasn't been well, and Ma asked me to check on her. I rode the train." She raised her eyebrows. "I bought a ticket."

Mum continued. "Aunt Catherine is much better now." She hesitated, gazing out over the crowd. "We...we had a nice visit. So, now I'm going back to Summervale."

"So are we." Joe clenched his hands. *Surely she will get us train tickets. Not leave us here like orphans. She's Mum. She'll do that.*

"I'll see you there then. You've become world travelers, I'm sure you'll find a way. Without even a goodbye, she headed toward the ticket booth, leaving the boys gape mouthed.

They looked at each other. *Mum? Deserting them on a train track?*

She took maybe ten steps. Joe wondered later whether she had counted them before turning and returning to them. Her eyes shone.

"By the way, do you know a man named Mr. Cain? He called me, said you had given him our telephone number, and that you should be arriving back here today."

"It's true Mum." Joe mumbled. "He was a good guy. He fed us and helped us get going, after…everything else had happened."

Itz continued. "Joe gave him the phone number because he said he wanted to check on us after we got home. Seemed like a good idea. He did a lot for us."

"It was a good idea. The world's full of good people and not so good. You have to learn, sometimes guess, which ones to trust. You made the right guess."

The boys stood, still embarrassed but beginning to brighten.

"Well, c'mon then. I guess it's time you learned to ride a train the proper way. Course in those awful clothes and smelling like you do, we probably won't have trouble finding a seat!" She laughed again and Joe's hands relaxed. *Mum is back and she's going to take us home.*

After a ride very different than all those of the last week, where the boys interrupted each other telling Mum their slightly edited tales from the road, they stepped onto the train platform in Summervale. *Much better than rolling.* As they approached their house, Itz said, "Give me your dime."

"Why?"

"Because I have an idea and it might help appease him."

"And you're not going to tell me what it is, right?""

"You'll see. Trust me."

Joe hooted so hard he started to cough, and it took some effort to contain himself.

Itz thought they should sneak back into the house at night, just be there in the morning when they all woke up, but Joe had had enough of sneaking. They waited down at the river. Eileen told them later that Mum went in, removed her hat and started cooking, just like an ordinary day when no one has had any adventures. The boys came in through the back door two hours later. Mum stood in the kitchen smiling and rolling out dough. She'd made soup and the pot gurgled softly on the stove. They hugged her, all of them holding their secret.

She stepped back, said "Nice to see you." Joe could feel that happiness in her he'd seen only a few times before. She pointed toward the living room where Pup sat reading the paper and Andras sprawled in the chair near the window.

No one spoke for a minute, then Pup's voice came from behind the paper as Joe and Itz stood trembling.

"You owe me ten cents. You stole ten cents."

Itz pulled their two dimes out of his pocket, placed them on the table by his father's chair and said, "We doubled our profits."

Joe couldn't believe the audacity of it. Two ragged boys, torn pants, dirty faces.

Pup lowered the paper and stared at them. No reaction.

"Leave those clothes on for a few days," he said. "It will be a good reminder." He raised the paper again and the boys felt relief all through their bones.

Then both pairs of eyes went toward Andras, who rose and moved toward them, his arms swinging. Joe thought he seemed a little smaller. Their big brother stopped a foot away and lowered his arms.

"I had it harder than you," he announced, and without another word he headed out the door and into the street.

Acknowledgements

"Write without fear. Edit without mercy." The second dictum is by far the more difficult, but I have learned from this process and from the many friends who have read, commented on and helped edit this text.

Writing must enable the reader to see a picture that is borne in the author's experience or imagination. This seems to me to be the greatest task: to clearly communicate so that the reader can paint their own picture. Friends and editors are an enormous help in this endeavor. They can say, "I don't see how that character got from there to there," or "If that happened then, how can this have happened later?"

First, my thanks to my writing partner: Heather Marshall, who not only helped shape this novel, but also taught me much about writing.

People who gave valued opinions: Karen Brown, Jon Grier, Marion Grier, Merridee Harper, Pat Jobe, and Greta Little.

Keller Freeman gently suggested that I remove a few characters, which made the story imminently more readable.

Jessica Brandon designed the cover and somehow managed to visualize and reveal the story truly and beautifully.

Peter Van Gieson helped with chronology and grammar, but more importantly supported my writing process by getting me out to ride bikes when it was crucial to do so.

Special thanks to Nancy Gore, who has been a source of practical suggestions as well as a foundation of encouragement.

It does take a village to raise a book. At least this book. Thanks to all of you.